Echoes in the Stone

A Journey of Discovery and Renewal

Sebastian X Cade

Copyright © 2024 Sebastian X Cade
All rights reserved.
ISBN: 9798340597922

1

The symphony of Sydney Harbour, a harmonious blend of ferry horns groaning, gulls echoing their calls, and the distant hum of traffic crossing the Harbour Bridge, floated up to Martin's flat window. It was the comforting soundtrack to his meticulously crafted life. Late summer sunlight, tinged with gold, filtered through sheer curtains, casting a warm glow over the minimalist décor: clean lines, neutral tones, and carefully curated art books lining the shelves, a testament to his love for simplicity and order.

Seated at his sleek glass desk, Martin inhaled the rich, dark-chocolatey aroma of freshly brewed espresso. This was his daily ritual: two precisely measured shots in his favourite ceramic mug, the one with a tiny imperfection on the rim. Each morning, his index finger traced the almost imperceptible bump, finding quiet satisfaction in acknowledging beauty within imperfection. The mug was a memento from his first solo trip overseas to Hong Kong years ago.

He recalled the overwhelming energy of the city, the neon lights, the cacophony of sounds, the crush of humanity. Down a narrow alleyway, he'd stumbled upon a tucked-away market stall, an oasis of calm amid the chaos. Earthenware pots in muted greens and blues lined the shelves, the air rich with sandalwood incense curling like wisps of ancient dragons. Behind the counter sat a small, wizened woman, her face etched with a thousand stories, eyes the colour of jade gleaming with wisdom.

Drawn to a simple mug glazed the colour of a stormy sky, Martin hesitated as his fingers traced a single imperfection marring its surface. The woman smiled softly, her eyes crinkling at the corners.

"Even the moon has its shadows," she said in halting English, her voice as gentle as the chime of a temple bell carried on the wind.

Her words resonated with him long after he'd left the market. The mug became a talisman, a reminder that true beauty often lay in the unexpected, in embracing flaws and imperfections. It was a lesson he'd carried with him; one he'd desperately needed after David.

Scanning his digital calendar displayed on the tablet, team meetings shaded in blue, project deadlines marked in urgent red, a workout session with Alex highlighted in motivating green, and a scheduled call with his mum in comforting purple, everything was in its place. Each event was meticulously categorised and colour-coded, a reflection of his need for control honed to a fine point after the emotional earthquake that had been David.

A notification chimed, breaking his focus. An email from GreenEarth Innovations, a prominent sustainable design firm he frequently collaborated with, sat in his inbox. The subject line, bold and attention-grabbing, practically screamed:

Exclusive Project Opportunity – Confidential

He'd been expecting this email, a tantalising whisper of a rumour that had circulated for weeks. Indulging his investigative instincts, he'd scoured the internet for clues. GreenEarth was notoriously tight-lipped about upcoming projects, preferring a dramatic reveal once everything was set in stone. He'd narrowed down the possibilities to a handful of historic properties across Europe, a crumbling palazzo in Venice, a faded manor house in the Cotswolds, and, notably, the Château de Valmont in the Loire Valley.

He'd spent hours poring over architectural plans and historical documents, each property igniting a different kind of excitement, presenting a unique challenge. He'd allowed himself to fantasise about living in each place, strolling through cobblestone streets, sipping espresso in charming cafés, his life a blend of historical elegance and modern sustainability.

As he scanned the email, his heart skipped a beat. It was the château.

Dear Mr Longman,

I hope this email finds you well.

GreenEarth Innovations is currently considering potential project leads for a unique and challenging restoration project. The endeavour involves the historic Château de Valmont in the Loire Valley, France, a region renowned for its rich heritage and architectural significance. Our vision is to transform the château into a state-of-the-art sustainability centre while meticulously preserving its historical integrity.

Given your exemplary work in sustainable design and your passion for architectural preservation, we believe you would be an ideal candidate to lead this project.

We understand that this is short notice; however, we are eager to assemble the best possible team for this endeavour.

Please do not hesitate to contact me at your earliest convenience to discuss the project in greater detail.

Sincerely,

Isabella Reed

Project Manager

GreenEarth Innovations

A familiar ache bloomed in his chest as images flickered across the screen, the château's elegant façade, overgrown gardens hinting at past glory, the crumbling grandeur of its interior. He'd spent a whirlwind 48 hours in the Loire Valley with David, a lifetime ago. David, with his fluent French and infectious passion for history, had swept him away on a tour of châteaux and vineyards, their laughter echoing through empty halls.

He recalled a photo he'd snapped of David, ever the theatrical one, pretending to be a knight guarding the crumbling entrance of the Château de Valmont. They'd stood there, hand in hand, the sun setting over rolling hills, the air thick with the scent of grapes and the promise of forever. Back then, life had felt full of possibilities, untainted by the weight of expectation and disappointment.

Now, viewing the château through the lens of a potential project, a potential life change, he felt a wave of apprehension wash over him. Living in a place was a different beast entirely. It meant settling, establishing a routine, confronting the mundane realities of daily life, and navigating conversations in a language he'd struggled with even when David was translating. His French, he thought ruefully, extended to ordering croissants and coffee, and even then, his pronunciation probably made David cringe.

"Don't overthink it, Longman," he muttered, echoing Alex's voice. He liked to think of himself as a traveller, not just a tourist, someone who embraced new experiences and immersed himself in different cultures. Besides, he could practically hear Sarah's delighted shriek if she knew he was even considering this.

"France! Château! Wine!" he imagined her exclaiming. "This is your destiny!"

His tablet buzzed again, an incoming video call. Sarah's smiling face, framed by her sleek brown bob and the familiar, comforting clutter of her home office, filled the screen.

"Morning, sunshine! Did you get the mysterious email?" she chirped, eyes sparkling with mischief.

"You mean the one about Château de Valmont?" Martin replied, attempting nonchalance, as if he hadn't spent the last hour immersed in the château's history.

"So, you did! Isn't it incredible? France! Imagine: baguettes, Bordeaux, and brooding, handsome Frenchmen!" Sarah exclaimed, already planning his social calendar. "You always did love a good château."

"It's... a lot to process," he admitted, rubbing a hand over his face, the weight of the decision pressing on him.

"But exciting, right?" She tilted her head, her expression softening. "I know you, Martin. You thrive on challenges. Remember when we almost got arrested for accidentally crashing that wedding in Thailand?"

He chuckled. How could he forget? It had been one of the most chaotic, exhilarating months of his life, that backpacking trip through Southeast Asia. They'd been lured into the wedding by the sounds of music and laughter spilling from a brightly decorated marquee beside a dusty road. One minute they were sipping Mekong whisky with giggling bridesmaids; the next, they were being ushered away by stern-faced uncles, all while Sarah insisted on honouring local customs. Terrifying and hilarious in equal measure.

"Or the time we convinced that bus driver in Laos to take us to a hidden waterfall, even though we didn't speak a word of Lao?" she continued, eyes twinkling.

He remembered the rickety, brightly painted bus, crammed with chickens clucking beneath their seats and Thai pop music blaring from the radio. Sarah had bartered with the driver using hand gestures and smiles, her infectious enthusiasm transcending the language barrier. The waterfall had been worth it, a hidden oasis of turquoise water and lush vegetation, like a scene from an adventure film. They'd spent the afternoon swimming, their laughter echoing through the jungle, everyday stresses a million miles away.

"We lived on instant noodles and slept on buses and in dodgy hostels, and you complained about your perfectly organised packing cubes being redundant every five minutes, but you secretly loved every minute," she finished, her tone laced with playful accusation.

"We were younger then," he said wistfully. "More... spontaneous. Or reckless, depending on how you look at it." He'd been different then, hadn't he? Before David, before the walls went up, before control became his default setting.

"Exactly! That's what you need, a good dose of spontaneity. France is calling, Martin! Think of the cheese, the wine, the architecture! You'll be in your element!"

He conceded, a smile tugging at his lips. She always knew how to reframe his anxieties. Maybe a change of scenery was exactly what he needed.

After ending the call, a text from Alex popped up: *You coming to the gym today? Don't go getting soft on me, Longman. Consistency is key!*

He glanced at his reflection in the window, a flicker of doubt crossing his features. Perhaps a workout would clear his head. He needed to talk to someone who wouldn't launch into a travelogue at the mere mention of France.

An hour later, amidst the clanging weights and rhythmic grunts of the gym, Martin confided in Alex, outlining the email, the château project, and his conflicting emotions.

Alex, perched on a weight bench, biceps gleaming with sweat, shrugged. "Sounds like an amazing opportunity, mate. Don't overthink it."

"Easy for you to say," Martin countered, wiping his forehead with a towel. "You're not the one being asked to relocate across the globe."

"Maybe you're right," Alex conceded, a flicker of something unreadable in his eyes. "But you've always talked about wanting to make a bigger impact with your work. This sounds like your chance. You'd be bloody good at it, you know? GreenEarth wouldn't offer it if they didn't think you could handle it."

"And what about your big plans?" Martin's gaze fell on the silver band adorning Alex's ring finger. He'd been surprised when Alex announced his engagement to Jennifer, a sensible and successful lawyer radiating quiet capability. For some reason, he'd always pictured Alex as a confirmed bachelor.

A shadow crossed Alex's face, the easy smile slipping. "Yeah, well, Jennifer's not exactly thrilled about the idea of me staying in Sydney," he mumbled, avoiding Martin's gaze. "Her firm's offered her a partnership in Newcastle. Closer to her parents, you know? But I don't know... I like my life here, my work, my mates. It's a big ask, moving three hours away." He trailed off, shaking his head. "I guess long-term relationships are all about compromise, right?"

Something about his tone didn't sit right with Martin. Was Alex truly happy? He'd never mentioned wanting to get married. Martin had always assumed Alex was content with his carefree existence. He decided to let it go. His own anxieties felt insurmountable without taking on his friend's relationship woes.

That evening, assembling his dinner salad, Martin's mind replayed the day's conversations. He arranged carefully washed greens in a bowl, rocket, baby spinach, a handful of watercress for bite, and began adding his usual array of colourful toppings. Cherry tomatoes, halved with precision, formed a neat circle around the edge. Thinly sliced cucumber overlapped in tidy rows. He added toasted walnuts for crunch, crumbled feta for saltiness, and a drizzle of homemade balsamic vinaigrette. The salad, like most things in his life, was a study in order and balance. Yet, as he ate, his appetite remained elusive, his thoughts a jumble of châteaux, career moves, and an uncertain future.

He decided to call his mum. They hadn't spoken in weeks, and he knew she'd have a fresh supply of local gossip to distract him.

"Martin! About time you called," his mother chided, her voice a mix of relief and reproach. "I was beginning to think you'd forgotten your dear old mum."

"You could've called me too, you know," he countered, unable to keep a slight edge out of his voice.

"Don't get cheeky with me, young man," she retorted, tone softening. "I raised you better than that. Now, tell me, what's new in your world? Anything exciting happening?"

He found himself telling her about the email, the project, and the possibility of relocating to France.

"France!" Her voice rose in excitement. "Oh, Martin, that's wonderful! You've always loved that country. Remember when we took you to Europe and you spent the entire trip with your nose in a guidebook, lecturing us about flying buttresses and Romanesque architecture?"

He chuckled. It was true, he'd been a painfully precocious teenager, desperate to impress with his burgeoning knowledge of architectural history.

"It's just... a big decision," he hedged. "Leaving Sydney, starting over... in another language."

"Life is all about taking chances, love," she said softly. "Don't be afraid to spread your wings. You'll be surprised what you can achieve when you step outside your comfort zone. Besides, what's so exciting happening in Sydney that you can't bear to leave?" She chuckled mischievously. "You wouldn't believe what that Peterson woman has gone and done!"

And just like that, she launched into a detailed account of Mrs Peterson's scandalous elopement with the owner of the local kitchen renovation company.

"Can you imagine?" Her voice was a mix of shock and delight. "Ran off to Bali with him, apparently. Left poor Richard with nothing but a broken heart and a half-finished kitchen renovation. Such a nice man, Richard. Deserves better, really. Now, who gets the house? You know it's worth a fortune! Imagine poor Richard having to cook in that kitchen of sin, all those marble surfaces and fancy appliances. It's practically a monument to their affair!"

Martin listened patiently, picturing Mrs Peterson in her leopard-print kaftans and oversized sunglasses, swanning off to Bali with her hunky renovator. He felt a bit sorry for Richard, the quiet, unassuming bloke who kept mostly to himself.

The gossip flowed, from the neighbour's new sunroom ("They're having issues with council approval, something about height restrictions.") to his sister's latest romantic drama ("Another new boyfriend! At this rate, she'll have gone through the entire eligible male population of Sydney by forty!"). He even offered titbits of his own, the latest office rumour about his boss's impending divorce, the gossip about the new intern who'd accidentally sent a rather racy text to the entire team.

By the time he hung up, his earlier anxieties had subsided somewhat, replaced by comforting familiarity. His mum, despite her gentle chiding and endless gossip, always had a way of grounding him, reminding him that life, for all its complexities, went on.

He sat down at his desk, the Château de Valmont beckoning from his laptop screen. He reread Isabella Reed's email, her words sparking a flicker of excitement. He thought of Sarah's infectious enthusiasm, Alex's pragmatic advice, his mother's unwavering faith, and even the old woman in the Hong Kong market, her words echoing in his mind: "Even the moon has its shadows."

Taking a deep breath, his fingers hovered over the keyboard. Maybe it was time to step into the shadows, to embrace the unexpected. Maybe it was time to rediscover the man he used to be, the one who craved adventure, unafraid to take a chance on happiness.

Dear Ms Reed,

Thank you for your email and for considering me for this incredible opportunity. I am very interested in the Château de Valmont restoration project and would welcome the chance to discuss it further at your convenience.

Sincerely,

Martin Longman

He hit send, the click echoing in the quiet flat. The die was cast.

The insistent honking of a taxi driver, impatient in Sydney's traffic snarl, jolted Martin back to reality. He'd been lost in a daydream, picturing the graceful turrets of Château de Valmont rising above a mist-shrouded Loire Valley, a stark contrast to the grimy reality of peak hour on George Street. He checked his watch, a vintage Omega passed down from his grandfather, its ticking a constant reminder of time's relentless march. He was running late.

The past week had been a whirlwind, a flurry of meetings with Isabella Reed, endless phone calls, mountains of paperwork, and a frantic scramble to organise his life before leaving for France. What had seemed like an eternity before the email had turned into a heart-stoppingly short timeframe to get his affairs in order.

Isabella, ever the efficient project manager, had wasted no time. They'd met twice at GreenEarth's headquarters, poring over architectural plans, historical documents, and projected budgets. She was a force of nature, her American accent a clipped counterpoint to his measured tones, her enthusiasm both infectious and slightly intimidating. She'd peppered him with questions, probing his design philosophy, his approach to sustainable practices, his thoughts on blending the old with the new.

"This project is more than just bricks and mortar, Martin," she'd said, eyes flashing with conviction. "It's about preserving history, creating a legacy, building a sustainable future for generations to come."

He found himself nodding, drawn in by her passion. He admired GreenEarth's commitment to sustainable design, their innovative approach to blending environmental responsibility with architectural integrity. This project was the culmination of everything he'd been working towards, a chance to leave his mark, to create something meaningful.

But alongside the excitement, a hum of anxiety thrummed beneath the surface. He wasn't sure he was ready for such a monumental undertaking, the pressure, the responsibility, the upheaval of relocating to a foreign country. He'd always been a creature of habit, finding comfort in routines, in the predictability of his curated life. The thought of uprooting himself, navigating a new culture and language, filled him with unease that bordered on panic.

He tried to quell the anxiety with meticulous planning. Hours were spent researching the Loire Valley, compiling detailed itineraries, booking accommodation, even brushing up on his rudimentary French. His flat, usually a haven of order, was now a chaotic jumble of half-packed suitcases, scattered guidebooks, and lists scribbled on every surface. He'd meticulously labelled boxes, sorted his wardrobe, and invested in colour-coded packing cubes, determined to maintain order amidst the chaos of relocation.

His attempts at mastering French were less successful. He'd downloaded a language app, diligently working through vocabulary lists and grammar exercises.

"Bonjour, je m'appelle Martin. Où est la boulangerie?" he'd practised in the shower, his pronunciation more akin to a strangled cat than a charming Parisian. He sighed. David would have been fluent by now, effortlessly charming locals with impeccable accent and witty observations. He pushed the thought away, a familiar ache settling in his chest.

He'd called his accountant, lawyer, bank, ensuring all financial and legal affairs were in order. Arranged for his mail to be forwarded, plants to be watered, flat to be cleaned. He'd even written detailed instructions for his neighbour on operating his complicated coffee machine ("Three scoops of beans, grind on setting five, preheat the milk frother..."). He knew he was being overly meticulous, but the need for control was a reflex, a way to cope with the uncertainty gnawing at him.

Glancing at his reflection in the taxi window, his face appeared pale and drawn, eyes shadowed with fatigue. He'd barely slept in a week, nights consumed by restless anticipation and apprehension.

He needed to get a grip. This was an incredible opportunity, a chance to prove himself, to step out of his comfort zone, to embrace a new challenge.

He closed his eyes, taking a deep breath, trying to quell the flutter in his stomach. He could do this. He had to do this.

Earlier in the week, Martin met Sarah for a farewell dinner at their favourite Thai restaurant, the one with the kitschy décor and potent cocktails. They ordered their usual feast, green curry, pad see ew, spring rolls, washed down with copious amounts of Singha beer.

Sarah, fuelled by nostalgia and beer, regaled him with tales of their backpacking adventures. "Remember when we convinced those monks in Chiang Mai to give us a blessing for good luck?" she said, eyes sparkling, words slightly slurred. "You were convinced they'd shave your head!"

He laughed, the memory vivid. They'd explored Chiang Mai's ancient temples, marvelled at intricate carvings, towering golden Buddhas, the sense of history permeating every stone. Sarah had been determined to receive a blessing from the monks at Wat Phra That Doi Suthep, a temple perched high on a mountain. He'd been hesitant, terrified of losing his carefully styled hair, but Sarah's charm had won them over. They emerged from the ceremony giggling, heads adorned with jasmine garlands, a blessing for safe travels.

"And that full moon party on Koh Phangan? You swore you'd never drink from a bucket again," she continued, dissolving into giggles. "But then you ended up dancing on the beach with that dreadlocked fire dancer until sunrise!"

He shuddered, recalling the hazy night of pounding music, glowing body paint, and questionable decisions. Koh Phangan had been a whirlwind of neon lights and thumping basslines. They'd danced until their feet ached, bodies covered in fluorescent paint, inhibitions lost in collective euphoria. He'd woken with a throbbing headache, sand in his hair, and a vague recollection of declaring his undying love for a coconut. He'd sworn off buckets forever after that.

Sarah recounted their adventures with gusto, their haggling for souvenirs in Bangkok markets, their hair-raising motorbike ride through Vietnamese rice paddies, even mimicking the gruff bus driver in Laos who'd taken them to a hidden waterfall.

He listened, his heart warming with each story. He'd almost forgotten how carefree he'd been, open to new experiences, willing to embrace the unexpected. It was before David, before the need for control consumed him.

He shared his anxieties about navigating French bureaucracy, his attempts to learn basic French ("Seriously, how many ways are there to say 'hello'?"), and the daunting task of restoring a crumbling 16th-century château. Sarah, ever supportive, offered encouragement and witty asides.

"Don't worry about the French," she said, waving a dismissive hand. "Just smile a lot, nod your head, and throw in a few 'oui oui's and 'merci's, you'll be fine. And as for the château, it's your dream project! You were born to restore crumbling historical buildings!"

He smiled, her unwavering faith both comforting and slightly embarrassing.

"Just promise me you'll send lots of photos, and that you won't forget about your old mate when you're surrounded by French wine and charming men," she said, raising her glass in a mock toast.

He promised, grateful for her friendship, her ability to make him laugh even when his world felt tilted.

By night's end, they were comfortably tipsy, their conversation a mix of shared memories, heartfelt confessions, and drunken promises to stay in touch. Sarah, even drunk, was the most caring person he knew. He hugged her goodbye, knowing that no matter the distance, their bond would remain, a constant source of support and laughter.

Two days before his farewell dinner with the GreenEarth team, Martin met Alex for their usual workout at the building's gym. It was Wednesday afternoon, the gym relatively quiet, the only sounds the rhythmic clang of weights and occasional grunts. They'd fallen into a comfortable routine over the past year, pushing each other, sharing a companionable silence.

Today, however, the usual rhythm felt off. Alex, usually a whirlwind of energy and banter, was uncharacteristically quiet, movements mechanical, gaze distant. Martin knew about the Newcastle situation, the tension between Alex's desire to stay in Sydney and Jennifer's career aspirations. He'd tried to offer support, but Alex mostly brushed it aside.

They finished their workout, bodies slick with sweat, muscles pleasantly fatigued. As they headed to the café for their usual post-workout ginger beers, Martin tried again.

"How are things with you and Jennifer?" he asked gently.

Alex shrugged, taking a long swig of his ginger beer, the one brewed by a small company in Canberra. "It's complicated," he mumbled, gaze fixed outside, watching people hurry past, each carrying their own stories. "She's been offered a partnership at her firm, a big deal. But it's in Newcastle. Her parents are there, and she wants to be closer. She wants to buy a place near the beach, start a family..." He trailed off, voice losing energy.

Martin nodded, understanding the difficult decision. He thought about his own impending move, the uncertainty ahead. Was he being selfish, pursuing this opportunity? What about his responsibilities here?

"What about you?" he asked. "What do you want?"

Alex sighed, shoulders slumping. "I don't know, mate. Part of me thinks I should just go for it, support her, make her happy. Compromise. That's what you do in a relationship, right?"

Martin hesitated. He thought about his relationship with David, the compromises, the sacrifices, all in the name of love. It hadn't ended well. He'd learned that compromising one's own happiness was a recipe for resentment.

He looked at Alex, his friend's eyes clouded with doubt, shoulders hunched under the weight of his decision.

"Maybe," Martin said carefully, "but maybe it's also about being honest, with yourself and with her. Figuring out what you both want, finding a way to make it work without giving up everything."

Alex nodded slowly, taking another swig, the ice clinking against the glass. He looked up, a flicker of gratitude in his eyes. "Yeah, you're right. It's just... a lot to think about. Moving away, starting over... It's scary, you know?"

Martin smiled genuinely. He knew exactly how Alex felt. "Tell me about it," he said empathetically. "I'm about to move to another bloody continent."

They shared a moment of silence, a shared understanding of life's complexities.

Martin placed a reassuring hand on Alex's arm. "You'll figure it out," he said firmly. "Just... be true to yourself. Don't lose sight of what makes you happy."

Alex nodded, a faint smile crossing his face. He raised his bottle in a toast. "To new beginnings," he said, voice regaining energy.

"To new beginnings," Martin echoed, clinking his bottle.

But even as he said the words, doubt lingered. He hoped, for Alex's sake, that this new beginning wouldn't come at the cost of his own happiness.

The insistent chirping of his phone alarm dragged Martin from restless sleep. He'd tossed and turned all night, mind a jumble of packing lists, flight itineraries, and half-remembered French phrases. He'd finally drifted off just before dawn, only to be jolted awake.

He glanced at the clock, 5:30 am. His flight to Paris wasn't until 10:00 am, but Alex insisted on picking him up at 6:30. "Wouldn't want you missing your flight and screwing up this once-in-a-lifetime opportunity," he'd said, voice a little too forceful.

Martin accepted the offer, grateful for the distraction. But as he showered and dressed, unease lingered.

Pulling on his socks, aligning the seams, the doorbell rang. He glanced at his reflection, hair a mess of sleep-tousled waves, eyes bloodshot, face pale. He looked like he'd just stepped off a red-eye flight.

Opening the door, he found Alex on the doorstep, suitcase in hand, travel mug in the other. Dressed in gym attire, track pants, T-shirt, trainers, hair damp from a workout. He looked reassuringly normal.

"Ready to go, mate?" Alex asked, smile a little strained. "Wouldn't want you to miss that croissant and baguette buffet in the business class lounge."

Martin chuckled, stepping back to let him in. "Always thinking of my stomach."

"What can I say? I'm a good mate." Alex winked, his usual demeanour returning momentarily.

Martin grabbed his laptop bag, the familiar weight a comforting anchor. He'd packed it carefully, ensuring essential work documents, laptop, noise-cancelling headphones were secure. Even included a travel-sized first aid kit. One couldn't be too prepared.

They headed to the car park, the predawn air cool and crisp. Alex's sporty Audi gleamed red under the dim lights. Martin loaded his suitcase, the sound echoing.

As they navigated the deserted streets, Alex, in a rare moment of vulnerability, commented, "Might have to trade this in for a people mover soon, you know, when the kids come along." He glanced at Martin, uncertainty in his eyes, seeking reassurance.

Martin, unsure how to respond, simply murmured, "Yeah, kids change everything."

Alex didn't respond, gaze fixed ahead, jaw clenched, knuckles white on the wheel. The rest of the drive was heavy with unspoken words.

At the airport, they exchanged an awkward hug.

"Take care, mate," Alex said gruffly. "And send me a postcard."

"Will do," Martin replied, forcing a smile. He wanted to say more, to offer advice, but words caught in his throat.

"And you..." he started, hesitating. "You sort things out, alright?"

Alex nodded, eyes distant, smile strained.

As Martin watched him drive away, concern washed over him. He hoped his friend would be okay, hoped he'd navigate love and commitment, and find his own happiness.

Turning towards the terminal, footsteps echoing on the polished floor, he felt a mix of relief, anticipation, lingering sadness, and burgeoning freedom. He was stepping into the unknown, embarking on a journey that would challenge him, test him, and, he hoped, lead him back to himself.

He checked in, laptop bag over his shoulder. Navigated security with practised ease, the routine oddly soothing. Good at routines, at compartmentalising, at keeping emotions in check. But beneath the surface, anticipation stirred.

In the sanctuary of the airline lounge, a world of plush armchairs, complimentary snacks, and hushed anticipation, the air was thick with the aroma of coffee, the gentle clinking of glasses, murmurs in multiple languages. He found a secluded corner, settling into a comfortable armchair. Ordered a cappuccino from the attentive waiter.

Reaching into his bag, fingers brushed against the smooth leather of the journal Sarah had given him. He pulled it out, the weight reassuring. Opening to the first page, blankness daunting. He took a deep breath, picked up a pen, hesitated.

He wasn't sure what to write. His mind was a jumble, excitement, apprehension, lingering sadness for what could have been with David, a flicker of hope for the future. He started with a date, grounding himself in the moment. Then, slowly, tentatively, words began to flow.

Sydney Airport, Departure Lounge. 7:15 am. About to embark on a new adventure. France. Château de Valmont. It all feels surreal, a dream I haven't quite woken from. I'm excited, terrified, a little bit lost... but also, strangely, free.

He paused, rereading, surprised by the rawness. He was a man of logic, of precision, of carefully crafted façades. Rarely delved into the messy depths of feelings, preferring to keep them hidden. But here, surrounded by strangers embarking on their own journeys, he felt liberated.

He continued writing, the pen flowing, thoughts taking shape. He wrote about Isabella's email, the opportunity disrupting his meticulously planned existence. About the château, the history and possibility it evoked. About Sarah's enthusiasm, Alex's quiet struggle, his mother's faith, and even the old woman in Hong Kong.

He wrote about David, the ghost of a love that still haunted him, the memory of shared laughter and whispered promises, the pain of a future that never happened. He hadn't allowed himself to think about David for years, burying the memories beneath work and routine, afraid to confront the raw ache of loss. But here, the emotions surfaced, a bittersweet tide washing over him, reminding him he was still capable of feeling, of hurting, of loving.

He closed the journal, fingers lingering on the leather, a sense of completion washing over him. He wasn't sure where this journey would lead, what challenges he'd face, what triumphs he might achieve. But he was ready. Ready to embrace the shadows, to face the moon, to discover beauty in imperfection. Ready to let go of the past and embrace the uncertainty of the future.

Taking a sip of his cappuccino, warmth spreading through him, he gazed out the window at planes taking flight, soaring into the vast blue sky.

It was time to spread his own wings.

2

The wheels of the aeroplane touched down with a gentle thud on the tarmac of Charles de Gaulle Airport, the subtle jolt pulling Martin from a restless doze. He blinked awake, momentarily disoriented by the unfamiliar surroundings. The muted hum of the engines winding down, the soft chime of the seatbelt sign turning off, and the murmured conversations of fellow passengers in a symphony of languages all served as a reminder: he was no longer in Sydney.

As he stepped off the plane and into the bustling terminal, a crisp autumn air greeted him, carrying with it the scent of damp leaves, distant woodsmoke, and a hint of something sweet, perhaps chestnuts roasting from a street vendor he couldn't yet see. Gone was the familiar humidity of Sydney's spring, replaced by the cool embrace of a European autumn. He shivered involuntarily, regretting not having his coat more accessible in his carry-on luggage. Pulling his recently acquired scarf, a last-minute purchase he'd been dubious about, tighter around his neck, he tried to acclimatise to the sudden change in climate.

The airport was a hive of activity, a chaotic symphony of motion and sound. Announcements echoed through the vast space in rapid-fire French, a language that flowed like music but left him grasping at only a few familiar words. The air buzzed with conversations, families reuniting with joyous embraces, business travellers rushing to their next connection, tourists fumbling with maps and luggage. Martin felt a pang of anxiety tighten in his chest, the sheer scale of the unfamiliar threatening to overwhelm him.

He paused near a large window overlooking the tarmac, taking a moment to centre himself. Planes taxied in the distance, their lights blinking against the overcast sky. *You can do this*, he reminded himself. *You've travelled before, navigated foreign cities, managed without knowing the language.* But this time felt different. This wasn't a holiday or a business trip with a defined end date. This was the start of something new, something uncertain.

He pulled out his phone, momentarily tempted to call Sarah or his mum for a reassuring word. The thought of hearing a familiar voice was comforting, but he hesitated. It was early morning in Australia, and they'd likely be asleep. Besides, he'd promised himself he would embrace this adventure wholeheartedly, without immediately retreating to the safety net of home.

Adjusting the strap of his laptop bag, a comforting weight against his side, he made his way to the baggage claim. The carousel was already crowded with passengers jostling for position. He spotted his suitcase, a sleek, navy hard-shell adorned with a discreet Australian flag sticker and manoeuvred through the throng to retrieve it. The familiar heft of his meticulously packed belongings offered a small measure of solace.

Navigating through customs was mercifully straightforward, and soon he found himself in the arrivals hall. He scanned the sea of faces, half-expecting someone to be there to greet him, even though he knew there wouldn't be. A flicker of loneliness sparked within him but was quickly extinguished by a surge of determination. *This is your choice*, he reminded himself. *Your opportunity.*

He approached a kiosk displaying rental car options but hesitated. Driving in a foreign country, especially after a long flight and with jet lag setting in, didn't seem wise. Opting instead for a pre-booked car service, a small indulgence to ease his transition, he located the designated meeting point.

"Bonjour, Monsieur Longman?" A driver approached, holding a sign with his name neatly printed.

"Oui, c'est moi," Martin replied, grateful for the familiar sight.

The driver, a middle-aged man with salt-and-pepper hair and a neatly trimmed moustache, offered a polite smile. "Bienvenue en France. Allow me to assist you with your luggage."

"Merci," Martin said, handing over his suitcase.

They made their way to a sleek black sedan parked just outside the terminal. The driver loaded the luggage with practised efficiency before opening the passenger door for Martin.

As they pulled away from the airport, Martin settled into the back seat, watching as the urban sprawl of Paris began to fade, giving way to the rolling countryside of the Loire Valley. The landscape unfolded like a painting, fields dotted with hay bales, vineyards stretching towards the horizon, and quaint villages with their distinctive stone houses and slate roofs.

"First time in France?" the driver asked in lightly accented English, glancing at Martin in the rear-view mirror.

"Not quite, but first time spending more than a few days," Martin replied. "I visited briefly years ago."

"Ah, very good. The Loire Valley is beautiful this time of year. You will enjoy it, I think."

"I hope so," Martin said, offering a polite smile.

The conversation lapsed into a comfortable silence. Martin watched as the scenery passed by, the vibrant autumn colours painting the landscape in shades of gold, crimson, and amber. He felt a mix of excitement and trepidation. The reality of his decision was sinking in, he was in France, about to undertake a monumental project, far from the familiar comforts of home.

His thoughts drifted to the Château de Valmont, the images he'd studied online and the plans he'd meticulously prepared. The château had captivated him from the moment he'd seen it, a grand structure steeped in history but marred by neglect. He recalled the detailed architectural plans he'd reviewed, the potential he saw in blending sustainable design with historical preservation. The idea of breathing new life into such a place filled him with a sense of purpose.

Yet, beneath the surface, doubts lingered. Would he be able to navigate the complexities of French bureaucracy? Would his ideas be accepted by the team, many of whom had deep roots in the region? And then there was the language barrier, a significant obstacle for someone whose French was, at best, rudimentary.

He pulled out his notebook, flipping through pages filled with sketches, notes, and to-do lists. Among them was a folded piece of paper, a handwritten note from Sarah slipped into his bag before he left. He unfolded it, smiling at her familiar scrawl.

Remember, embrace the imperfections. They're what make life interesting. And don't forget to try the cheese!

He chuckled softly, tucking the note back into his notebook. Sarah always knew how to lighten his mood.

As they continued south, the driver switched on the radio, tuning into a station playing soft classical music. The soothing melodies blended with the rhythmic hum of the tyres on the road, lulling Martin into a state of relaxed contemplation.

A sign indicated they were nearing Chenonceaux. The driver caught Martin's eye in the mirror. "We will arrive shortly, Monsieur."

"Thank you," Martin replied, straightening in his seat.

They turned onto a narrow lane flanked by towering plane trees, their branches arching overhead to form a natural canopy. The leaves, starting to fall, drifted lazily in the breeze, creating a carpet of orange and gold on the road.

"Le Clos des Roses, correct?" the driver confirmed.

"Yes, that's right," Martin said.

They pulled up in front of a charming stone building, ivy climbing its walls and window boxes overflowing with late-blooming flowers. A wrought-iron sign swung gently in the breeze, proclaiming the name of the guesthouse.

"Here we are," the driver announced, stepping out to retrieve Martin's luggage.

"Thank you for the smooth journey," Martin said, offering a tip.

"Merci, Monsieur. Enjoy your stay."

As the car pulled away, Martin stood for a moment, taking in his surroundings. The guest house exuded warmth and character, a stark contrast to the sleek modernity of his Sydney flat. The air was fresh and crisp, carrying the distant sound of church bells chiming the hour.

He approached the heavy wooden door, adorned with an intricately carved brass knocker in the shape of a rose. Before he could lift it, the door swung open.

"Bonjour! Vous devez être Monsieur Longman," a woman greeted him, her voice rich and welcoming.

"Oui, c'est moi," Martin replied, smiling.

"Bienvenue! I am Madame Dubois. Please, come in."

She stepped aside, allowing him to enter a cosy reception area. The interior was a delightful blend of rustic charm and understated elegance. Exposed wooden beams crisscrossed the ceiling, and a stone fireplace crackled invitingly in one corner. The scent of baking, perhaps cinnamon and apples, filled the air.

"Your journey was pleasant, I hope?" she inquired, her eyes bright with genuine interest.

"Yes, very comfortable, thank you," Martin replied.

"Excellent. Let me show you to your room. After you have settled in, perhaps you would like some tea? I have just made tarte tatin."

"That sounds wonderful," Martin said, his stomach rumbling in agreement.

She led him up a winding staircase to the second floor. "This is our Rose Suite," she announced, opening a door to reveal a charming room bathed in soft light. A large bed with a wrought-iron frame was adorned with a quilted bedspread in shades of cream and blush. French doors opened onto a small balcony overlooking the garden, where roses still bloomed despite the chill.

"This is lovely," Martin said sincerely.

"I am glad you like it. The en-suite is just through there, and if you need anything, please do not hesitate to ask."

"Merci beaucoup, Madame Dubois."

"De rien, Monsieur. I will leave you to settle in."

After she left, Martin took a moment to absorb the ambience of the room. It was worlds away from the minimalist decor he favoured at home, but he found the difference refreshing. Setting his suitcase on the luggage rack, he began unpacking, hanging his clothes in the antique armoire and arranging his toiletries in the bathroom.

He moved to the balcony, pushing open the doors to step outside. The garden below was a riot of colour, roses in full bloom, neatly trimmed hedges, and a small fountain trickling water into a stone basin. Beyond the garden walls, he could see the rooftops of Chenonceaux and, in the distance, the silhouette of the Château de Valmont. The sight stirred a mix of excitement and apprehension.

A soft knock at the door interrupted his thoughts. "Come in," he called.

Madame Dubois entered, carrying a tray laden with tea and a generous slice of tarte tatin. "I thought you might like to enjoy this on the balcony," she suggested.

"That's very kind of you," Martin said, helping her set the tray on the small table.

She hesitated for a moment. "If I may say, it is not often we have guests from Australia. What brings you to our little corner of France?"

"I'm here to work on the restoration of the Château de Valmont," he explained.

Her eyes widened with interest. "Ah, the old château! It has been waiting a long time for someone to care for it again. You have a big task ahead."

"Indeed," Martin agreed. "But I'm looking forward to it."

She smiled warmly. "I am sure you will do great things. If you need any assistance or have any questions about the area, please ask."

"Thank you, I appreciate that."

After she left, Martin poured himself a cup of tea, savouring the fragrant steam that rose from the delicate china cup. The tarte tatin was divine, the pastry buttery and crisp, the apples sweet and caramelised to perfection. He allowed himself a moment to simply enjoy the tranquillity, the sounds of the garden, and the distant murmur of village life.

Feeling the weight of travel settle over him, he decided to rest before exploring. He set an alarm on his phone, stretched out on the comfortable bed, and was soon enveloped in a deep sleep.

The alarm chimed softly, rousing Martin from a dreamless slumber. He blinked, momentarily disoriented by the unfamiliar surroundings, before the events of the day came rushing back. Stretching, he felt more refreshed and ready to face the rest of the day.

He changed into casual clothes, jeans, a comfortable jumper, and sturdy walking shoes, anticipating a few hours of exploration. Grabbing his camera, he headed downstairs. The guest house was quiet, the soft ticking of a grandfather clock in the hallway the only sound.

Stepping outside, he was greeted by the late afternoon sun casting long shadows across the cobblestone street. The air was cooler now, but invigorating. He set off towards the village centre, eager to acquaint himself with his new surroundings.

Chenonceaux was picturesque, the kind of place that seemed lifted from the pages of a travel magazine. Narrow streets wound between buildings of stone and timber; their shutters painted in cheerful colours. Window boxes overflowed with flowers, and vines climbed trellises in a tangle of green.

He wandered without a specific destination, allowing curiosity to guide him. A small market square opened before him, stalls laden with fresh produce, cheeses, and artisanal goods. The vendors chatted amiably with customers; their exchanges punctuated by laughter.

Approaching a stall displaying an array of cheeses, Martin's interest was piqued. An elderly man behind the counter greeted him with a toothless smile. "Bonjour, Monsieur! Fromage? The best in the region!"

"Bonjour," Martin replied. "They look wonderful."

"Ah, English!" the man exclaimed. "I have some English, yes. You are visiting?"

"Yes, I've just arrived today."

"Then you must try this," the vendor said, selecting a small wheel wrapped in vine leaves. "Saint Maure de Touraine. Goat cheese, very good."

"Sounds perfect," Martin agreed.

The vendor expertly sliced a piece and handed it to Martin on a small piece of crusty bread. The cheese was tangy and creamy, the flavour complex.

"Delicious," Martin said appreciatively.

"You like? Good! I make you a special price."

Martin purchased the cheese, along with a fresh baguette and some olives. "Merci beaucoup," he said.

"Enjoy, Monsieur! And welcome to Chenonceaux!"

Continuing his exploration, Martin found himself drawn towards the river. The Cher flowed gently, its surface reflecting the colours of the sky as the sun began its descent. A stone bridge arched gracefully across the water, and he paused midway to take in the view.

He pulled out his camera, framing shots of the river, the reflections of the trees, and the play of light on the water. Photography had always been a passion, a way to capture moments and details that might otherwise be overlooked.

As he reviewed the images, a movement caught his eye. Across the river, a group of children were playing, their laughter carrying on the breeze. They chased each other in a game of tag, their carefree joy infectious. Martin smiled, a pang of nostalgia tugging at him. He thought of his own childhood adventures, simpler times when the world seemed full of endless possibilities.

A nearby bench offered a place to sit and enjoy his impromptu picnic. He settled down, breaking off a piece of baguette and assembling it with the cheese and olives. The flavours melded beautifully, a simple yet satisfying meal.

As he ate, his phone buzzed, a message from Sarah: *How's France? Met any charming locals yet? Remember, life begins at the end of your comfort zone!*

He chuckled, typing a quick reply: *France is beautiful. The cheese is incredible. No charming locals yet, unless you count an enthusiastic cheese vendor. Will keep you posted.*

Her response was immediate: *Cheese vendors definitely count. Don't forget to try the wine. And send pictures!*

He smiled, snapping a photo of the river, and attaching it to the message.

Wish you were here to share this view, he wrote.

Me too. Take care, Longman. And don't work too hard.

Pocketing his phone, Martin leaned back, allowing the peacefulness of the moment to wash over him. The doubts and anxieties that had plagued him seemed distant now, replaced by a quiet optimism.

As dusk approached, he made his way back through the village. The streets were beginning to empty, the shops closing for the day. Warm light spilled from windows, and the aroma of cooking drifted on the air, garlic, herbs, roasting meats.

Passing a small bistro, he considered stopping for dinner but decided to return to the guest house instead. Madame Dubois had mentioned offering meals to guests, and he was curious to experience more of her hospitality.

Back at Le Clos des Roses, he found her in the kitchen, humming softly as she stirred a pot on the stove.

"Ah, Monsieur Longman! Did you enjoy your walk?"

"Very much. Chenonceaux is charming."

"I am glad to hear it. Are you hungry? I am making coq au vin."

"That sounds wonderful. Can I help with anything?"

She waved a hand dismissively. "Non, non. You are a guest. But if you would like to keep me company, I would not object."

"Then I will pour us some wine," he suggested, spotting a bottle of red on the counter.

"An excellent idea."

They settled into an easy conversation as she cooked. She shared stories of the village, local legends, notable residents, and the annual festivals that brought everyone together.

"The Château de Valmont has always been a source of fascination," she said, slicing mushrooms with practised ease. "There are stories of hidden passages, secret romances, even ghosts."

"Ghosts?" Martin raised an eyebrow, intrigued.

She chuckled. "Ah, every old building has its ghosts, non? But perhaps they are just echoes of the past, waiting for someone to listen."

He considered her words. "I suppose restoring the château is, in a way, giving voice to those echoes."

"Exactly. You have a poetic soul, Monsieur."

"Perhaps," he conceded, sipping his wine.

Dinner was a leisurely affair, the coq au vin rich and flavourful. They ate in the cosy dining room, candles casting a warm glow over the table. Martin found himself opening up more than usual, sharing stories of his work, his travels, and even his apprehensions about the project.

"You will do well," Madame Dubois assured him. "You have passion, and that is more important than anything."

"Thank you," he said sincerely. "Your kindness means a lot."

"Bah, it is nothing. Now, would you like some dessert? I have crème brûlée."

"How can I refuse?"

They lingered over dessert and coffee, the conversation meandering comfortably. By the time he retired for the evening, Martin felt a deep sense of contentment. The guesthouse had begun to feel like a home away from home.

The next morning dawned bright and clear, sunlight filtering through the lace curtains to cast intricate patterns on the wooden floor. Martin woke early, anticipation buzzing through him. Today he would meet the rest of the team at the château, a crucial step in turning plans into reality.

He dressed carefully, opting for attire that balanced professionalism with practicality. Dark trousers, a light blue shirt, and a tailored jacket that offered warmth without bulk. He checked his reflection, noting the subtle signs of jet lag still lingering but overall satisfied with his appearance.

Downstairs, Madame Dubois had prepared a hearty breakfast, fresh croissants, fruit, yoghurt, and strong coffee.

"Good morning!" she greeted him cheerfully. "You look ready to conquer the world."

"Perhaps just a château," he replied with a grin.

"One step at a time. Eat well, you will need your strength."

As he ate, she handed him a small paper bag. "For later," she said. "A snack in case you get hungry."

"You're spoiling me," Martin protested lightly.

"Nonsense. It is my pleasure."

Leaving the guesthouse, he felt a renewed sense of purpose. The walk to the château was pleasant, the morning air crisp but not biting. Birds chirped in the trees, and the village was beginning to stir with activity.

Approaching the château, he was struck once again by its imposing presence. Even in disrepair, it held a certain majesty. The façade was adorned with intricate stonework, gargoyles, reliefs, and archways hinting at the craftsmanship of a bygone era.

In the courtyard, a group of people stood engaged in conversation. He recognised Isabella immediately, her vibrant red hair and confident stance unmistakable.

"Martin!" she called out, waving him over. "Welcome to Château de Valmont!"

"Good morning, everyone," he greeted as he joined the group.

Isabella began introductions. "This is Sophie Dubois, our architectural historian."

"Enchantée," Sophie said, offering her hand. She was elegant, with dark hair pulled back and sharp, intelligent eyes. "I've heard much about your work."

"Likewise," Martin replied. "I'm looking forward to collaborating."

"Jean-Claude Boucher, our lead architect," Isabella continued.

Jean-Claude was tall and lean, with an air of meticulous precision. "Pleasure," he said, his handshake firm. "Your reputation precedes you."

"All good, I hope," Martin said lightly.

"Of course," Jean-Claude replied, a hint of a smile playing at the corners of his mouth.

"Marie Laurent, junior architect and sustainability specialist," Isabella introduced next.

Marie was younger, perhaps in her late twenties, with an open, friendly expression. "Hello! I'm so excited to work with you. Your ideas on sustainable design are inspiring."

"Thank you. It's great to have someone passionate about sustainability on the team," Martin said.

"And this is Antoine Rousseau, our stonemason extraordinaire," Isabella concluded.

Antoine was stocky, with strong hands and a face weathered by years of outdoor work. "Bonjour," he said simply, his gaze assessing.

"Bonjour," Martin replied. "I've heard your family's history with the château goes back generations."

"Oui," Antoine confirmed. "It is in my blood."

"Well, I hope to honour that legacy," Martin said earnestly.

Antoine gave a curt nod, and Martin sensed that earning his respect would take time.

They moved into the château, the group dynamic settling into a professional rhythm. The interior was a mix of faded grandeur and evident neglect. Dust motes floated in shafts of sunlight, and the air held a slight chill.

Gathered around a large table in what had once been a grand hall, they spread out plans and sketches. Martin began outlining his vision, referencing the materials he'd prepared.

"I believe we can restore the château's historical features while integrating modern sustainable technologies," he explained. "For example, we can use geothermal heating to reduce energy consumption without altering the building's exterior."

Jean-Claude examined the plans thoughtfully. "It's ambitious, but feasible," he acknowledged.

Sophie added, "Preserving the architectural integrity is paramount, but we must also consider the building's future viability."

Marie chimed in, "I've researched grants and incentives for sustainable restoration projects. We may have access to additional funding."

Antoine remained silent, his focus seemingly elsewhere. Martin made a mental note to engage him directly later.

As the discussion progressed, ideas flowed freely. They debated materials, techniques, and timelines, each bringing their expertise to the table. Martin found himself energised by the collaboration, the initial apprehensions fading.

During a break, he approached Antoine, who was examining a section of stonework.

"It's remarkable craftsmanship," Martin observed.

"Oui," Antoine agreed. "But time is unforgiving."

"True. But with your skills, we can restore it."

Antoine glanced at him. "Restoration is not just about skills. It's about respect."

"I understand," Martin said. "Respect for the materials, the history, and the people who built it."

Antoine considered his words. "Perhaps you do," he conceded.

They stood in a companionable silence, the weight of the château's history palpable around them.

By the end of the day, they had outlined a preliminary plan. Isabella was pleased. "This is an excellent start," she declared. "I think we're all on the same page."

As they prepared to depart, Martin felt a sense of accomplishment. He lingered for a moment in the courtyard, watching as the team dispersed. The sun was setting, casting the château in warm hues of gold and rose.

"Beautiful, isn't it?" Sophie remarked, joining him.

"Very much so," Martin agreed. "It's easy to see why people fall in love with this place."

She smiled. "Be careful. The Loire Valley has a way of capturing hearts."

"I'm beginning to see that," he admitted.

They walked back towards the village together, conversation flowing easily. Sophie pointed out landmarks and shared anecdotes about the area's history.

"You know," she said thoughtfully, "I think you're going to fit in here."

"I hope so," Martin replied. "It's starting to feel like home already."

As they parted ways, he reflected on the day's events. The initial meeting had gone better than he could have hoped. There was a long road ahead, but he felt ready to face the challenges.

Back at the guesthouse, he found a letter waiting for him, a note from his mum, forwarded by Sarah.

Dear Martin,

I hope this finds you well. We're all so proud of you taking this leap. Remember, even the longest journeys start with a single step. Take care of yourself, and don't forget to call once in a while.

Love, Mum

He smiled, touched by her words. Sitting at the small desk in his room, he opened Sarah's journal and began to write, capturing the experiences and emotions of his first days in France.

In the weeks that followed, Martin settled into a routine. Days were spent at the château, overseeing the initial stages of restoration. He worked closely with the team, their professional relationships deepening into friendships.

He found himself embracing the local culture, improving his French, participating in village events, and even trying his hand at pétanque with the locals. Madame Dubois continued to be a source of warmth and wisdom, her guesthouse a haven at the end of long days.

One evening, as he sat on the balcony watching the stars emerge, he realised how much had changed. The tightness in his chest that had once accompanied thoughts of the future was gone. In its place was a quiet confidence and a sense of belonging.

He thought of Alex and wondered how his friend was faring. Making a mental note to reach out, he felt a surge of gratitude for the people who had supported him on this journey.

The château's restoration was progressing steadily. Challenges arose, as expected, but each was met with determination and creativity. Antoine had become more open, sharing stories of his family's connection to the château. Marie's enthusiasm was infectious, and Jean-Claude's expertise invaluable.

One afternoon, as they stood on scaffolding examining the roof, Martin felt a moment of clarity.

"What's on your mind?" Isabella asked, noticing his contemplative expression.

"Just thinking about how far we've come," he said. "And how much there is still to do."

She nodded. "It's a monumental task, but we're making history here."

He smiled. "I suppose we are."

As they descended, the sun casting long shadows, Martin felt a sense of contentment he hadn't known in years.

That evening, back at the guesthouse, he penned a letter to his mum.

Dear Mum,

France is becoming a second home. The project is challenging but rewarding. I've met some incredible people, and every day brings something new.

I think you'd love it here. Maybe you can visit once the château is restored.

Thank you for your support. It means more than you know.

Love, Martin

He sealed the letter, placing it on the desk. Looking out the window at the moon rising over the village, he remembered the words of the old woman in Hong Kong: *Even the moon has its shadows.*

He understood now. Embracing imperfections, facing fears, and stepping into the unknown had led him to this moment. And it was only the beginning.

3

The days following Martin's arrival at Château de Valmont unfolded in a whirlwind of activity, a blend of meticulous planning, unexpected discoveries, and a growing camaraderie among the team. The initial assessment of the château's condition was a daunting task, requiring a delicate balance between Martin's ingrained need for order and the inherent unpredictability of a centuries-old building. He was accustomed to working with clean lines, precise measurements, and predictable materials. The château, however, was a living, breathing entity, its walls whispering secrets, its floors creaking under the weight of history, the air thick with the scent of time's passage.

He found himself constantly adjusting his expectations, adapting his meticulous approach to accommodate the château's quirks and inconsistencies. Measurements that should have been straightforward were complicated by uneven floors, crumbling walls, and hidden alcoves. Architectural plans, meticulously drawn by long-dead architects, often proved inaccurate; the château's structure had been altered and adapted over the centuries, its history a palimpsest of additions, renovations, and improvisations.

"This is not a building that likes to be rushed," Jean-Pierre had warned, his voice laced with a mixture of amusement and respect. "She has her own rhythm, her own secrets. You must listen to her, Monsieur Longman, or she will make your life very difficult."

Martin, accustomed to controlling every aspect of a project, found this advice both frustrating and intriguing. He'd always approached his work with meticulous precision, relying on detailed plans, accurate measurements, and a strict adherence to deadlines. But the château, he was beginning to realise, demanded a different approach, a willingness to embrace the unexpected, to adapt to the unpredictable, to listen to the whispers of the past.

He started each day with a walk through the château, his camera and notebook in hand, documenting its every detail. He captured the intricate carvings on the stone fireplace in the grand salon, the delicate frescoes fading on the ceiling of the formal dining room, the worn grooves in the oak staircase polished smooth by generations of footsteps. He sketched the layout of each room, noting the placement of windows, doorways, and fireplaces, trying to understand the flow of space, the way the château's inhabitants had lived and moved within its walls.

Drawn to the building's imperfections, the cracks in the plaster, the crumbling stonework, the faded paint, he saw beauty in these flaws, a story etched into the château's very fabric. It was a testament to its resilience, its endurance. A growing sense of responsibility settled over him, a duty to honour the château's history, to preserve its essence even as he prepared to usher it into a new era.

He spent hours poring over old architectural plans, comparing them to the château's current state, trying to decipher the changes made over the centuries. He discussed his findings with Sophie, the architectural historian, their shared passion for the château's past forging a bond between them.

"It's like peeling back the layers of an onion," Sophie said, her eyes sparkling with excitement. "Each discovery reveals a new story, a new perspective on the château's history."

He found himself increasingly drawn to the château's hidden corners, the forgotten spaces that whispered of a time long past. He explored the dusty attics, their rafters filled with cobwebs and the faint scent of lavender, the floors littered with discarded furniture and forgotten toys. He ventured into the dark cellars, the air thick with the smell of damp earth and mildew, the walls lined with empty wine bottles and rusty tools. He even climbed the rickety ladder to the top of one of the towers, its stone walls offering a panoramic view of the surrounding countryside, a vista that hadn't changed much in centuries.

He felt a sense of connection to the people who had lived and worked in the château, their presence lingering in the worn stone floors, the faded tapestries, the dusty portraits lining the walls. He imagined their lives, their loves, their losses, their dreams. He felt a responsibility to honour their memories, to ensure their stories were not forgotten, that their legacy lived on.

Restoring a historic building, he realised, was a delicate dance. It wasn't simply about fixing what was broken or replacing the old with the new. It was about understanding the building's essence, its spirit, its history. It was about finding a balance between preserving the past and embracing the future, about creating a space that honoured its heritage while adapting to the needs of the present.

As he delved deeper into the château's mysteries, uncovering its secrets, feeling its history seep into his bones, he knew that this project was more than just a job. It was a calling, a chance to make a meaningful contribution to the world, a chance to leave his mark on a place that had already touched so many lives.

One crisp autumn afternoon, Martin felt drawn to the château's library, a room he'd glimpsed during his initial exploration but hadn't yet had the time to fully explore. Situated on the second floor, at the end of a long, dimly lit corridor, its heavy oak door was slightly ajar, as if inviting him in. He pushed the door open, the hinges groaning in protest, the sound echoing in the stillness.

The library was a cavernous room, its high ceilings adorned with intricate plasterwork, its walls lined with floor-to-ceiling bookshelves, the dark wood gleaming softly in the filtered sunlight streaming through tall, arched windows. The air was thick with the scent of old paper and leather, a musty, comforting aroma that evoked a sense of history, of forgotten knowledge, of untold stories waiting to be discovered.

He stepped inside, his footsteps muffled by a thick, faded rug covering the floor, its intricate patterns barely visible beneath a layer of dust. He ran his hand along the back of a leather-bound chair, the upholstery worn smooth by countless hours spent in quiet contemplation within these walls. He imagined generations of the de Valmont family, their guests, scholars, dreamers, sitting in these chairs, surrounded by the wisdom of the ages, their minds lost in thought, their imaginations ignited by the power of words.

Moving towards the bookshelves, he was drawn to the silent presence of the books, their spines a kaleidoscope of colours and textures, their titles a tantalising glimpse into a world of knowledge and imagination. He ran his fingers along the dusty spines, the titles a mix of French, Latin, and English, subjects ranging from philosophy and history to poetry and botany. He saw first editions of classic novels, leather-bound volumes of scientific treatises, faded copies of travelogues describing far-off lands, and even a collection of children's fairy tales, their illustrations whimsical and charming.

A sense of awe washed over him, a humbling awareness of the vastness of knowledge, the endless capacity of the human mind to explore, imagine, create. He thought of his own carefully curated collection of architecture books, their sleek spines and modern typography a stark contrast to the chaotic beauty of this ancient library. He realised, with sudden clarity, that his own world, his own knowledge, was but a tiny fragment of a much larger tapestry, a single thread in a vast and intricate web of human experience.

He pulled a random volume from the shelf, a thick, leather-bound book with a worn spine and faded gilt lettering. It was a history of the Loire Valley, written in French, its pages filled with engravings of castles and châteaux, maps of ancient roads and waterways, and portraits of noblemen and women gazing out from the past. He carefully turned the brittle pages, the paper crackling softly in the silence of the library, his fingers tracing the faded ink as if trying to connect with the hand that had written these words.

He spent hours lost in the library, moving from shelf to shelf, book to book, each volume a portal to another time, another world. He discovered journals written in elegant script, detailing the lives of the château's previous inhabitants, noble families, wealthy merchants, artists, intellectuals. He read entries describing lavish balls, political intrigues, romantic trysts, and philosophical debates. He felt a sense of intimacy with these long-dead strangers, their hopes and fears, their joys and sorrows leaping from the pages, their voices whispering across the centuries.

He found architectural plans dating back to the 16th century, meticulously drawn by hand, revealing the château's original design, its evolution over the centuries, the hidden secrets concealed within its walls. He studied the intricate details, the elegant lines, the meticulous craftsmanship, marvelling at the ingenuity of the architects and builders who had created this masterpiece. Evidence of alterations, renovations, improvisations, a testament to the château's ongoing evolution, was fascinating.

Thinking of his own plans for the château, his vision for its transformation, his desire to blend modern sustainability with historical integrity, he realised, with a renewed sense of humility, that he was but one small part of a much larger story. A single chapter in a narrative that had begun centuries before him and would continue long after he was gone. A weight settled on his shoulders, a responsibility to honour the château's past, to ensure its future, to be a worthy custodian of its legacy.

As the sun began to set, casting long shadows across the library floor, Martin reluctantly closed the book he was reading, his mind buzzing with new knowledge, new ideas, new possibilities. He stood up, stretching his stiff muscles, the silence of the library a stark contrast to the bustling activity of his mind. Glancing around the room, its shadows deepening, its bookshelves a silent army of witnesses to the passage of time, he knew he would be spending many more hours in this room, lost in the whispers of the past, seeking inspiration, guidance, and a deeper understanding of the château he was tasked with restoring.

Martin and Sophie huddled over a dusty leather-bound journal in the library, sunlight filtering through the tall windows, illuminating the faded ink and delicate script of a bygone era. Martin, his brow furrowed in concentration, attempted to decipher a particularly cryptic passage, his rudimentary French struggling to keep pace with Sophie's rapid translations.

"It speaks of a hidden room," Sophie explained, her voice hushed with excitement. "A secret chamber concealed behind a tapestry in the main salon. It's said to have been used as a hiding place during the Revolution, a refuge for the de Valmont family and their loyal servants."

She pointed to a faded sketch in the journal, a crudely drawn diagram depicting a hidden door behind a tapestry showing a hunting scene. The sketch wasn't detailed, but it was enough to pique Martin's curiosity, igniting a sense of adventure stirring beneath his usually controlled exterior.

"Do you think it's still there?" he asked, his voice tinged with excitement.

"There's only one way to find out," Sophie replied, her eyes sparkling with mischief. She closed the journal, a cloud of dust rising from its ancient pages. "Come on, let's go investigate."

They made their way to the main salon, a grand room on the first floor, its high ceilings adorned with ornate plasterwork, its walls lined with faded tapestries and portraits of stern-faced ancestors. The room was in a state of disrepair, its furniture covered in dust sheets, the air thick with the scent of dampness and decay.

They found the tapestry depicted in the journal, a faded scene of hounds chasing a stag through a dense forest. It hung on the wall between two tall windows, its colours muted with age, the fabric threadbare in places. Martin ran his hand over the rough texture, tracing the outlines of the embroidered figures, his mind imagining the secrets hidden behind its woven threads. A shiver ran down his spine, a blend of anticipation and apprehension.

He glanced at Sophie, her eyes shining with excitement. She seemed unfazed by the prospect of uncovering a hidden chamber, her academic curiosity outweighing any apprehension. He, on the other hand, was acutely aware of the weight of history within these walls, the countless lives that had unfolded within these rooms, the stories whispered in the shadows.

He stepped back, allowing Jean-Pierre, who had joined them with his toolbox in hand, to take charge. Jean-Pierre, with his decades of experience working on the château, seemed to possess an innate understanding of its structure, its secrets, its hidden rhythms. He had already uncovered a number of surprises during the initial assessment, a concealed doorway behind a bookcase, a bricked-up fireplace revealing a small storage room, and a series of underground tunnels that once connected the château to the nearby village.

Approaching the tapestry with cautious respect, Jean-Pierre gently probed the wall behind it. He tapped lightly, listening for a change in sound, a hollow echo that might indicate a hidden space.

"Ah, voilà!" he exclaimed, a triumphant grin spreading across his weathered face. "There's definitely something behind here."

He produced a small crowbar from his toolbox and carefully inserted it between the tapestry and the wall. With gentle but firm pressure, he pried the tapestry away, revealing a small wooden door, its paint cracked and peeling, its hinges rusted with age. A musty smell wafted from the opening, the scent of dust and damp earth, a whiff of a forgotten world. Martin felt a prickle of unease, his rational mind struggling to quell the superstitious whispers rising within him. He'd heard the stories, the rumours of the château's resident ghost, a heartbroken lady in white who roamed the halls at night, searching for her lost love.

He glanced at Sophie, her eyes wide with anticipation, her smile unwavering. She seemed oblivious to his apprehension, her focus entirely on the mystery unfolding before them.

Jean-Pierre, sensing their curiosity, reached out and slowly pushed the door open, the hinges groaning in protest. A narrow, stone staircase spiralled downward into darkness, the air growing colder, the scent of damp earth and dust intensifying.

"Well," Jean-Pierre said, his voice a low rumble, "shall we see what secrets the château has been hiding?"

The narrow staircase, its stone steps worn smooth by the passage of time, descended into a darkness that felt both ancient and oppressive. The air grew colder, the scent of damp earth and dust intensifying with each step. Martin followed Jean-Pierre, his hand trailing along the rough stone wall, his flashlight beam cutting through the gloom, illuminating cobwebs and the occasional scuttling spider. A shiver ran down his spine, a primal fear of the unknown mixed with a thrill of anticipation.

Sophie, ever the intrepid historian, followed close behind, her own flashlight illuminating the walls, her eyes scanning for any clue, any inscription, any whisper from the past. She seemed unfazed by the darkness, the musty air, the oppressive silence that hung heavy around them. Her academic curiosity, her thirst for knowledge, outweighed any trepidation.

"Be careful, Monsieur Longman," Jean-Pierre warned, his voice a low rumble echoing in the confined space. "The steps are uneven. And watch your head."

Martin ducked instinctively as they reached the bottom of the staircase, finding themselves in a small, rectangular chamber, its stone walls damp and cold, its ceiling low and vaulted. The air was thick with the scent of dust and mildew, a faint aroma of lavender lingering beneath the more pungent smells of decay.

"It appears to be a storage room," Martin observed, shining his flashlight around the chamber, revealing shelves lining the walls, their surfaces covered in a thick layer of dust. "But what were they storing down here?"

"Let's find out," Sophie said, her voice buzzing with excitement. She moved towards a shelf, her flashlight beam illuminating a collection of dusty boxes, their shapes and sizes varying, their contents obscured by years of neglect.

Martin joined her, his heart quickening with anticipation. He'd always loved uncovering hidden treasures, the thrill of discovery, the sense of connecting with the past, the feeling that he was holding a piece of history in his hands. He carefully lifted one of the boxes from the shelf, the wood dry and brittle beneath his fingers. Placing it on the floor, he brushed the dust from its lid, revealing a faded label written in elegant script, "Correspondance de la Famille de Valmont."

He glanced at Sophie; his eyebrows raised in question. She nodded, her eyes shining with excitement. He carefully lifted the lid, the hinges creaking in protest, as if reluctant to reveal their secrets.

Inside, nestled among layers of tissue paper yellowed with age, lay a collection of letters, their ink faded but still legible, the handwriting a mix of elegant script and hurried scrawl. He picked up one of the letters, the paper thin and fragile, its edges browned with age. The letter, dated 1789, was written by a young woman named Celeste de Valmont to her brother, Henri, who was away fighting in the French Revolution.

He began to read, his French rusty but adequate, the words transporting him back in time, immersing him in Celeste's world, her hopes and fears, her love for her brother, her anxieties about the revolution tearing France apart.

My dearest Henri, the letter began, *It has been weeks since I last received word from you, and my heart aches with worry. The streets of Paris are filled with unrest, the air thick with fear and suspicion. The people are hungry, desperate for change, and the whispers of revolution grow louder each day...*

He continued reading, captivated by Celeste's words, her vivid descriptions of the tumultuous events unfolding around her, her longing for her brother's safe return, her unwavering belief in the ideals of liberty, equality, and fraternity. He could almost hear her voice, a delicate whisper across the centuries, her emotions, fear, love, hope, despair, resonating through the fragile paper, bridging the gap between past and present.

Sophie, peering over his shoulder, gasped. "Martin, this is incredible! These letters could be a treasure trove of information about the château's history, about the lives of the people who lived here during one of the most turbulent periods in French history. We could learn so much about their daily lives, their thoughts, their feelings, their hopes and dreams..."

He nodded, his heart pounding with excitement. This wasn't just a restoration project, it was an archaeological dig, a journey into the past, a chance to uncover the hidden stories of the Château de Valmont and its inhabitants. He felt a surge of gratitude towards the de Valmont family, towards Celeste and Henri, for leaving behind these fragments of their lives, a glimpse into a world long gone.

They spent the next few hours carefully examining the chamber's contents, their excitement growing with each discovery. They found boxes filled with old photographs, faded sepia-toned images of families posing stiffly in front of the château, their expressions serious, their clothes formal, their eyes a window into a bygone era. They discovered rolled-up tapestries, their colours muted with age, their intricate designs depicting scenes of hunting, courtly love, and pastoral landscapes, a testament to the artistry and craftsmanship of a time when beauty and functionality were intertwined.

Unearthing a collection of porcelain dolls, their faces painted with delicate features, their clothes meticulously crafted, their tiny limbs frozen in time, Martin felt a shiver run down his spine. Holding one of the dolls in his hands, its glass eyes stared back at him, its porcelain skin cold and smooth, a tangible link to a child who had once played within these walls, whose laughter and tears had echoed through these halls. He imagined a little girl, her hair in ringlets, her dress a miniature replica of her mother's finery, carefully arranging the dolls in a grand salon, lost in a world of make-believe.

He placed the doll carefully back in its box, a wave of sadness washing over him. He wondered about the child who had owned it, their life, their fate, their story now lost to the mists of time. He realised, with sudden poignancy, that the château wasn't just a building, it was a repository of memories, a silent witness to the joys and sorrows, the triumphs and tragedies of countless lives.

They unearthed a wooden chest, its surface carved with intricate floral designs, its lock rusted shut. Jean-Pierre, ever resourceful, produced a small crowbar and, with gentle but firm pressure, pried the chest open. Inside, nestled among layers of yellowed linen, they found a collection of old photographs, their edges frayed, their images faded but still discernible.

They spread the photographs out on the floor, their flashlight beams illuminating the faces gazing back at them across the decades. Family portraits, stern-faced men in military uniforms, elegant women in elaborate gowns, children with wide eyes and mischievous smiles. Photos of the château in its prime, gardens meticulously manicured, fountains sparkling in the sunlight, windows gleaming with life. Even a few candid shots, a group of friends picnicking by the river, a young couple sharing a stolen kiss beneath a tree, a solitary figure standing on the château's balcony, gazing out at the vast expanse of the Loire Valley, their expression a mixture of longing and hope.

Martin felt a connection to these people, their hopes and dreams, their joys and sorrows, their connection to this place that had endured through the centuries. He imagined their voices, their laughter echoing through the halls, their footsteps on the worn stone floors, their spirits lingering in the very air he breathed. He realised that the château wasn't just a building, it was a living, breathing entity, a repository of memories, a testament to the enduring power of the human spirit.

As they worked, they talked, their voices hushed with excitement, their shared passion for the château's history forging a bond between them. Sophie, her academic reserve melting away, shared anecdotes and insights gleaned from her years of studying the Loire Valley and its rich history. She pointed out architectural details in the photographs, identified the fashions of the era, and speculated about the relationships between the people captured in the images.

Jean-Pierre, drawing on his own family's connection to the château, added his layer of knowledge, stories interwoven with local legends and tales passed down through generations. "My grandfather worked here as a gardener," he said, his voice a low rumble echoing in the dimly lit space. "He told me stories about the grand parties they used to hold, the elegant ladies, the handsome gentlemen, the music and dancing that filled the château with life. He said it was a magical place, a place where dreams came true."

He paused, his gaze fixed on a photograph of a young woman in a flowing white dress, her hair adorned with flowers, her eyes shining with a mischievous sparkle. "He was in love with one of the maids," he continued softly. "A beautiful girl with hair as black as a raven's wing and eyes like the summer sky. He used to sneak her flowers from the garden, hide love letters in the hollow of an old oak tree. They planned to run away together, to start a new life, but the war came, and he was called away to fight. He never saw her again."

Martin, captivated by Jean-Pierre's story, felt a lump form in his throat. He thought about his own lost love, the pain that had faded but never truly disappeared, the ache of what might have been. He understood the power of love, the way it could transcend time and circumstance, leaving an indelible mark on the soul, even when it ended in heartbreak.

He looked at Sophie, her eyes shining with unshed tears, her hand resting on Jean-Pierre's arm, a silent gesture of empathy. He realised that he wasn't the only one carrying the weight of the past, the burden of unfulfilled dreams and lost loves.

They packed up the artefacts carefully, their movements reverent, their voices hushed with respect for the lives that had touched these objects, the stories they held within their faded fabrics and tarnished surfaces. Carrying the boxes up the narrow staircase, their footsteps echoed in the silence of the château, their flashlight beams cutting through the darkness, illuminating the path back to the present.

As they emerged from the hidden chamber, blinking in the late afternoon sunlight, Martin felt a sense of exhilaration, a thrill of discovery that rivalled anything he'd experienced in his professional life. This wasn't just a job, it was an adventure, a journey into the heart of a place steeped in history and mystery. He had unearthed not just artefacts, but fragments of lives lived, echoes of dreams dreamed, whispers of love lost and found.

He looked at the château, its weathered walls now seeming less like a symbol of decay and more like a tapestry woven with the threads of countless lives, a testament to the enduring power of human connection, the resilience of the human spirit.

He couldn't wait to see what other secrets the château held, what other stories whispered in the shadows, waiting to be brought into the light.

4

The village of Chenonceaux was just beginning to stir as Martin stepped out of Le Clos des Roses. The church bells chimed softly in the distance, their melody a gentle reminder of the rhythm of life in this peaceful corner of France. The air was crisp and cool, carrying the scent of woodsmoke and damp leaves, a comforting aroma that hinted at the approaching winter. Above, the sky was a canvas of muted greys, heavy with clouds that promised a day of rain and quiet introspection, a welcome respite from the château's relentless demands.

It was Sunday, a day of rest when villagers gathered with family and friends, attended church, strolled through the market, and savoured the simple pleasures of life. For Martin, it was a day to step away from the Château de Valmont, to momentarily escape the weight of responsibility, the pressure of deadlines, and the constant hum of activity that had consumed him in recent weeks.

Over the past few months, he had immersed himself in the world of the château, its history, its architecture, its secrets whispering from the shadows. He had found a rhythm that both comforted and challenged him. Early morning walks, coffee on his balcony, camaraderie with the team, and late-night conversations with Sophie had become his new normal. Their shared passion for the château had forged a bond deeper than he had anticipated. He had even found solace in the physicality of the restoration work, the satisfaction of seeing the château slowly awaken from its slumber, its beauty re-emerging from beneath layers of neglect and decay.

Yet, the conversation with Alex lingered in his mind like a persistent cloud on the horizon. Worry gnawed at him, a dissonant note in the harmony he had found here. He had woken that morning with a knot in his stomach, a sense of foreboding that cast a shadow over the day's promise of peace.

Alex's forced cheerfulness, his focus solely on Jennifer's happiness and the wedding plans, unsettled Martin. He remembered the hesitation in Alex's voice, the uncertainty in his eyes, the way he had avoided certain topics, as if afraid to reveal the doubts that gnawed at him. Martin recognised that feeling all too well, the sense of being trapped in a life that wasn't truly your own, playing a role that felt hollow, suffocating under the weight of expectations.

He had been there before, years ago, with David. He had built his life around David's dreams, silencing his own voice until he lost himself. Escaping that labyrinth had been painful but necessary, a catalyst for self-discovery and a re-evaluation of his priorities. He had constructed a safe, predictable life in Sydney, revolving around work and a carefully curated circle of friends who accepted but never truly challenged him.

But the email from Isabella Reed had changed everything, a siren song whispering of history, beauty, and a chance to create something meaningful. Despite his fears, he had leapt into the unknown, and now he stood in a small French village, the rain beginning to fall in a gentle drizzle. The scent of damp earth rose from the cobblestones, and the sound of his own footsteps echoed in the quiet morning air.

He needed this day, a chance to step away from the château, to clear his head, to untangle the thoughts and emotions swirling within him. He needed to find balance between the demands of the project, the weight of history, the echoes of the past, and the simple beauty of the present moment.

Wandering down the cobblestone streets, he passed the boulangerie with its tempting display of pastries, the fromagerie exuding the pungent aroma of aged cheese, and the flower shop bursting with vibrant autumn blooms. The florist was arranging a display of chrysanthemums, deep reds, vibrant oranges, and sunny yellows, that seemed to defy the grey day. Martin paused to admire the arrangement, the colours lifting his spirits momentarily.

"Bonjour, Monsieur," the florist greeted him with a warm smile. "Would you like to buy some flowers? They brighten even the gloomiest of days."

"Bonjour," Martin replied. "They're beautiful, but not today, thank you."

She nodded, her eyes kind. "Perhaps another time. Enjoy your day."

"Merci," he said, continuing his walk.

Reaching the village square, he paused by the centuries-old fountain at its centre. Its waters were still now, the once-grand sculptures worn smooth by time. His gaze lingered on the intricate carvings and faded inscriptions; layers of history etched into stone. He traced his fingers over a weathered engraving, the stone cool and damp beneath his touch. He felt connected to this place, to the people who had walked these streets, their lives a tapestry woven into the very fabric of the village.

Children's laughter drew his attention. A group of kids, bundled in colourful scarves and hats, chased each other around the square, their boots splashing in puddles. Their joy was infectious, and Martin found himself smiling, the sound of their laughter momentarily easing his worries.

He continued his walk, the rain falling steadily now, a soft, persistent drizzle that cleansed the air and brought renewed vibrancy to the colours around him. His shoulders hunched against the damp; Martin's thoughts remained tangled with worry about Alex.

Crossing the square, his attention was drawn to a small café nestled in the corner, its faded blue awning a beacon of warmth amidst the grey. "Café de la Place" proclaimed the sign above the entrance, its lettering chipped and faded, a testament to the café's long history. A wave of warmth enveloped him as he pushed open the heavy wooden door, the aroma of coffee and freshly baked pastries wrapping around him like a comforting blanket.

Inside, the café buzzed with a gentle hum of activity, the rhythmic hiss of the espresso machine, the clinking of cups and saucers, the murmur of conversations in French, and the occasional burst of laughter. The interior was a blend of rustic charm and homely comfort. Exposed wooden beams crisscrossed the ceiling, and vintage posters adorned the walls, faded images advertising absinthe, chocolate, and travel destinations from a bygone era.

He scanned the room, taking in the mismatched tables and chairs, the worn wooden counter, and the shelves lined with bottles of liqueurs and jars of homemade jams. The space exuded a cosy charm, a sanctuary from the chill outside.

He found an empty table by the window, its surface a mosaic of worn wood, the edges softened by years of use. Settling into the chair, he shrugged off his damp coat and took a moment to simply breathe, letting the warmth seep into his bones. Outside, the rain streaked the window, and he watched as droplets traced erratic paths down the glass.

A young woman approached, her dark hair pulled back in a ponytail, an apron tied neatly around her waist. Her cheeks were flushed from the warmth of the café, and her eyes held a friendly spark.

"Bonjour, Monsieur," she greeted with a warm smile. "Que puis-je vous servir?"

"Bonjour, Mademoiselle," Martin replied, summoning his limited French. "Un cappuccino, s'il vous plaît. Et un pain au chocolat."

"Tout de suite, Monsieur," she said, her smile widening before she disappeared behind the counter.

He leaned back, observing the café's patrons. A young couple sat nearby, fingers intertwined, whispers shared over steaming mugs. The girl's head rested lightly on the boy's shoulder, their contentment palpable. A group of elderly men huddled in a corner, engaged in a lively debate over a game of cards, their laughter rising above the ambient noise. They gestured animatedly, teasing each other in good-natured camaraderie. A solitary woman with silver hair sat engrossed in a book, her expression one of serene contentment. A small dog curled at her feet, occasionally lifting its head to survey the room before settling back down.

Martin felt a pang of longing, a desire for that ease of connection, the comfort of belonging. He had spent so many years building walls around himself, seeking solace in solitude and the predictability of his work. But here, amidst the aroma of coffee and the murmur of conversations in a language he barely understood, he felt those walls begin to crack.

The young woman returned with his order, placing the cappuccino and pastry on the table. "Voilà, Monsieur. Bon appétit."

"Merci," he replied, offering a genuine smile.

He sipped the cappuccino, the rich, creamy flavour warming him from the inside. The pain au chocolat was divine, the flaky layers melting in his mouth, the chocolate a decadent indulgence. For a moment, he allowed himself to simply enjoy, the tastes, the sounds, the ambience. He watched the steam rise from his cup, curling and dissipating into the air.

His gaze drifted to the counter, where a young man worked efficiently, his dark hair falling over his forehead, obscuring his eyes. He moved with quiet intensity, preparing orders with meticulous care. There was something about him that caught Martin's attention, a subtle grace, a hint of melancholy. He noticed the way the young man seemed both present and distant, his focus on his tasks yet his mind seemingly elsewhere.

Watching as the young man cleared a table, Martin noticed the way his fingers lingered on a book left behind by a customer, his touch gentle, almost reverent. An artist's hands, Martin thought, sensitive and expressive.

Impulsively, he approached the counter. "Excusez-moi," he began, his French hesitant but his smile encouraging. "I couldn't help but notice your efficiency. It's impressive."

The young man looked up, surprise flickering in his eyes before he offered a shy smile. His eyes were a deep brown, flecked with hints of amber. "Merci, Monsieur. It's important to keep things in order."

"Indeed," Martin agreed. "I'm Martin, by the way. I'm an architect working on the restoration of the château."

"Ah, the château," the young man replied, his eyes lighting up with genuine interest. "It's a magnificent place."

"Do you have an interest in it?" Martin asked, sensing a shared enthusiasm.

The young man hesitated before nodding. "Yes. I like to draw it sometimes, the way the light hits the stone, the shadows in the evening."

"You're an artist?"

He shrugged modestly. "I suppose so. I'm Luca."

"Nice to meet you, Luca." Martin felt a spark of excitement. "I'd love to see your work sometime."

Luca's cheeks flushed slightly. "It's nothing special."

"I'm sure that's not true," Martin insisted gently. "Art has a way of revealing truths that words cannot."

Luca studied him for a moment before reaching beneath the counter and pulling out a worn sketchbook. "If you like," he said, sliding it across the counter.

Martin opened the sketchbook carefully. The pages were filled with charcoal sketches of the château, each one capturing its essence with a depth and sensitivity that took his breath away. There were detailed studies of the façade, the turrets reaching skyward, the ivy clinging to ancient stone. Interior sketches depicted the grand staircase, the library, the ballroom, all rendered with an artist's eye for detail and emotion.

He lingered on a sketch of the library. The play of light and shadow was masterful, the way the sunlight filtered through the tall windows, casting elongated patterns on the floor. The shelves, filled with aged books, seemed almost alive. In another sketch, Luca had captured the reflection of the château in the still waters of the moat, the image rippled gently, giving it an ethereal quality.

"These are incredible," Martin said sincerely, looking up to meet Luca's gaze. "You have a real talent."

Luca's eyes met his, a mixture of pride and vulnerability. "Thank you."

"Have you ever considered exhibiting your work?" Martin asked.

Luca shook his head, tucking a stray lock of hair behind his ear. "It's just a hobby. Something I do to relax."

"I think your drawings could play a significant role in the restoration project," Martin mused aloud. "They capture the spirit of the château in a way that plans and photographs can't."

Luca's eyes widened. "You think so?"

"Absolutely. Perhaps we could collaborate, use your art to showcase the château's history, maybe even include them in the interpretive materials."

A hesitant smile spread across Luca's face. "I'd like that."

"Great," Martin said, feeling a surge of enthusiasm. "Why don't we meet up later this week? I can show you around the château, and we can discuss ideas."

"I'd like that very much," Luca agreed. "I'm usually off on Thursdays."

"Perfect. Let's plan for then."

They exchanged contact information, and Martin left the café feeling lighter than he had in days. The rain had eased, and a sliver of sunlight broke through the clouds, casting a golden glow over the village. He walked back towards the château, his mind buzzing with ideas.

Passing the market stalls that were beginning to open, he paused to admire the array of fresh produce, plump tomatoes, vibrant peppers, and fragrant herbs. The vendors greeted him with friendly nods, their conversations peppered with laughter and animated gestures. He purchased a small bouquet of lavender from an elderly woman, the scent reminding him of the château's hidden corners where the fragrance lingered.

He couldn't wait to share his discovery with Sophie and the rest of the team, to see their reactions to Luca's sketches, to explore how his art could enrich their project. The possibility of collaboration ignited a renewed sense of purpose.

As he approached the château, its turrets rising above the trees, a beacon amidst the rolling hills of the Loire Valley, he spotted Sophie standing by the fountain. Her dark hair caught the light, and she was sketching in a notebook, her brow furrowed in concentration. She wore a deep green scarf that accentuated her eyes, and her cheeks were flushed from the cool air.

"You're back early," she remarked as he approached.

"I had an interesting encounter," he replied, a hint of excitement in his voice.

"Oh?" She looked up, curiosity shining in her eyes.

He told her about Luca, the café, the sketches, and the unexpected talent he had discovered. Handing her the sketchbook, he watched as she flipped through the pages, her expression shifting from interest to admiration.

"These are remarkable," she breathed. "He captures the château's soul."

"That's exactly what I thought," Martin agreed. "I was thinking we could incorporate his work into the project."

Sophie nodded enthusiastically. "We could create an exhibition space, use his art to tell the château's story. It would add a personal, emotional layer to the restoration."

"That's what I was hoping," Martin said, relieved that she shared his enthusiasm. "I'm meeting him on Thursday to show him around."

"Wonderful. I'd love to join you, if that's alright."

"Of course," he replied, pleased by her interest.

They spent the afternoon discussing possibilities, how Luca's art could be integrated into the visitor experience, and how it could bring the château's history to life in a way that was both authentic and engaging. They walked through the château, envisioning where his sketches might be displayed, debating the merits of various locations.

In the grand hall, Sophie gestured to the high ceilings and expansive walls. "Imagine a series of his drawings here, perhaps enlarged, juxtaposed with historical artefacts. It would create a dialogue between past and present."

"Yes," Martin agreed. "And perhaps interactive displays where visitors can compare the current state with Luca's interpretations."

They climbed the worn steps to the second floor, their footsteps echoing in the quiet. In one of the smaller salons, they found Antoine carefully restoring a fireplace mantle, his tools spread out meticulously. He looked up as they entered, his expression guarded but curious.

"Bonjour, Antoine," Sophie greeted him warmly. "We have something we'd like to show you."

Antoine wiped his hands on a cloth and approached them. Martin handed him the sketchbook, explaining about Luca and the potential collaboration.

Antoine flipped through the pages slowly, his rough hands handling the delicate pages with surprising gentleness. His eyes softened as he studied the drawings. "Il a un don," he murmured. "He has a gift."

"Do you think his work could complement the restoration?" Martin asked.

Antoine nodded thoughtfully. "Oui. It brings a human touch. It reminds us that the château is not just stone and wood, but a vessel of memories."

Martin felt a surge of satisfaction. Gaining Antoine's approval was significant; the stonemason's deep connection to the château lent weight to his opinions.

They continued their tour, gathering input from other team members. Marie was enthusiastic, suggesting that Luca could also contribute to the educational programmes they planned to offer. "Art workshops, perhaps," she proposed. "He could teach visitors to sketch the château, fostering a deeper appreciation."

As the day waned, they gathered in the courtyard, the setting sun casting long shadows. The air was crisp, and the scent of woodsmoke drifted from nearby chimneys. Martin felt a deep sense of contentment, a feeling that he was exactly where he was meant to be.

"You know," Sophie said thoughtfully, "sometimes the most meaningful connections happen when we least expect them."

He glanced at her, noting the way the fading light softened her features. "I think you're right."

She smiled softly. "I'm glad you found Luca. I think he'll be an invaluable addition to our team."

"Me too," Martin agreed. "It's amazing how an unexpected encounter can open up new possibilities."

They stood in comfortable silence for a moment, the weight of the day settling into a peaceful calm. The château seemed to breathe with them, its old stones basking in the quiet energy of their shared purpose.

"By the way," Sophie began hesitantly, "have you heard anything more from your friend Alex?"

Martin sighed, the earlier worry creeping back in. "Not since our last conversation. I can't shake the feeling that something's not right."

"Maybe you should reach out again," she suggested gently. "Sometimes people need a reminder that they're not alone."

"Perhaps you're right," he conceded. "I'll try contacting him tonight."

She placed a reassuring hand on his arm. "I hope everything works out."

"Thank you," he said, grateful for her support.

As they parted ways, Martin walked back to the guest house, the evening air cool against his skin. He felt a mixture of hope and apprehension, the excitement of new collaborations tempered by concern for his friend.

Settling into his room, he composed a message to Alex, choosing his words carefully: *Hey mate, just wanted to check in. Met someone today who reminded me of the importance of following one's passion. Hope everything's going well with the wedding plans. Let me know if you fancy a chat.*

He sent the message and set the phone aside, pulling out Sarah's journal. Opening to a fresh page, he began to write, capturing the day's events, his reflections, his hopes. The act of writing brought clarity, a way to process the swirl of emotions.

As he closed the journal, a soft ping signalled a new message. His heart skipped as he saw Alex's name: *Hey Martin, good to hear from you. Things are hectic but okay. Might be good to talk soon. Let me find a time. Cheers.*

It was brief, but it was something. A door left ajar.

Martin smiled softly, a sense of relief washing over him. Perhaps there was hope yet, for Alex, for the château, for himself.

The following days were a flurry of activity. Martin immersed himself in preparations for Luca's visit, coordinating with the team to ensure that the young artist would feel welcomed and inspired. He arranged for some of Luca's sketches to be displayed in the temporary office, hoping to spark further ideas among the team.

On Thursday morning, the sky was a clear expanse of blue, a stark contrast to the previous day's gloom. The air was crisp, carrying the faint scent of autumn leaves. Martin arrived at the café early, a spring in his step. He spotted Luca through the window, seated at a table, a cup of coffee before him and his sketchbook open.

"Bonjour, Luca," Martin greeted as he approached.

"Bonjour, Martin," Luca replied, standing to shake his hand. He seemed more relaxed today, a hint of excitement in his eyes.

"Ready to explore the château?" Martin asked.

"Absolutely."

They walked to the château, the conversation flowing easily. Luca shared stories of growing up in Chenonceaux, his love for drawing sparked by the village's picturesque surroundings.

"My grandmother used to bring me here," Luca said as they approached the gates. "We'd sit under that oak tree, and she'd tell me stories about the château, ghosts, hidden treasures, tragic romances."

"Sounds like she had quite the imagination," Martin remarked.

"She did," Luca agreed wistfully. "She passed away last year, but I feel close to her when I'm here."

"I'm sorry for your loss," Martin said sincerely.

"Thank you. She lived a full life."

They entered the château, and Martin guided Luca through the grand entrance hall. Sunlight streamed through the tall windows, illuminating the space with a warm glow.

"This is even more magnificent up close," Luca said, his eyes wide as he took in the intricate details.

Martin introduced him to the team, who greeted him warmly. Sophie was particularly enthusiastic, engaging Luca in a discussion about his artistic influences.

They spent the day exploring the château, Luca sketching intermittently, his eyes alight with inspiration. In the library, he paused before a large portrait of Celeste de Valmont.

"She's beautiful," Luca commented, studying the painting. "There's a sadness in her eyes."

"That's Celeste," Sophie explained. "She lived during the French Revolution. Her story is quite tragic."

"Tell me," Luca urged.

Sophie recounted Celeste's tale, the love letters they had found, her hopes and fears, her untimely fate. Luca listened intently, his expression thoughtful.

"Perhaps I could create a series based on her life," he mused. "Bring her story to life through art."

"I think that would be wonderful," Martin said. "It would add a personal dimension to the château's history."

As the afternoon waned, they gathered in the courtyard. The team discussed plans for integrating Luca's work, the excitement palpable.

"I feel honoured to be a part of this," Luca said quietly to Martin as the others chatted.

"We're glad to have you," Martin replied. "Your perspective brings something unique to the project."

Luca smiled, a genuine warmth in his eyes. "Thank you for believing in me."

Later, as they walked back towards the village, Martin felt a sense of fulfilment. The day had been productive, but more importantly, it had reaffirmed his belief in the power of collaboration and connection.

"Would you like to join me for dinner?" Martin asked. "There's a little place by the river that serves the best coq au vin."

"I'd like that," Luca agreed.

They dined at a small restaurant with a terrace overlooking the Cher River. The water reflected the colours of the setting sun, creating a tapestry of gold and pink.

"This place is magical," Martin said, taking a sip of his wine.

"It is," Luca agreed. "I'm glad you found your way here."

"Me too," Martin said, meaning it.

They talked about art, life, and their hopes for the future. Luca opened up about his aspirations, his desire to attend art school, and his fears about leaving the familiar comforts of home.

"Change can be daunting," Martin acknowledged. "But sometimes stepping into the unknown leads to the most rewarding experiences."

"Like you coming here," Luca pointed out.

"Exactly," Martin smiled.

As they parted ways that evening, Martin felt as though he had made a true friend. Luca's passion and openness were refreshing, a reminder of the importance of following one's heart.

Back at the guesthouse, Martin checked his phone to find a message from Alex: *Hey mate, free to chat tomorrow? Could use a friendly ear.*

Martin's heart lifted. He quickly replied: *Absolutely. Call me anytime.*

He settled into bed, a sense of peace washing over him. The threads of his life, once frayed and disconnected, were beginning to weave together into a tapestry rich with possibility.

As he drifted off to sleep, his thoughts lingered on the connections forged, the threads that tied the past to the present, that bound people together in unexpected ways.

He was learning to embrace the unexpected detours, to open himself to new experiences, to find beauty in imperfections. The château was not just a restoration project, it was a journey of self-discovery, of healing, of finding one's place in the world.

And perhaps, he mused as sleep claimed him, that was the most valuable restoration of all.

5

The morning sun cast a golden hue over the rolling hills of the Loire Valley as Martin stepped out of Le Clos des Roses, the quaint guest house he had come to think of as home. The aroma of freshly baked bread wafted through the air, mingling with the scent of blooming lavender from Madame Dubois's well-tended garden. Clutching his ever-present journal, he took a deep breath, savouring the tranquillity that had become a cherished part of his daily routine.

Today marked the beginning of his fourth week in Chenonceaux, and the restoration of the Château de Valmont was well underway. The initial phases had progressed smoothly, structural assessments completed, sustainable materials sourced, and preliminary designs approved by his team. Yet, beneath the surface of this progress, Martin sensed an undercurrent of unease that he could no longer ignore.

As he walked towards the château, he replayed recent interactions in his mind. There was the baker, Monsieur Laurent, who had greeted him warmly upon his arrival but now offered only curt nods. The cheerful waves from villagers during his morning runs had diminished to polite but distant acknowledgments. Even the children who once eagerly approached him to practise their English now kept a respectful distance, their parents watching cautiously from nearby.

"Bonjour, Martin!" a voice called out, pulling him from his thoughts.

He turned to see Sophie cycling towards him, her auburn hair gleaming in the sunlight. She dismounted gracefully, her satchel brimming with rolled-up parchments and notebooks.

"Good morning, Sophie," he replied with a smile. "Ready for another day of unearthing secrets?"

"Always," she grinned, adjusting her scarf against the crisp autumn air. "But first, I wanted to discuss something with you."

They began walking together along the cobblestone path leading to the château. Birds chirped melodiously from the trees overhead, and the river nearby whispered softly as it flowed.

"I've noticed that some of the villagers seem... hesitant around me lately," Martin began, voicing the concern that had been gnawing at him. "Have you observed anything?"

Sophie's smile faded slightly. "Yes, I have. It's something I've been meaning to bring up."

"What do you think is causing it?" he asked, genuinely perplexed.

She glanced at him, her hazel eyes thoughtful. "Chenonceaux is a village deeply rooted in tradition. Change isn't always readily welcomed here, especially when it involves something as significant as the Château de Valmont."

"But we're restoring it," Martin protested. "Preserving its history, not altering it beyond recognition."

"I understand that, and so do the others on our team," Sophie replied gently. "But to many villagers, the château is more than a historical building; it's a symbol of their heritage and identity. There's a fear that the restoration might lead to commercialisation or bring in outsiders who don't respect their way of life."

Martin frowned, considering her words. "I hadn't realised they felt that strongly. I've been so focused on the technical aspects that perhaps I overlooked the personal impact."

Sophie nodded. "It's not that they dislike you personally. They just need reassurance that their traditions will be honoured."

As they approached the château's grand entrance, Martin paused to take in the sight. The morning light bathed the ancient stone walls, highlighting the intricate carvings and time-worn statues that stood as silent guardians. He felt a renewed sense of purpose but also a growing awareness of the responsibility he carried, not just to the project, but to the community that held the château dear.

"Thank you for bringing this to my attention," he said earnestly. "I need to find a way to connect with them."

"Perhaps start by listening," Sophie suggested. "Attend local events, engage in conversations, show them that you're invested in more than just the project."

"I'll do that," Martin agreed. "Are there any events coming up?"

She smiled. "As a matter of fact, there's a market fair this weekend. It's a perfect opportunity to mingle and experience the local culture."

"I'll be there," he promised.

They entered the château, the cool air inside a stark contrast to the warmth outside. The team was already assembled in the great hall, Jean-Claude reviewing blueprints, Marie cataloguing artefacts, Jean-Pierre inspecting masonry samples, and Antoine organising tools.

"Good morning, everyone," Martin greeted them. A chorus of "Bonjour" and nods responded.

"Before we dive into today's agenda, I wanted to discuss something important," Martin began, addressing the group. "I've become aware that some villagers may have concerns about our restoration work. I believe it's crucial for us to engage with the community and address any apprehensions they might have."

Jean-Claude adjusted his glasses, his expression thoughtful. "It's true. I've heard murmurs at the café about worries over potential changes."

Jean-Pierre crossed his arms, his weathered face serious. "The people here value their traditions. They need to know that we're not here to disrupt but to preserve."

"Agreed," Martin said. "I intend to attend the market fair this weekend to start building those connections. Any advice on how best to approach this?"

Marie chimed in, her eyes bright. "Participate actively! Perhaps set up a small stall showcasing some of our restoration plans and how we're incorporating sustainable practices."

"That's an excellent idea," Martin said, his spirits lifting. "We can display sketches, photographs, and maybe even some of the artefacts we've found."

Antoine, who had been quietly listening, spoke up. "Food is a universal language. Perhaps offering some treats could draw people in."

"Now you're speaking my language," Martin laughed. "Though I might need some guidance on local delicacies."

The team exchanged glances, a collective warmth spreading through the group.

"I can help with that," Jean-Pierre offered. "My wife makes the best tarte tatin in the village. I'm sure she'd be happy to contribute."

"Thank you," Martin replied gratefully. "I appreciate all your support."

The day proceeded with renewed camaraderie. As they worked, Martin couldn't help but feel a shift in the atmosphere, a subtle but significant change that signalled unity and shared purpose.

Later that afternoon, Martin decided to take a stroll through the village. The sun hung low in the sky, casting long shadows that danced along the narrow streets. He observed the daily rhythms of Chenonceaux, the laughter of children playing, elders conversing on benches, shopkeepers arranging their displays.

At the corner of Rue des Fleurs, he noticed an elderly woman struggling with a basket of groceries. Without hesitation, he approached her.

"Permettez-moi de vous aider, madame," he offered, his French still tinged with an Australian accent.

She looked up, surprise flickering in her eyes before a gentle smile formed. "Merci, monsieur."

As they walked together, she introduced herself as Madame Lefèvre. "You are the architect working on the château, are you not?" she inquired.

"Yes, I am. My name is Martin Longman."

"A pleasure to meet you, Monsieur Longman," she said graciously. "The château holds many memories for our village."

"I've come to understand that" he replied thoughtfully. "It's a privilege to work on such a cherished landmark. I hope to honour its history and the community's connection to it."

She studied him for a moment. "It is good to hear you say that. Many are wary of outsiders, but perhaps they simply need to see your sincerity."

"I intend to show them," Martin said earnestly. "Starting with attending the market fair this weekend."

"Then I shall see you there," she nodded approvingly. "And thank you again for your kindness."

They parted ways, and Martin felt a spark of hope. Each interaction was a step toward bridging the gap.

As evening approached, he returned to Le Clos des Roses. Madame Dubois was tending to her rose bushes, humming a melody that carried on the breeze.

"Good evening, Madame Dubois," Martin greeted her.

"Ah, Martin! How was your day?" she asked, wiping her hands on her apron.

"Productive and enlightening," he replied. "I've realised I need to engage more with the village, to understand their perspectives and share ours."

She smiled knowingly. "The heart of a community beats in unison when each person listens to the other. It's wise of you to seek that harmony."

"I was hoping you might offer some guidance," Martin ventured. "I plan to participate in the market fair, perhaps with a stall showcasing our project. Any suggestions on how to make it appealing?"

Madame Dubois tapped her chin thoughtfully. "Visuals are always captivating. Displaying before-and-after images could be impactful. And perhaps sharing stories of the château's history that you've uncovered."

"That's a wonderful idea," Martin agreed. "I also thought about offering some local treats to attract visitors."

Her eyes twinkled. "Then you must let me contribute my lavender honey madeleines. They're quite popular, if I may say so."

"That would be incredible," he said gratefully. "Thank you."

She waved a hand dismissively. "It's the least I can do. You're a guest in our village, but more importantly, you're showing respect for our heritage."

They chatted a while longer, with Madame Dubois sharing anecdotes about past market fairs and the villagers' fondness for music and dance.

"Perhaps we could arrange for some live music at our stall," Martin mused.

She clapped her hands. "Now you're thinking like a true Chenonceaux resident! Music brings joy and breaks down barriers."

As night settled in, Martin retreated to his room. He opened Sarah's gifted journal and began to write:

Today, I took the first steps toward truly connecting with the people of Chenonceaux. I've been so immersed in the restoration that I neglected the living history around me, the people who breathe life into this village. Their traditions, fears, hopes, they are as much a part of the château's story as the stones and artefacts. I realise now that to restore the château authentically, I must also become a part of this community, however humble my role may be.

I feel a renewed sense of purpose, not just as an architect but as a steward of something greater than myself. The journey ahead may be challenging, but I am not alone. With the support of my team, new friends like Madame Dubois, and perhaps in time, the villagers themselves, I believe we can create something truly meaningful.

Closing the journal, Martin felt a mixture of anticipation and calm. The path forward was clearer now, illuminated by the understanding that connection and collaboration were the true foundations upon which lasting change was built.

❖ ❖ ❖

The weekend arrived with clear skies and a gentle breeze that carried the mingled scents of fresh produce, flowers, and baked goods throughout the village square. Colourful stalls lined the cobblestone plaza, their canopies fluttering in the wind. Lively chatter and laughter filled the air as villagers greeted one another, children darting between stalls with joyous abandon.

Martin stood before their own stall, a collaborative effort that showcased the château's past, present, and future. Large boards displayed photographs and sketches, some depicting the château in its former glory, others highlighting the restoration work underway. Luca's evocative drawings added a personal touch, capturing the soul of the château through his artistic lens.

A table was adorned with an array of local delicacies: Jean-Pierre's wife's famous tarte tatin, Madame Dubois's lavender honey madeleines, and an assortment of cheeses and breads contributed by other team members. A small area was set aside for live music, where a local trio played traditional melodies on accordion, violin, and flute.

"Everything looks fantastic," Sophie remarked, adjusting a display of antique tools they'd found during the restoration. "I think this will really draw people in."

"Let's hope so," Martin replied, straightening his shirt. "I'm a bit nervous, to be honest."

She smiled reassuringly. "You'll do great. Just be yourself."

As the fair commenced, villagers began to approach their stall, curiosity evident in their expressions. Martin greeted each visitor warmly, offering samples of the treats and inviting them to explore the displays.

"Bonjour, Monsieur Longman," Madame Lefèvre said, appearing with a friendly smile. "Your stall is quite the attraction."

"Madame Lefèvre, it's lovely to see you," Martin replied. "Please, help yourself to some madeleines."

"Merci," she said, taking one. "My husband is around here somewhere. He's eager to see what you've put together."

"Ah, I'd be happy to speak with him," Martin said, a hint of apprehension in his voice.

"Don't worry," she whispered conspiratorially. "He may seem stern, but he's a softie at heart."

Throughout the morning, Martin and his team engaged with villagers, discussing the restoration plans and addressing concerns. Many were intrigued by the sustainable practices being implemented, while others were fascinated by the historical artefacts on display.

"This is a letter from 1789," Marie explained to a group of elderly women, pointing to a carefully preserved document. "Written by Celeste de Valmont to her brother Henri during the French Revolution."

"Mon Dieu," one of the women gasped. "Such beautiful penmanship. It's like touching a piece of history."

Luca stood nearby, sketching portraits of children who eagerly lined up for their turn. His gentle demeanour and talent quickly endeared him to both young and old.

As the day progressed, Martin noticed a figure standing at the edge of the crowd, Monsieur Lefèvre, observing quietly. Gathering his courage, Martin approached him.

"Bonjour, Monsieur Lefèvre," he greeted respectfully.

"Monsieur Longman," the elder replied, his eyes steady. "You've created quite a display here."

"Thank you. We're hoping to share our vision for the château and involve the community in our efforts."

Monsieur Lefèvre glanced around the stall. "I've heard many promises from outsiders over the years. Few have been kept."

"I understand your scepticism," Martin acknowledged. "But I assure you, our intention is to honour the château's history and the village's heritage. We welcome your input."

The older man studied him for a moment. "Words are easy, young man. It's actions that matter."

"Perhaps you'd be willing to visit the château," Martin suggested. "See the work we've done so far, meet the team. Your experience and knowledge would be invaluable."

Monsieur Lefèvre raised an eyebrow. "You wish to include me?"

"Yes," Martin said earnestly. "Your insight could help ensure the restoration aligns with the village's traditions."

There was a pause before Monsieur Lefèvre nodded slowly. "Very well. I will come by tomorrow."

"Thank you," Martin replied, relief washing over him.

As the afternoon wore on, the atmosphere around their stall grew increasingly convivial. The music drew people in, and the shared food fostered a sense of community.

"Martin," Isabella called out, approaching with a bright smile. "This is fantastic. The villagers seem genuinely engaged."

"That's the idea," he grinned. "I'm glad you could make it."

"Wouldn't miss it," she said, taking a madeleine. "Mmm, these are divine."

"Madame Dubois's special recipe," Martin noted. "She's been incredibly supportive."

"She has a way of bringing people together," Isabella observed. "Speaking of which, have you considered organising a community event at the château? Something that invites everyone to participate."

"That's a brilliant idea," Martin said. "Perhaps a harvest festival or a historical reenactment."

"Exactly. It would demonstrate our commitment to integrating the château into village life."

"I'll discuss it with the team," he agreed. "Thank you for the suggestion."

As the fair drew to a close, Martin felt a sense of accomplishment. The day's efforts had not only increased awareness of the restoration project but also fostered connections that felt genuine and promising.

❖ ❖ ❖

The following morning, Martin stood at the entrance of the château, awaiting Monsieur Lefèvre's arrival. The air was crisp, leaves crunching underfoot as a gentle breeze rustled through the trees.

"Are you nervous?" Sophie asked, joining him.

"A bit," he admitted. "This feels like an important step."

"It is," she agreed. "But you've prepared well. Just be honest and open."

He nodded, appreciating her steady presence.

Soon, Monsieur Lefèvre appeared, walking with measured steps along the gravel path.

"Good morning, Monsieur Lefèvre," Martin greeted him.

"Good morning," the elder replied, his expression neutral.

"Shall we begin the tour?" Martin suggested.

"Lead the way."

They entered the château, the grand foyer echoing softly with their footsteps. Sunlight streamed through the tall windows, casting patterns on the polished floor.

"This is the main hall," Martin explained. "We've restored the flooring and repaired the stained glass to its original splendour."

Monsieur Lefèvre surveyed the space thoughtfully. "I remember attending dances here in my youth," he said quietly. "The hall was filled with laughter and music."

"Perhaps it will be again," Martin said. "We're considering hosting community events once the restoration is complete."

They continued through the various rooms, Martin highlighting the work done and plans ahead. In the library, they paused before a portrait of Celeste de Valmont.

"She was a remarkable woman," Martin noted. "Her letters provide a vivid glimpse into the past."

"Indeed," Monsieur Lefèvre agreed. "My family has roots connected to the Valmonts. Stories passed down through generations."

"Would you be willing to share them?" Martin asked. "We aim to include personal histories in our exhibits."

A hint of a smile touched the elder's lips. "Perhaps. It would be good for others to know the legacy."

As they concluded the tour, they stepped onto the terrace overlooking the gardens.

"The view has always been breathtaking," Monsieur Lefèvre remarked.

"It's one of my favourite spots," Martin admitted. "I often come here to think."

There was a moment of comfortable silence before the elder turned to him.

"You've done well, Monsieur Longman. I see now that your intentions are sincere."

"Thank you," Martin said earnestly. "It means a great deal to hear that."

"I will speak with the village council," Monsieur Lefèvre offered. "Encourage them to support your efforts."

"I appreciate your advocacy."

He nodded. "Our heritage is precious. It seems it's in capable hands."

As Monsieur Lefèvre departed, Martin felt a surge of optimism. The elder's approval could pave the way for broader acceptance within the community.

❖ ❖ ❖

Over the next few weeks, the relationship between the restoration team and the villagers blossomed. Collaborative workshops were held, with local artisans contributing their skills to the project. Children visited the château on field trips, their eyes wide with wonder as they learned about their history.

One evening, as the sun dipped below the horizon, casting a warm glow over the vineyards, Martin found himself walking through the village. The streets were quiet, the day's activities winding down.

He passed by the café where Luca sat sketching, the soft glow of lamplight illuminating his focused expression.

"Mind if I join you?" Martin asked.

"Not at all," Luca smiled. "I was just finishing up."

Martin sat down, glancing at the sketch, a delicate rendering of the château framed by autumn leaves.

"That's beautiful," he commented. "You have a real gift."

"Thank you," Luca said, a hint of colour rising in his cheeks. "I've been thinking about compiling my drawings into a book. Perhaps sell it to raise funds for the restoration."

"That's a wonderful idea," Martin said. "I'd be happy to help you with that."

"I appreciate it," Luca replied. "This project has given me purpose."

"You're not the only one," Martin admitted. "Being here has changed me in ways I didn't expect."

"How so?" Luca inquired.

"I came here focused solely on the technical aspects," Martin explained. "But I've learned that architecture is as much about people as it is about structures. Connecting with the community has been incredibly fulfilling."

Luca nodded thoughtfully. "I feel the same. Art was always a solitary pursuit for me but sharing it has been rewarding."

They sat in companionable silence for a while, the quiet of the evening wrapping around them like a comforting blanket.

"By the way," Martin said, breaking the silence. "Isabella suggested organising a community event at the château. I was thinking of a harvest festival. What do you think?"

"That would be amazing," Luca said enthusiastically. "I could help with decorations and activities."

"Fantastic. Let's bring it up at the next team meeting."

❖ ❖ ❖

The idea of a harvest festival was met with enthusiasm from both the team and the villagers. Plans were swiftly put into motion, local musicians volunteered to perform, artisans prepared stalls to showcase their crafts, and families offered to contribute food and beverages.

On the day of the festival, the château grounds were transformed into a vibrant celebration. Colourful banners adorned the entrance, lanterns hung from trees, and the air was filled with the enticing aromas of freshly cooked dishes.

Martin stood at the heart of the festivities, watching as people danced to lively tunes, children played games on the lawn, and friends gathered in joyous conversation.

"This is incredible," Sophie said, joining him with a glass of cider. "Look at everyone, they're so happy."

"It's everything I hoped for," Martin replied, a contented smile spreading across his face. "The château feels alive again."

Isabella approached, her eyes reflecting the warm glow of the lanterns. "Congratulations, Martin. You've achieved something truly special."

"Thank you," he said. "But it's been a collective effort."

"Modest as always," she teased gently. "You should be proud."

"I am," he admitted. "And grateful, for all of you."

As night fell, fireworks lit up the sky, their vibrant colours mirrored in the delighted eyes of the spectators. Laughter and applause echoed through the grounds, a testament to the unity that had been forged.

Madame Dubois found Martin amidst the crowd. "A marvellous event," she praised. "You've brought the village together in a way I haven't seen in years."

"It's been an honour," Martin replied sincerely. "I feel fortunate to be a part of this community."

"You've become more than a part," she said kindly. "You've become family."

Her words touched him deeply. "That means more than I can express."

As the festivities wound down, Martin took a moment to himself, standing on the terrace overlooking the peaceful gardens. The moon cast a silver sheen over the landscape, and a gentle breeze carried the distant sounds of merriment.

"Mind some company?" Isabella's voice drifted softly behind him.

"Not at all," he replied, turning to face her.

They stood side by side, the quiet enveloping them.

"You seem reflective," she observed.

"Just taking it all in," he said. "It's been quite a journey."

"It has," she agreed. "You've accomplished so much."

He glanced at her, a hint of wistfulness in his eyes. "I couldn't have done it without you."

She smiled softly. "I'm glad I could help."

They held each other's gaze for a moment, unspoken sentiments lingering in the air.

"What's next for you?" she asked gently.

"Continuing the work here," he replied. "There's still much to be done."

"And beyond that?"

He considered her question. "I honestly don't know. For the first time in a long while, I'm content not having everything mapped out."

She nodded understandingly. "Sometimes the best paths are the ones we discover as we walk them."

"Wise words," he remarked.

She laughed lightly. "I've picked up a few along the way."

They shared a comfortable silence, the weight of the day settling into a peaceful calm.

"Would you like to dance?" Martin asked impulsively, gesturing towards the faint strains of music still playing.

"I'd love to," Isabella accepted.

They moved slowly, the world fading away as they swayed to the gentle melody. The moment was simple yet profound, a culmination of shared experiences and unspoken possibilities.

As the night was ending, Martin felt a deep sense of fulfilment. The bridges he had built extended beyond the project, connecting hearts, fostering friendships, and perhaps, opening doors to new beginnings.

Returning to his room at Le Clos des Roses, he opened his journal, the pages filled with memories of his journey.

Tonight was a testament to what can be achieved when people come together with open hearts. The château stands not just as a restored structure but as a symbol of unity and hope. I've found a home here, in ways I never expected. The future remains unwritten, but for now, I am exactly where I need to be.

Closing the journal, he felt at peace. Sleep came swiftly, filled with dreams of sunlit halls, laughter, and the gentle whisper of possibilities yet to unfold.

❖ ❖ ❖

Over the following weeks, the restoration continued with renewed vigour. The advisory council, including Monsieur Lefèvre, met regularly, providing valuable insights that enriched the project. The château's transformation was not just physical but emblematic of the community's revitalised spirit.

One afternoon, as Martin oversaw the installation of refurbished stained-glass windows, his phone rang. Recognising the number, he stepped aside to answer.

"Martin Longman speaking."

"Martin, it's Alex."

A rush of emotions surged through him. "Alex! It's great to hear from you."

"I'm sorry it's taken me so long to call back," Alex said, his tone hesitant. "Things have been... complicated."

"It's alright," Martin assured him. "How are you holding up?"

"Honestly? Not great," Alex admitted. "I needed someone to talk to, and I realised I've been avoiding reaching out."

"I'm here," Martin said softly. "Whatever you need."

They spoke for over an hour, Alex sharing his doubts and fears about his impending wedding and the direction of his life.

"I feel like I'm living someone else's dream," Alex confessed. "I don't know how to fix it."

"Have you spoken to Jennifer about how you feel?" Martin asked gently.

"Not yet. I'm afraid of hurting her."

"Honesty is difficult, but it's necessary," Martin advised. "You deserve to live authentically, and so does she."

There was a pause before Alex sighed. "You're right. I need to face this."

"Let me know if there's anything I can do," Martin offered. "Even if it's just to listen."

"Thank you, mate," Alex said sincerely. "I appreciate it more than you know."

After they hung up, Martin felt a mix of concern and relief. Reconnecting with Alex reminded him of the importance of supporting those we care about, even from afar.

That evening, he shared his thoughts with Sophie and Isabella over dinner.

"Sounds like he's at a crossroads," Sophie remarked. "It's brave of him to confront it."

"Agreed," Isabella said. "And it's good that he has a friend like you to lean on."

"I just hope he finds his way," Martin said thoughtfully.

❖ ❖ ❖

As winter approached, the château stood resplendent against the backdrop of frosted fields and snow-dusted trees. The restoration was nearing completion, and plans were made for a grand reopening ceremony.

On the day of the event, dignitaries, villagers, and visitors gathered to celebrate. Speeches were made, ribbons cut, and glasses raised in honour of the collaborative achievement.

Martin stood before the assembled crowd, emotions welling within him.

"Today marks not just the restoration of a building but the culmination of a shared dream," he began. "The Château de Valmont stands as a testament to what we can accomplish when we come together with respect, dedication, and heart. I am humbled and grateful to have been a part of this journey."

Applause filled the air, and as Martin stepped down, he was enveloped by the warmth of the community he now called home.

❖ ❖ ❖

That night, as stars glittered in the clear winter sky, Martin found himself once again on the terrace, the château glowing softly behind him.

Isabella joined him, her breath forming delicate clouds in the cold air.

"You did it," she said quietly. "The château is restored, and so much more."

"We did it," he corrected with a smile. "I couldn't have done it without you."

She looked at him, a question in her eyes. "What's next for Martin Longman?"

He took a deep breath, considering his response. "I'm not sure. For the first time, I'm okay with that uncertainty. Maybe I'll stay here a while longer. There's still work to be done."

She nodded. "I think you'll make the right choice, whatever it is."

He met her gaze. "What about you?"

She smiled softly. "I go where I'm needed. But perhaps I'll stay a bit longer too."

A comfortable silence settled between them, the unspoken possibilities lingering in the crisp night air.

"Isabella," he began hesitantly. "I've been meaning to tell you..."

She placed a gentle hand on his arm. "You don't have to say anything now. Let's just enjoy this moment."

He nodded, a sense of peace enveloping him.

As they stood together under the vast expanse of the night sky, Martin knew that while the future remained uncertain, the bridges he had built, between himself and others, between past and present, would guide him toward whatever lay ahead.

6

The morning sun filtered through the tall, narrow windows of Château de Valmont, casting elongated rectangles of golden light across the stone floor of the grand hall. Dust particles danced in the beams, stirred by the gentle movements of the restoration team as they prepared for the day's work. The atmosphere was one of quiet anticipation, a collective eagerness to delve deeper into the mysteries the château held within its ancient walls.

Martin stood at the base of the grand staircase, his fingers tracing the intricate carvings of the oak banister. The events of the past weeks had invigorated him; the successful town meeting and the burgeoning collaboration with the villagers had infused new life into the project. Now, another opportunity beckoned, the exploration of a hidden chamber they had stumbled upon during initial surveys.

"Ready to unlock some secrets?" Sophie asked, approaching him with a smile. She carried a leather-bound notebook, and a set of delicate brushes tucked into the pocket of her khaki field jacket.

"More than ever," Martin replied, his eyes reflecting the excitement he felt. "I've been thinking about that room constantly. It's time we see what stories it holds."

Luca joined them, his sketchpad under one arm and a camera slung over his shoulder. "I brought the equipment we might need to document everything," he said, adjusting his glasses nervously. "I hope that's alright."

"Perfect, Luca," Martin assured him. "Your attention to detail will be invaluable."

They made their way through the labyrinthine corridors of the château, their footsteps echoing softly against the stone walls adorned with faded tapestries and framed portraits of stern-faced nobles. The air grew cooler as they descended a spiral staircase leading to the lower levels, where the hidden chamber awaited.

"Hard to believe this place has been standing for centuries," Luca mused, his eyes tracing the vaulted ceilings overhead. "Imagine all the people who've walked these halls."

Sophie nodded. "Every stone has a story. We're just the latest chapter in a very long book."

They arrived at an unassuming door, its wooden surface weathered, and iron hinges rusted with age. Martin produced an old-fashioned key they had found nearby, fitting it carefully into the lock. With a creak and a sigh, the door yielded, revealing a dimly lit space beyond.

"Here we are," Martin whispered, almost reverently.

The hidden chamber was larger than it had first appeared. Shelves lined the walls, laden with books whose spines bore titles in faded gold lettering. In the centre stood a large table cluttered with objects draped in cloth stiffened by time. The air was thick with the scent of aged paper and a hint of something herbal, perhaps dried lavender or rosemary long forgotten.

"Let's be cautious," Sophie advised. "Some of these items could be extremely fragile."

They donned gloves and began to carefully remove the coverings from the table. Underneath lay a collection of artefacts that immediately captured their attention: a stack of letters tied with a frayed ribbon, a leather-bound journal, an antique quill alongside dried-up inkwells, and a small locket tarnished with age.

Luca gently lifted the locket, examining the intricate filigree design. "It's beautiful," he murmured. "I wonder who it belonged to."

"Perhaps we can find out," Martin suggested, nodding toward the journal. "Let's start documenting everything."

They set up a workstation, arranging the items methodically. Sophie took charge of cataloguing, assigning numbers to each artefact and noting their conditions. Martin photographed the items from various angles, ensuring they had detailed records. Luca began sketching the room's layout, annotating where each object was found.

As they worked, the initial silence gave way to subdued conversation, each discovery sparking questions and theories.

"Look at this," Sophie said, holding up one of the letters. "It's sealed with wax bearing a unique crest, a rose intertwined with a compass."

Martin examined the symbol. "That doesn't match any of the known family crests associated with the château. Could it be a personal emblem?"

"Possibly," Sophie replied. "We'll need to research it further."

Luca, flipping through one of the books from the shelves, looked up thoughtfully. "I think I found something. This book is a collection of poems and essays, but it's not attributed to any author. And there's a handwritten note on the inside cover."

He read aloud: "'To those who seek refuge in words when the world offers none.'"

A chill ran down Martin's spine. "That's a powerful sentiment."

They continued exploring, and as the hours passed, a pattern began to emerge. Many of the letters and documents contained recurring phrases and symbols, the rose and compass emblem appeared frequently, along with coded messages that hinted at secret meetings and safe passages.

"These aren't just personal belongings," Sophie concluded. "They suggest the existence of a clandestine network."

"A secret society operating from the château?" Luca speculated, his eyes wide with intrigue.

Martin considered this. "It would explain why the chamber was hidden and why the contents have remained undisturbed."

Sophie carefully unfolded another letter, this one more fragile than the rest. The ink was faded but still legible.

"'Dear Emilie,'" she read softly. "'The night is darkest before the dawn. Trust in the path we've set and know that the compass will guide you home. Yours in solidarity, A.'"

"Emilie and A.," Martin repeated. "Who were they?"

Luca scanned the room. "Perhaps there's more here that can tell us."

In a small drawer beneath the table, they found a bundle of documents wrapped in cloth. Inside were maps marked with routes and locations, some crossing national borders.

"These are escape routes," Martin realised. "Look, this one leads to Switzerland, another to Spain."

"During times of conflict, perhaps?" Sophie suggested. "World War II, or even earlier?"

They exchanged glances, the gravity of their discovery sinking in.

"This château may have been part of an underground network," Martin said. "A place of refuge for those fleeing persecution."

The atmosphere grew solemn as they contemplated the implications. The hidden chamber was not just a forgotten room; it was a silent witness to acts of courage and compassion.

"We need to handle this with the utmost care," Sophie stated firmly. "These artefacts are historically significant."

"Agreed," Martin said. "We should consult with experts, historians, archivists, who can help us preserve and interpret what we've found."

Luca hesitated before speaking. "Do you think the villagers know about this? It seems like such an important part of the château's history."

"It's possible that the knowledge was lost over time," Sophie speculated. "Or perhaps it was intentionally kept secret to protect those involved."

"Either way, we have a responsibility to uncover the truth and honour the legacy of those who were here before us," Martin affirmed.

They spent the rest of the day immersed in their work, the initial excitement giving way to a profound respect for the stories unfolding before them. Each item they handled felt like a thread connecting them to the past, weaving a tapestry of human experiences that transcended time.

As the afternoon light waned, casting long shadows across the chamber, Martin suggested they take a break.

"We've made incredible progress," he said. "Let's reconvene tomorrow with fresh eyes."

"Good idea," Sophie agreed, stretching her back. "I could use some rest."

Luca carefully packed away his sketches. "I'll secure the room before we leave."

They ascended the staircase, emerging into the château's main hall where the warmth of the setting sun greeted them. The colours outside had shifted to hues of amber and crimson, painting the sky in a breathtaking display.

"Days like this remind me why I love what we do," Sophie remarked, gazing out a window. "Uncovering hidden histories, connecting with the past, it's extraordinary."

Martin smiled. "It's certainly not your typical nine-to-five job."

They parted ways for the evening, each carrying with them the weight and wonder of their discoveries.

Back at Le Clos des Roses, Martin settled into a comfortable armchair by the window of his room. The village below was coming alive with the soft glow of lanterns and the distant murmur of evening conversations. He opened his journal, intending to document the day's findings, but found himself reflecting instead.

Today, we stepped into a hidden world, a sanctuary preserved in silence. The artefacts we uncovered speak of courage in the face of oppression, of solidarity among strangers. I can't help but feel a connection to those who once walked these halls, who sought refuge within these walls. Their stories are a reminder of the resilience of the human spirit.

A knock at the door pulled him from his thoughts.

"Come in," he called.

Luca peeked his head in. "I hope I'm not disturbing you."

"Not at all," Martin assured him. "What's on your mind?"

"I was thinking about everything we found today," Luca began, entering the room hesitantly. "It's been... stirring."

Martin gestured to the chair opposite him. "Have a seat."

Luca sat down, fidgeting slightly with the edge of his sketchpad. "Reading those letters, seeing the personal items, it made me wonder about the people behind them. What they went through, what they felt."

"I've been thinking the same," Martin admitted. "It's one thing to study history in abstract terms, but quite another to touch the tangible remnants of individual lives."

Luca hesitated before continuing. "I was particularly moved by the diary we found; the one written by Antoine."

"Antoine?" Martin asked, recalling the name from one of the documents.

"Yes," Luca confirmed. "His entries were so personal, so raw. He wrote about hiding who he was, about finding solace among others like him in secret."

Martin felt a pang of empathy. "It's heartbreaking to think of the fear and isolation he must have experienced."

Luca nodded, his gaze distant. "It makes me grateful for the progress we've made, but also aware of how much those before us sacrificed."

They sat in contemplative silence for a moment.

"Do you think we can do justice to their stories?" Luca asked quietly.

"I believe we can," Martin replied with conviction. "By bringing their experiences to light, we honour their memories and contribute to a more understanding world."

Luca offered a small smile. "I'm glad we're on the same page."

"Me too," Martin said warmly. "Your insights are important, Luca. Don't hesitate to share them."

"Thank you," he replied, standing up. "I should let you get back to your evening."

"Have a good night," Martin said as Luca left the room.

Turning back to his journal, Martin added:

Luca's perspective brings depth to our work. His sensitivity and thoughtfulness are assets I hadn't anticipated. Together, perhaps we can ensure that the voices from the past are heard once more.

❖ ❖ ❖

The next morning, the team reconvened in the hidden chamber. This time, they were joined by Marie, who brought her expertise in archival preservation.

"I've contacted a colleague at the National Archives," she informed them. "She can assist us with proper conservation techniques and might be able to help identify some of the symbols and codes."

"Excellent," Martin said. "The more resources we have, the better."

They resumed their work with renewed focus. Marie carefully examined the materials, offering guidance on handling the most delicate items.

"Look at this," she said, pointing to a ledger bound in cracked leather. "It's a register of names and dates."

"Could it be a record of those who sought refuge here?" Sophie speculated.

"Possibly," Marie agreed. "But some entries are written in cipher."

"Another mystery to unravel," Martin remarked.

As they delved deeper, they discovered a hidden compartment within one of the bookshelves. Inside was a small box containing a ring bearing the rose and compass emblem, along with a parchment bearing a motto: *'In unity, strength. In secrecy, survival.'*

"This confirms it," Sophie said. "There was indeed a clandestine organisation operating from the château."

Martin's mind raced with possibilities. "We need to cross-reference these findings with historical events. If we can pinpoint the time periods involved, we might uncover a significant piece of history."

Throughout the day, the team worked tirelessly, their efforts fuelled by a shared sense of purpose. The atmosphere in the chamber shifted from one of mere curiosity to solemn dedication.

As afternoon turned to evening, they gathered their notes and secured the chamber.

"Tomorrow, we'll visit the local archives," Martin announced. "Perhaps the town records can shed more light on what we've found."

"Agreed," Sophie said. "And I'll reach out to some academic contacts who specialise in secret societies and resistance movements."

Luca packed away his sketches, his expression thoughtful. "I have a feeling we're only scratching the surface."

"Which makes our work all the more important," Martin affirmed.

Leaving the château, they walked together under a sky streaked with the colours of dusk. The village lights twinkled below, and the distant sound of church bells marked the hour.

"Do you think the villagers will be receptive to what we've uncovered?" Luca asked.

"It's hard to say," Sophie replied. "Some may welcome the revelation, while others might prefer to keep the past buried."

"Either way, we must approach it with sensitivity," Martin said. "These are their ancestors, their history. We need to honour that."

They parted ways for the evening, each carrying the weight of their discoveries and the responsibility that came with them.

Back at Le Clos des Roses, Martin found himself restless. He decided to take a walk through the village, the quiet streets offering a peaceful backdrop for his thoughts.

Passing by the café, he noticed Monsieur Lefevre seated alone at an outdoor table, a cup of steaming tea before him.

"Bonsoir, Monsieur Lefevre," Martin greeted him.

"Ah, Monsieur Longman," the elder replied. "Good evening."

"May I join you?" Martin asked.

"Please do," Monsieur Lefevre gestured to the empty chair.

They sat in comfortable silence for a moment before Martin spoke.

"I wanted to thank you again for your support at the town meeting," he began.

"It was a necessary step," Monsieur Lefevre replied. "For the good of the village."

"Indeed," Martin agreed. "We've been uncovering some fascinating aspects of the château's history. I believe it may have served as a sanctuary during difficult times."

Monsieur Lefevre raised an eyebrow. "Interesting. Chenonceaux has many secrets."

"Do you know anything about this?" Martin inquired cautiously.

The elder sipped his tea thoughtfully. "Stories passed down, whispers of courageous acts. But memory fades, and some prefer the past to remain undisturbed."

"I understand," Martin said. "I want to approach this with respect."

"That is wise," Monsieur Lefevre acknowledged. "History can be a double-edged sword."

They continued their conversation, the exchange deepening Martin's appreciation for the complexities of revealing hidden histories.

As Martin returned to the guest house, he felt a renewed sense of purpose. The journey ahead would not be easy, but it was a path worth pursuing.

He settled into bed, the echoes of the day weaving through his mind. The château's secrets were unfolding, and with them, the opportunity to honour those who had sought refuge within its walls.

❖ ❖ ❖

The morning sun broke through a veil of clouds, casting a soft, diffused light into the hidden chamber where Martin, Sophie, and Luca had spent countless hours since their initial discovery. The atmosphere was a blend of hushed reverence and intellectual fervour, each team member acutely aware that they were not merely handling objects but touching the remnants of human lives long past.

"Look at this inscription," Sophie whispered, carefully holding up a delicate piece of parchment with tweezers. The document was fragile, edges frayed, the ink faded yet legible. "'Pour ceux qui cherchent la liberté', 'For those who seek freedom.'"

Martin leaned in; his brow furrowed in concentration. "It seems to be a recurring theme. Many of these items are inscribed with similar phrases."

Luca, seated at a makeshift desk fashioned from an old crate, was surrounded by an array of letters and diaries. His eyes scanned the looping cursive of an old journal, fingers tracing the embossed initials on the cover: 'A.D.'

"I've been going through this diary," Luca said softly, almost as if speaking too loudly might disturb the echoes of the past. "It's written by someone named Antoine Dubois. His entries are... deeply personal."

Sophie glanced over, intrigued. "What does he write about?"

Luca hesitated, choosing his words carefully. "He speaks of his journey to the château, fleeing from persecution. There's a profound sense of isolation but also hope. He found solace here."

Martin exchanged a meaningful look with Sophie. "It corroborates our theory that the château served as a refuge."

"Indeed," Sophie agreed. "I've found letters that reference safe passages and coded messages. It appears the château was part of a larger network."

They worked in companionable silence for a while, each absorbed in their tasks. Martin photographed documents, ensuring they had digital records for further analysis. Sophie meticulously catalogued each item, noting any symbols or markings that might be significant. Luca continued to immerse himself in Antoine's diary, his expression reflecting a mixture of empathy and introspection.

"Listen to this entry," Luca said after some time, his voice tinged with emotion. "'April 12, 1942. The walls here are thick, but they cannot shield me from the memories. I am safe, but at what cost? To live in the shadows is to forsake the light of truth. Yet, among these hidden faces, I have found a kind of family, united not by blood, but by the shared burden of our existence.'"

A heavy silence followed his words.

"Antoine was here during World War II," Sophie noted. "It's likely he was part of the Resistance or perhaps a target of the Vichy regime's oppressive policies."

"His writings suggest he was hiding not just from political persecution but also because of who he was," Luca added, his eyes meeting Martin's.

Martin nodded thoughtfully. "It's important that we handle this sensitively. These are deeply personal accounts."

Sophie continued sifting through the documents. "Here's a letter addressed to 'Mademoiselle Colette.' It mentions arranging passage to England and references a contact in Paris."

"Colette..." Martin mused. "Perhaps another person who sought refuge here."

They began to notice patterns, the same names recurring, mentions of clandestine meetings, and references to safe houses. Symbols like the rose and compass appeared frequently, possibly serving as identifiers within this secret network.

"I think we should start constructing a timeline," Martin suggested. "It might help us understand the broader context."

"Agreed," Sophie said. "We can plot the dates from the letters and diaries, see how they align with historical events."

Luca stood up, stretching his legs. "I'll start mapping out the names and connections we've found."

They laid out a large sheet of paper on the floor, anchoring the corners with old books. Using coloured markers, they began to plot the information:

- 1939: The earliest dated letter, referencing the onset of war.
- 1940: Antoine's arrival at the château.
- 1941-1944: Frequent mentions of safe passages, coded messages, and increasing danger.
- 1945: The final entries, filled with cautious optimism about the war's end.

"These documents span the entirety of World War II," Sophie observed. "But some items seem even older."

"Yes," Martin agreed, holding up a parchment dated 1793. "This is from the time of the French Revolution."

"Perhaps the château's role as a sanctuary predates the war," Luca suggested.

They delved into the older documents, discovering that the château had a long history of offering refuge:

- French Revolution (1789-1799): Letters indicating that aristocrats and those targeted by revolutionary forces hid within the château.
- Religious Wars (16th century): Evidence suggesting that Protestants sought sanctuary during periods of Catholic-Protestant conflict.

"This place has been a beacon for the marginalised throughout history," Martin said, awe evident in his voice.

Sophie pointed to a name that appeared in both 1793 and 1942 documents: 'Lafayette.'

"Could this be a familial connection?" she pondered.

"Possibly," Martin replied. "We should research the lineage of the families associated with the château."

As the day progressed, the team became increasingly engrossed in the lives unfolding before them. Each letter, diary entry, and artefact were a window into another time, another soul.

Luca returned to Antoine's diary, feeling a personal connection he couldn't quite articulate. He read silently; his heart heavy yet uplifted by the resilience expressed in the pages.

"'June 5, 1943,'" he read quietly to himself. "'The liberation forces are near. Hope stirs in our hearts, yet I cannot shake the feeling that my journey is far from over. The world outside these walls may not be ready for someone like me, but I must try. Perhaps freedom lies not just in survival, but in living openly.'"

Luca closed the diary momentarily, reflecting on the courage it must have taken for Antoine to pen those words, knowing the risks.

Meanwhile, Sophie and Martin examined a collection of photographs they had uncovered. The sepia-toned images depicted groups of people, some smiling cautiously, others with solemn expressions. They were gathered in the château's gardens, the familiar architecture serving as a backdrop.

"These must be some of the individuals who stayed here," Sophie surmised. "Look at their eyes, there's so much emotion captured."

Martin pointed to a figure at the edge of one photo. "That could be Antoine."

"Possibly," Sophie agreed. "If we can verify identities, it would add depth to our understanding."

They decided to digitise the photographs and use software to enhance the images, hoping to reveal more details.

As evening approached, they took a brief respite, gathering around a small table where Marie had laid out sandwiches and tea.

"This is some of the most meaningful work I've ever done," Sophie admitted between sips of tea.

"Agreed," Martin said. "It's as if we're giving voice to those who were forced into silence."

Luca looked up from his plate. "Do you think we can find out what happened to them after the war?"

"It's worth investigating," Martin replied. "Perhaps local records or archives in Paris might hold some answers."

Reinvigorated, they returned to their tasks. Sophie began cross-referencing names with public records, while Martin reached out via email to contacts at historical societies. Luca continued his deep dive into the personal narratives.

"Here's something interesting," Sophie announced. "I've found a record of a Colette Bernard who emigrated to England in 1943. She became a renowned painter known for her depictions of wartime France."

"That's incredible," Martin said. "Maybe her time at the château influenced her work."

"Possibly," Sophie agreed. "I'll dig deeper."

Luca approached Martin hesitantly. "There's a passage in Antoine's diary that might shed light on his fate."

"Would you like to share it?" Martin asked gently.

Luca nodded. "'August 15, 1944. The liberation forces are near. Hope stirs in our hearts, yet I cannot shake the feeling that my journey is far from over. The world outside these walls may not be ready for someone like me, but I must try. Perhaps freedom lies not just in survival, but in living openly.'"

"Powerful words," Martin said, his eyes meeting Luca's.

"I think he might have left the château after the liberation," Luca speculated. "Maybe he sought a life where he could be himself."

"Let's see if we can trace him," Martin suggested. "He deserves to be remembered."

They searched through immigration records, wartime registries, and any documents that might provide a clue. Hours passed with little success.

"Wait," Sophie exclaimed suddenly. "I found an Antoine Dubois who emigrated to Canada in 1946. He became a writer known for his works on identity and belonging."

"That could be him," Luca said excitedly.

"Let's see if we can find a photograph for confirmation," Martin proposed.

They located an old author bio with a grainy image. The man in the photo had kind eyes and a gentle smile, a face that seemed to match the spirit captured in the diary.

"It's him," Luca affirmed, a sense of closure washing over him.

"This adds a new dimension to our findings," Martin said. "Not only did the château provide sanctuary, but it also served as a starting point for new beginnings."

They compiled their findings into a comprehensive report, noting the connections and narratives they had uncovered. The scope of their discovery extended beyond the walls of the château, touching lives across continents and generations.

As they wrapped up for the day, Martin addressed the team. "I think it's time we consider how to integrate this history into our restoration project."

"You mean share these stories publicly?" Sophie asked.

"Yes," Martin confirmed. "Perhaps create an exhibit or a dedicated space within the château."

"I believe it's essential," Luca agreed. "Their stories can inspire and educate others."

"Agreed," Sophie said. "But we'll need to approach the community first. This history is part of their heritage."

"Absolutely," Martin affirmed. "We'll present our findings to the advisory council and seek their input."

❖ ❖ ❖

That evening, they gathered at Le Clos des Roses to discuss their proposal in more detail. Madame Dubois joined them, her wisdom and connection to the village invaluable.

"Madame Dubois," Martin began, "we've uncovered significant aspects of the château's history that we believe should be shared with the community and visitors."

She listened attentively as they outlined their discoveries, her expression contemplative.

"This is indeed profound," she said after a moment. "The château has always held secrets, but perhaps it's time for them to see the light."

"We want to honour those who found refuge here," Luca added. "Their stories deserve to be told."

She nodded. "I agree. However, some in the village may be resistant. The past can be painful, and not everyone wishes to revisit it."

"That's why we wanted to consult with you first," Martin said. "Your guidance is crucial."

She smiled kindly. "You have my support. I will help you present this to the council."

Over the next few days, they prepared a presentation, carefully considering how to convey the sensitive nature of their findings. They emphasised the themes of courage, solidarity, and the château's role in protecting the vulnerable.

At the advisory council meeting, held in the same hall where they had once faced scepticism, Martin stood before the assembled villagers alongside Sophie, Luca, and Madame Dubois.

He began by recounting their journey of discovery, the meticulous work involved, and the significance of the artefacts. Sophie detailed the historical context, while Luca shared excerpts from Antoine's diary, his voice resonating with emotion.

The room was silent, the weight of the revelations palpable.

Monsieur Lefevre broke the silence. "These are remarkable findings. The château's history is richer than we knew."

"Indeed," Madame Dubois agreed. "It's a legacy of compassion and courage."

"How do you propose we share this history?" another council member asked.

"We'd like to create a dedicated exhibit within the château," Martin explained. "A space where visitors can learn about these individuals and the château's role in offering sanctuary."

There was a murmur of consideration among the council members.

One elderly woman raised a concern. "Some may not wish to expose these secrets. It could bring unwanted attention."

"We understand," Sophie replied gently. "Our intention is to honour the past, not exploit it. We can implement measures to ensure the exhibit is respectful and informative without sensationalism."

Monsieur Lefevre nodded thoughtfully. "Education is important. If we can preserve these stories, perhaps future generations will learn from them."

After further discussion, the council reached a consensus.

"We support your proposal," the council chairperson declared. "Let us work together to bring this history to light."

Relief and gratitude washed over the team.

As the meeting concluded, villagers approached them, some sharing stories passed down through their families, others expressing appreciation for their dedication.

Luca felt a hand on his shoulder and turned to see a middle-aged man with kind eyes.

"Thank you for sharing Antoine's story," the man said. "He was my great-uncle. Our family knew little of his time here."

Emotion welled in Luca's chest. "It's an honour to help tell his story."

❖ ❖ ❖

That night, the team celebrated modestly at the café, the atmosphere buoyant yet reflective.

"To unveiling hidden histories," Martin toasted, raising his glass.

"To honouring the past," Sophie added.

"To giving voice to those who came before," Luca said softly.

As they clinked glasses, Martin looked around at his companions. The journey had been transformative, not just professionally but personally. They had bridged time, connecting with lives long past, and in doing so, had forged deeper connections with each other.

He penned his thoughts later that night:

Today, we took a significant step in honouring the château's legacy. The stories we've uncovered are not just echoes of the past but lessons for the present. In revealing them, we pay tribute to the resilience of the human spirit and the enduring power of compassion. I am humbled to be part of this journey and look forward to the path ahead.

Sleep came peacefully, the weight of responsibility balanced by the satisfaction of purpose. The château stood silhouetted against the night sky; a sentinel of history now ready to share its secrets with the world.

7

The sun had just begun to set over Chenonceaux, casting a warm, golden glow over the village as Martin sat at his desk, immersed in yet another architectural report. Outside the window, the gardens of Château de Valmont were bathed in the soft light of dusk, with a gentle breeze swaying the autumn leaves. The restoration project was progressing well, and although there were still challenges to overcome, Martin felt a sense of accomplishment with how far they had come.

It was in these quiet moments that Martin often found his mind drifting. The château's grandeur, its hidden stories, and the meticulous care required to bring it back to life all felt intertwined with his own journey. But tonight, as he typed up notes and cross-referenced architectural plans, the sharp chime of his phone snapped him back to reality.

He glanced at the screen, expecting a message from Sophie about the next day's site inspection or a reminder from Isabella about an upcoming meeting. Instead, he saw a name he hadn't expected, David.

Martin stared at the notification for several seconds, his heartbeat quickening. David, his ex-partner. It had been years since their last contact, and even longer since they had seen each other in person. Yet, here was his name, lighting up Martin's phone screen as if no time had passed at all. The simplicity of the message, "Just checking in. How are you?", belied the complicated emotions it stirred within him.

He felt a tug in his chest, a blend of nostalgia, unease, and something else he couldn't quite place. Memories of his time with David came rushing back, uninvited but vivid, as though the years between them had dissolved in an instant.

Their relationship had been intense and passionate, but also marked by a sense of control that, in hindsight, had stifled Martin in ways he hadn't fully realised until it was over. They had spent countless hours together, both in Sydney and abroad, including a memorable trip to the Loire Valley, the very place Martin now called home. It was during that trip that Martin had first laid eyes on Château de Valmont. At the time, it had been a romantic backdrop, an idyllic escape from the pressures of their careers and lives in Sydney. But now, standing at the centre of Martin's world, the château took on new meaning, one that had nothing to do with David.

Still, the memories lingered. Walking hand-in-hand through the château's gardens. Sharing quiet conversations over wine in a quaint French café. The way David had always known exactly what to say to make Martin feel special, but also, in retrospect, how he had a way of directing the course of their relationship with subtle manipulations that Martin had been too enamoured to notice.

"How are you?" Martin muttered aloud, staring at the text. It was such a simple question, but it carried the weight of unresolved emotions. He hadn't thought about David in any real depth since arriving in France. The château, the project, his burgeoning friendship with Luca, these things had kept him grounded, forward focused. And yet, here was his past, knocking on the door once again.

He debated responding. Part of him wanted to ignore the message, to let it fade into the background like so many others before it. After all, wasn't that the healthy thing to do? He had moved on, hadn't he? He was building something new, something meaningful, and David belonged in the past.

But another part of him, the part that still carried the scars from their relationship, felt compelled to respond. Maybe he needed closure. Maybe this was his chance to finally lay to rest the lingering questions and unresolved feelings that had haunted him since their breakup.

Martin set his phone down and leaned back in his chair, exhaling slowly. He wasn't ready to respond yet, not without thinking it through. He couldn't afford to get sucked back into a conversation that might reopen old wounds, especially now, when he was finally beginning to feel secure again, both in his work and in his growing relationship with Luca.

He stood up and walked to the window, looking out at the château's silhouette against the fading light. The history of the place always seemed to echo his own experiences, as though the château itself had its own stories of love and loss, of broken hearts and forgotten dreams. In a way, working on its restoration felt like a form of therapy, a way to piece together the fragmented parts of his life.

As he stood there, he thought about David and the effect their relationship had had on him. David had been charming, magnetic even. From the moment they met, Martin had been drawn to his confidence and ambition. But over time, that same confidence had turned into something more controlling. David had wanted things done a certain way, his way. And Martin, in his desire to please, had gone along with it. He had convinced himself that compromise was part of love, that giving up pieces of himself was worth it to maintain the relationship.

But eventually, the pieces he gave up became too many, and Martin had been left feeling hollow, like a shadow of his former self. It wasn't until the relationship ended that he realised how much of himself he had lost in the process. It had taken years to rebuild, to find his voice again, to rediscover the things that made him happy, things that had nothing to do with David's influence.

And now, with a single message, all of that felt like it was teetering on the edge of collapse.

His phone buzzed again, pulling him from his thoughts. It was a reminder about tomorrow's early morning site visit with Luca. The thought of Luca brought a smile to Martin's face, easing some of the tension that had built up since seeing David's name.

Luca was different. He wasn't flashy or overbearing like David had been. Instead, he was quiet, thoughtful, and unassuming. There was a simplicity to their relationship, if Martin could even call it that yet, that felt refreshing. Luca never pressured him for more than he was ready to give. He didn't need to control the conversation or direct their interactions. With Luca, things just flowed naturally, and that was something Martin hadn't realised he needed until now.

But was he ready for something more with Luca? And could he truly move forward with someone new while there were still parts of him tethered to his past with David?

He turned back to his desk, eyeing his phone again. The message from David stared back at him, waiting for an answer. Martin knew he couldn't ignore it forever. He needed to confront his past if he was ever going to move forward, both in his personal life and in his work.

Sitting down, Martin picked up his phone and typed a response.

"I'm doing well. How about you?"

He paused before hitting send, his thumb hovering over the screen. There was no going back once the message was sent. But perhaps this was the step he needed to take to finally close that chapter of his life.

With a deep breath, Martin pressed send.

The message was gone, and with it, a weight lifted from his shoulders. Whatever happened next, he knew he was ready to face it.

He placed his phone down again and glanced at the time. The day's work was far from over, but his thoughts were now more focused. He had a project to lead, a team to support, and a life to build. As the night crept in, Martin felt a sense of resolve. His past with David was just that, his past. And while the echoes of that relationship might still linger, they no longer held the power to dictate his future.

Tomorrow, he would meet Luca at the château, and they would continue their work together. And for the first time in a long while, Martin felt that he was truly ready to embrace whatever the future had in store.

The following morning, Martin arrived early at Château de Valmont, the sun still low in the sky, casting long shadows across the grounds. The air was crisp, and the chill of the late autumn morning felt invigorating, waking him up more effectively than the coffee he had hastily sipped on the drive over. He was grateful for the freshness of the day after the emotional weight of the previous night. His message to David had been sent, but there was no response, leaving a strange emptiness in its wake.

As he stepped into the château's main hall, Martin took a deep breath, allowing the grandeur of the space to centre him. The restoration work was progressing steadily, and there was still so much to uncover, both within the château and, it seemed, within himself.

Luca arrived shortly after, smiling warmly when he saw Martin. There was an easy familiarity between them now, a shared sense of purpose that had grown over the past weeks. Martin had come to appreciate Luca's presence, not only for his artistic talents but also for his calm, grounding influence. It was a contrast to the emotional turbulence Martin had been grappling with, particularly since David's message.

"Morning," Luca greeted, his voice soft in the quiet of the château.

"Morning," Martin replied, smiling back. "Ready to dive in?"

"Always," Luca nodded, setting his bag down near the grand staircase. "I was thinking about the new exhibit layout we discussed. I have a few ideas for how we could incorporate some of the older architectural plans we found in the library."

Martin nodded. "That sounds great. Let's take a look once we finish the site inspection. I also want to go through more of those old documents. There's a story here we're missing."

The château's library had been a treasure trove of historical documents, old blueprints, letters, journals, and personal mementos left behind by generations of the family who had once owned it. As Martin and Luca walked through the winding corridors to the library, their footsteps echoing on the stone floors, Martin felt the weight of history pressing down on him, as if the château itself had secrets to share, if only they knew where to look.

Once inside the library, the air felt different, cooler, more solemn, as though the room held its breath in anticipation of revealing something long hidden. Dust motes floated lazily in the streams of light pouring in through the tall windows, illuminating the towering shelves that held centuries of forgotten knowledge.

Martin moved to one of the long wooden tables, where several of the old journals had been laid out, their leather covers worn and cracked with age. Luca joined him, his eyes already scanning the titles, eager to unearth new insights.

"I was looking at some of these last night," Martin said, gesturing to a stack of journals bound with faded ribbon. "They belonged to one of the previous owners, Madame Elodie de Valmont, who lived here in the late 1800s."

"Any interesting discoveries?" Luca asked, leaning in closer.

Martin nodded, flipping open the top journal. The pages were yellowed but still intact, the handwriting elegant and flowing. "Madame de Valmont wrote extensively about her life here. But what caught my attention were her entries about a man she loved, Henri. He was someone she met long after her husband had passed, but they never had the chance to be together."

Luca raised an eyebrow. "Why not?"

"She writes about how society's expectations, her role as the widow of a nobleman, and the pressure to maintain the château's reputation kept her from pursuing her relationship with him," Martin explained, his finger tracing the delicate script. "It was clear that she loved him deeply, but she chose duty over happiness."

Luca frowned thoughtfully. "That's tragic. To be so close to something you want but feel like you can't have it."

Martin nodded slowly. "It made me think about my own choices. About how sometimes we convince ourselves that we have to sacrifice certain parts of our lives to meet other expectations, whether it's for a relationship, a career, or something else."

Luca looked at Martin curiously. "Are you talking about David?"

Martin hesitated, the question hanging in the air between them. He hadn't spoken to Luca about David in any detail before. It was a part of his life he had been content to leave in the past, at least until David's message had resurfaced those memories.

"Yes," Martin admitted after a moment, his voice quieter. "David and I... our relationship was complicated. When we were together, I thought I was doing the right thing, compromising, adjusting, trying to make it work. But looking back, I realise I gave up too much of myself in the process. I let him dictate things because I thought that's what love required."

Luca listened, his expression understanding but neutral, giving Martin the space to continue without pressure.

"He wanted control," Martin went on, his hands tracing the edge of the journal absently. "Not in a domineering way, but subtly. He wanted things to be a certain way, and I... I went along with it. By the time it ended, I barely recognised who I was anymore."

Luca nodded; his voice soft when he finally spoke. "It sounds like you've carried that weight for a long time."

"I have," Martin admitted. "I thought coming here, taking on this project, would give me the space I needed to move past it. And in some ways, it has. But then he messaged me last night, and suddenly, it feels like I'm right back there, questioning everything."

Luca's brow furrowed slightly. "Do you still have feelings for him?"

Martin shook his head quickly. "No. It's not about that. It's more about what he represents, what that relationship taught me about myself and what I want. Or don't want."

"Sometimes facing the past is the only way to really move forward," Luca said thoughtfully. "It's hard, though. Those old wounds can be tricky to heal."

Martin sighed, nodding. "That's what I'm realising. And then finding this journal, Madame de Valmont's story, it's like a reminder that history repeats itself. People, centuries apart, making the same sacrifices, the same choices. I don't want to be someone who looks back and realises they missed out on something important."

Luca was quiet for a moment, his eyes scanning Martin's face as if trying to gauge the depth of his emotions. Finally, he spoke, his voice gentle but firm. "You're not that person anymore, Martin. You've already started making different choices."

Martin met Luca's gaze, feeling a warmth in his chest that hadn't been there just minutes before. It was a simple statement, but it carried weight. He wasn't the same person he had been with David. He had grown, learned, and begun to rebuild. The fact that he was even here, in France, leading this restoration project and forming new connections, was proof of that.

"I think you're right," Martin said quietly. "But I need to make sure I don't fall back into old patterns."

Luca smiled slightly, a softness in his eyes. "You won't. Not if you keep listening to yourself."

They fell into a companionable silence, the quiet hum of the château surrounding them as they returned to the task at hand, sorting through the old journals and piecing together the history of the château's former residents.

As they worked, Martin couldn't help but reflect on how much his work at the château paralleled his own life. Each layer they uncovered, each hidden detail, was like another step in his own journey of self-discovery. Madame de Valmont's story, in particular, struck a chord with him. She had made choices that led to a life of unfulfilled love, a life where duty and expectation had outweighed her own desires.

Martin didn't want that to be his story. He didn't want to be someone who looked back with regret, wishing he had made different choices, wishing he had pursued the things that truly mattered to him. And as he glanced at Luca, who was quietly flipping through one of the journals with a look of deep concentration, Martin realised that this was his moment to choose differently.

The past didn't have to dictate the future. David didn't have to have a hold over him anymore. What mattered now was the choices he made going forward, the relationships he nurtured, the career decisions he embraced, and the life he wanted to build, free from the constraints of his old self.

Martin stood, stretching his arms as he looked down at the stacks of journals still waiting to be explored. "I think we're onto something with these," he said, his voice lighter now. "There's a story here that needs to be told."

Luca looked up, his eyes bright with curiosity. "Yeah, I think you're right. We're only scratching the surface."

Martin nodded, feeling a sense of purpose reignite within him. "Let's keep going. There's more to uncover."

They worked in tandem, sifting through the pages of history, uncovering personal truths not only about the château but about themselves. And as the day wore on, Martin felt a quiet certainty settle in his heart, he was no longer bound by the past. He was free to write his own story, on his own terms.

The sun had long since set by the time Martin and Luca wrapped up their work in the library. The soft glow of the lamps illuminated the scattered journals and documents on the table, but outside, the world was cloaked in darkness. The once bustling château now stood still, with only the occasional creak of old wood or the whisper of wind through the cracked window to break the silence.

"That's enough for today, I think," Martin said, closing the leather-bound journal he had been reading. His voice sounded louder in the quiet, making him feel oddly self-conscious.

Luca glanced up from his notebook, where he had been sketching ideas for a future exhibit. "Yeah, we've made good progress. There's still so much to uncover, though."

"Definitely," Martin agreed, stretching his arms as he stood. His body was stiff from sitting for hours, but his mind was more restless than fatigued. He could feel the weight of unspoken words pressing on his chest, and it had been growing heavier all day.

The conversation earlier about David had opened a door that Martin wasn't sure how to close, or if he even wanted to. He had been holding back for weeks, letting his past remain locked away, but the more time he spent with Luca, the harder it became to ignore the desire to be honest, not just about his past, but about his present feelings as well.

"You heading back to the village tonight?" Luca asked, standing and gathering his things.

"Yeah, I'll walk back," Martin said, his eyes following Luca's movements as he slid his sketchbook into his bag. He hesitated before speaking again. "Luca, before you go... do you have a minute? I wanted to talk about something."

Luca paused, his hand resting on the strap of his bag, his eyes curious. "Of course. What's on your mind?"

Martin's stomach twisted. He wasn't used to these moments, moments of vulnerability, of baring his soul. With David, it had always felt safer to keep his emotions in check, to not reveal too much of himself. But Luca was different. There was something about Luca that made him feel like he could finally exhale, let down his guard, and just... be.

"Let's sit for a minute," Martin said, motioning to the worn leather armchairs by the window. He walked over and sat down, feeling the cool leather beneath him. Luca followed, his eyes never leaving Martin's face.

Martin ran a hand through his hair, trying to find the right words. "I've been thinking a lot about what we talked about earlier. About David and about... well, everything."

Luca nodded, his expression open but patient, waiting for Martin to continue.

"I haven't really talked much about him since we broke up," Martin admitted, his voice quieter now, as though saying David's name aloud could summon the past back into the room. "And honestly, I didn't want to. It was easier to just move on, to focus on work, on the next project, on anything that wasn't... him."

Luca listened, his face soft with understanding. He didn't rush Martin or fill the silence with unnecessary words, and for that, Martin was grateful.

"But when I got that message from him last night, it just, " Martin paused, searching for the right way to explain what he was feeling. "It brought up everything I thought I'd already dealt with. All the doubts, all the mistakes. And it made me realise that maybe I haven't moved on as much as I thought I had."

Luca's brow furrowed slightly. "You said earlier that you don't have feelings for him anymore. Is that still true?"

Martin nodded quickly. "Yes, absolutely. It's not about that. I don't want to be with him. It's more about... what he represents, I guess. When I was with David, I let so much of myself go. I compromised on things that were important to me, things that I didn't even realise I cared about until it was too late."

He leaned forward slightly, his elbows resting on his knees. "It's not that David was a bad person. He wasn't. But he had this way of making everything about him, his career, his choices, his life. And I just... fit into that. I never stood up for what I wanted because I thought love was about making those kinds of sacrifices."

Luca was silent for a moment before he spoke. "And now you're realising that maybe it wasn't."

"Exactly," Martin said, his voice heavy with emotion. "I thought I was doing the right thing, but in the end, I lost myself. And after we broke up, I promised myself I'd never let that happen again."

Luca shifted slightly in his chair, leaning forward to mirror Martin's posture. "It sounds like you learned a lot from that experience. But it also sounds like you're still carrying the weight of it."

"I think I am," Martin admitted. "And it's affecting how I move forward. It's making me afraid to… to let anyone else in, I guess."

Luca's eyes were soft, his voice steady. "Do you think that's why you've been holding back? With me, I mean."

Martin's breath caught in his chest. There it was, the unspoken truth between them, laid bare.

He hadn't meant to keep Luca at a distance. In fact, the thought of pushing Luca away was the last thing he wanted. But there had always been something holding him back, a quiet fear that he wasn't ready, that he would make the same mistakes, that he would lose himself again.

"I think so," Martin said, his voice barely above a whisper. "I'm scared, Luca. Scared that I'll mess it up. Scared that I'm not ready. And scared that… maybe I'm still too tied to the past to move forward with anyone."

Luca's gaze never wavered. He sat there, absorbing Martin's words with a quiet intensity, before speaking softly. "I can't tell you what you should or shouldn't feel, Martin. But I do know that you're not the same person you were with David. You've grown, and you've learned from that experience. You're more aware now of what you want and what you don't want. And that's important."

Martin nodded, though his chest still felt tight. He had heard those words before, in some form or another. Friends, even Alex, had tried to reassure him that he was different now, that he had learned and grown. But the fear of repeating his past mistakes still gnawed at him.

"You don't have to be perfect," Luca continued, his voice gentle but firm. "None of us are. And I don't expect you to have it all figured out. But if there's one thing I've learned, it's that you can't let fear keep you from taking a step forward. If you do, you'll always be stuck in the same place."

Martin looked down at his hands, turning Luca's words over in his mind. He knew Luca was right. He had been holding himself back, not because he didn't want something with Luca, but because he was afraid of where it might lead, afraid of opening himself up again.

But what Luca was offering wasn't the same as what David had offered. Luca wasn't asking Martin to fit into some pre-constructed idea of a relationship. He wasn't pushing, wasn't controlling. He was simply… there. And that, Martin realised, was what made it different.

Luca wasn't trying to change him. He wasn't trying to dictate what their relationship should look like. He was giving Martin the space to be himself, to grow and explore without pressure. It was something Martin hadn't experienced before, something that, now that he thought about it, felt profoundly liberating.

"I don't want to be stuck in the past," Martin said, finally meeting Luca's gaze. "And I don't want to hold back with you. I've just… I've been scared."

Luca's lips curved into a small, understanding smile. "I get it. And for what it's worth, I've been scared too."

Martin blinked, surprised. "You have?"

"Of course," Luca said, his voice soft but steady. "I haven't exactly had the easiest time with relationships either. But I like being around you, Martin. And I don't want to let fear keep me from getting to know you more."

The vulnerability in Luca's words hit Martin like a wave, washing over him and dissolving the last of his reservations. Luca wasn't perfect, and neither was he, but maybe that was the point. Maybe relationships weren't about fitting into some idealised version of love, but about two people figuring it out together, imperfections and all.

"I like being around you too," Martin said, his voice quiet but sure. "And I don't want to hold back anymore."

Luca's smile widened slightly, his eyes reflecting a mix of relief and something deeper, something that made Martin's heart ache in the best possible way.

"Then let's not," Luca said simply.

They sat there in silence for a moment, the air between them lighter now, charged with a quiet sense of possibility. For the first time in a long while, Martin felt like he could breathe easily, like the weight of his past was finally starting to lift.

Luca stood first, extending a hand toward Martin. "Come on, let's walk back to the village. We could both use some fresh air."

Martin smiled, taking Luca's hand and letting him pull him to his feet. As they made their way out of the château and into the crisp night air, Martin felt a sense of clarity settling over him.

He wasn't defined by his past, and he wasn't bound to repeat the same mistakes.

For the first time in years, he felt like he was finally ready to move forward, one step at a time.

The sun had begun its steady rise over the Loire Valley, casting a soft, golden light across Château de Valmont. The mist that usually clung to the fields had dissipated, leaving the air crisp and clear. Inside the château, the sounds of daily activity were already beginning to stir, workers preparing for the day, tools clattering softly in the distance, and the faint hum of conversations from the project team.

Martin arrived early, his footsteps echoing in the grand hall as he took in the space around him. He felt lighter today, his mind clearer, as if the confession he had shared with Luca the previous night had lifted a burden he hadn't realised he had been carrying for so long. For weeks, his thoughts had been clouded by doubts, about his past, his relationship with David, and the nagging fear of repeating old mistakes. But now, he felt a renewed sense of direction.

This wasn't just about restoration anymore; it was about finding himself again. The château, with its history and secrets, had become a reflection of his own journey, both professional and personal. It was as though; in restoring the château, Martin was also restoring parts of himself.

As he stood in the hall, admiring the work they had accomplished so far, Isabella Reed, the passionate project manager from GreenEarth Innovations, approached him with a clipboard in hand.

"Morning, Martin," she greeted with a bright smile. "You're here early, as usual."

"Morning, Isabella," Martin replied, smiling back. "I guess I just couldn't stay away. There's always something to do."

Isabella nodded, her eyes scanning the notes on her clipboard. "Well, we've made great progress, but I wanted to talk to you about some updates. We're getting more attention from potential sponsors, especially after the success of the preliminary tours we've been offering. The château's story is really resonating with people."

"That's great news," Martin said, feeling a swell of pride. "The more support we get, the better we can ensure the château's long-term sustainability."

"Exactly," Isabella agreed. "But there's one thing I wanted to discuss with you. Some of the sponsors are interested in expanding the visitor experience to include more modern attractions, things like virtual reality tours and interactive digital exhibits. I know we've been focused on preserving the château's historical authenticity, so I wanted to get your thoughts on how we might balance that with these newer ideas."

Martin paused, considering her words. The idea of incorporating modern technology into the restoration had been something they'd discussed briefly at the beginning of the project, but he hadn't given it much thought since then. His initial instinct had always been to protect the integrity of the château, to preserve its history as authentically as possible. But now, as he looked around the space, he realised that this restoration wasn't just about looking back, it was also about moving forward.

"We'll need to be careful with how we integrate those elements," Martin said thoughtfully. "I think it's possible to find a balance between historical authenticity and modern innovation, but we'll have to make sure that whatever we add enhances the experience rather than detracts from it."

Isabella smiled, clearly pleased with his response. "That's exactly what I was hoping you'd say. I think with your leadership, we can create something really special here, something that bridges the past and the future."

Martin nodded, feeling a sense of excitement building within him. For so long, he had been focused on preserving the past, both at the château and in his own life. But now, with this new sense of purpose, he felt ready to embrace the possibilities of the future.

As Isabella continued with her updates, Luca arrived, his usual sketchbook in hand. He flashed Martin a warm smile, and Martin felt a flicker of something deeper, an unspoken understanding between them, a connection that had only grown stronger since their conversation the night before.

"Morning," Luca greeted, joining the conversation. "Did I miss anything important?"

"Just discussing some potential updates to the visitor experience," Martin explained. "We're thinking about adding some modern elements, virtual reality, interactive exhibits, while still keeping the focus on the château's history."

Luca raised an eyebrow, intrigued. "That could be interesting. If done right, it could really enhance the storytelling aspect of the restoration."

"That's what we're hoping for," Isabella said, handing Luca one of the brochures they had been using to promote the château's tours. "We're getting a lot of interest from people who want to see the château's history brought to life in new ways."

Luca glanced at the brochure, then back at Martin. "Sounds like you've got some big decisions to make."

Martin smiled. "Yeah, but I'm ready for it."

After Isabella left to attend to other matters, Martin and Luca made their way to the château's library, where they had been spending a lot of their time recently. The library was one of the most fascinating parts of the château, not just for its collection of old books and documents, but for the stories it held, stories that had been forgotten over the centuries.

As they entered the room, the familiar scent of aged paper and leather greeted them. Sunlight streamed through the tall windows, illuminating the dust motes that danced in the air. The library was quiet, almost reverent, as if the space itself was waiting to reveal its secrets.

"We've found so much here already," Luca remarked as they walked toward the table where they had left their research the previous day. "But I feel like there's still more to uncover."

"I think you're right," Martin agreed. "There's a depth to this place that goes beyond just its architecture. The people who lived here left their mark, and I want to make sure we capture that in the restoration."

They settled at the table, surrounded by stacks of journals, blueprints, and personal letters from the château's previous inhabitants. As they began sorting through the materials, Luca pulled out one of his sketches, an intricate drawing of the château's exterior, but with subtle details that hinted at the lives that had once filled its halls.

"This is beautiful," Martin said, admiring the sketch. "You've really captured the spirit of the place."

"Thanks," Luca replied, his voice soft. "I've been thinking a lot about how to convey the emotional history of the château, not just the physical details, but the stories behind them."

Martin glanced at Luca, feeling a wave of admiration. Luca's ability to see beyond the surface, to connect with the emotional layers of the château, was something Martin had come to deeply appreciate. It was also something that resonated with his own journey, his desire to move beyond the surface of his life and confront the emotions he had buried for so long.

"I think that's exactly what we need to do," Martin said. "The architecture, the restoration, it's all important. But what's really going to make this place come alive is the stories of the people who lived here. Their joys, their struggles, their sacrifices."

Luca nodded, his eyes thoughtful. "Like Madame de Valmont and her story about Henri. She lived here for years, and yet she never felt free to pursue the life she wanted. Her story needs to be told."

"Exactly," Martin agreed. "And it's not just her. There are so many others, people whose lives were intertwined with this place. If we can bring their stories to light, I think it will make the restoration that much more meaningful."

As they continued their work, Martin felt a growing sense of excitement. This project was no longer just about restoring a building, it was about restoring the emotional and personal history of the château, about giving voice to the people who had once called it home. And in doing so, it was also helping Martin restore parts of himself.

After a while, they took a break, stepping outside to the gardens to enjoy the fresh air. The day had warmed up, and the sun felt good on their faces as they walked through the carefully tended paths. The gardens, like the château, were a blend of old and new, restored to their original grandeur but with touches of modern landscaping that enhanced their beauty.

As they walked, Luca glanced over at Martin, his expression thoughtful. "You seem different today," he observed. "Lighter, somehow."

Martin smiled, feeling the truth of Luca's words. "I guess I just feel like I'm finally moving in the right direction. For a while, I wasn't sure what I was doing, whether I was holding on to the past or if I was ready to move forward. But after last night... I don't know. It feels like something clicked."

Luca nodded, his eyes warm. "I'm glad. You deserve to feel that way."

They continued walking in companionable silence, the sound of their footsteps mingling with the rustling of leaves and the distant hum of the château's activity. For the first time in a long time, Martin felt at peace, not just with his work, but with himself. The doubts that had plagued him, the fear of repeating past mistakes, seemed to have quieted. He was no longer afraid of what the future might hold. Instead, he was eager to embrace it.

As they reached the far edge of the garden, where the château's walls met the forest beyond, Martin turned to Luca, his expression serious but calm. "I know I've been holding back with you. I didn't realise how much until last night, but I see it now."

Luca didn't say anything, waiting for Martin to continue.

"I don't want to hold back anymore," Martin said, his voice steady. "I want to see where this goes, with us, with everything."

Luca's smile was slow and genuine, lighting up his face in a way that made Martin's heart ache with warmth. "Me too," Luca said simply.

They stood there for a moment, the connection between them solidifying in the quiet, natural way that had always defined their relationship. There was no pressure, no need to rush. Just an understanding that they were both ready to take the next step, whatever that might look like.

As they turned back toward the château, Martin felt a renewed sense of purpose, not just in his work, but in his life. The restoration project, his relationship with Luca, even his unresolved feelings about David, it all felt like pieces of a larger puzzle that were finally starting to fall into place.

The past would always be there, but it no longer had the power to hold him back. Martin was ready to move forward, to embrace the future with an open heart and a clear mind.

And for the first time in a long while, he felt truly free.

The following weekend, Martin and Luca decided to take a brief break from the hustle and bustle of the château's restoration work. After weeks of long hours spent uncovering historical treasures, drafting plans, and meeting with the various teams, they both felt the need for a change of scenery, a chance to step back and regain some perspective. Martin had suggested a trip to a nearby town, Amboise, known for its mediaeval charm, rich history, and quiet cafés along the river.

The drive through the Loire Valley was serene, the landscape stretching out before them like a series of postcards, vineyards, rolling hills, and quaint villages that seemed untouched by time. The autumn leaves, now in full bloom with fiery reds and oranges, swirled gently in the wind as they passed through narrow country roads.

Sitting in the passenger seat, Luca was quiet for most of the journey, his sketchbook resting on his lap as he occasionally glanced out the window. Martin, too, was content with the silence between them, allowing his mind to wander. The week had been filled with significant moments, both in terms of their work at the château and the personal shifts between them, and now, he felt like he was standing on the edge of something new.

As they approached Amboise, the sight of the town's famous château, Château d'Amboise, rose against the skyline, its towering spires and majestic stone walls reflecting in the calm waters of the Loire River. Martin parked the car near the riverbank, and the two of them stepped out into the crisp afternoon air.

"Wow," Luca murmured, gazing up at the château. "It's even more impressive in person."

"It is," Martin agreed, following Luca's gaze. "I've always found this place inspiring. There's something about the way history seems to linger in the air here."

They walked together along the river's edge, the sound of water lapping gently against the shore mingling with the distant chatter of tourists and locals enjoying their weekend. The tranquillity of the town felt like a welcome contrast to the intensity of their work at Château de Valmont.

After a while, they found a small café with outdoor seating, where they ordered coffee and settled in to watch the world go by. The tables around them were filled with people enjoying the afternoon sun, families, couples, friends, but there was an unhurried, peaceful atmosphere that allowed Martin to finally exhale. He realised, in that moment, just how much he had needed this break. The constant pressure of managing the château's restoration, combined with his own emotional journey, had weighed heavily on him, and now, here in Amboise, he could finally breathe freely again.

Luca seemed to sense this as well. "It's nice to just sit and take it all in, isn't it?" he said, sipping his coffee.

"Yeah," Martin replied, leaning back in his chair and letting the sun warm his face. "I didn't realise how much I needed this."

Luca glanced at him, his expression thoughtful. "You've been working hard. And not just on the restoration."

Martin raised an eyebrow. "What do you mean?"

"I mean," Luca said, setting his cup down, "that you've been working on yourself too. I've seen it, how you've been dealing with everything that's come up, especially with David and all the emotions that surfaced after his message. It's not easy to face those things, but you've been doing it."

Martin thought about that for a moment, realising that Luca was right. Over the past few weeks, he had been confronting parts of himself that he had buried for a long time, his past with David, the doubts he had about moving forward, and his fears of repeating old mistakes. It hadn't been easy, but it had been necessary.

"Yeah," Martin said softly. "I guess I have."

"And now," Luca continued, a smile tugging at the corner of his mouth, "you're in a different place. You've made choices, and you've allowed yourself to move forward. That's something to be proud of."

Martin looked at Luca, feeling a warmth spread through him that had nothing to do with the coffee or the sunlight. "Thanks, Luca. That means a lot coming from you."

Luca's eyes sparkled with quiet understanding. "I'm just glad I get to be here with you, seeing it happen."

The conversation fell into a comfortable silence after that, each of them lost in their own thoughts as they watched the river flow by. Martin couldn't help but think about how far he had come, not just in the months since starting the château's restoration, but in his journey as a whole. The project had become a metaphor for his life, something that required care, patience, and attention to detail. It was about preserving the past, yes, but also about finding ways to build something new, something lasting.

After their coffee, they wandered through the town's cobblestone streets, exploring the local shops and admiring the mediaeval architecture that lined the narrow alleys. As they strolled through the market square, Luca spotted an art gallery tucked away in a small corner of the square.

"Let's check it out," Luca said, his face lighting up with curiosity.

The gallery was modest in size but filled with vibrant works of art, paintings, sculptures, and mixed-media pieces that reflected both the historical and modern influences of the region. As they wandered through the space, Luca gravitated toward a series of abstract paintings that depicted the Loire Valley in sweeping, vivid colours.

"This is incredible," Luca murmured, his eyes fixed on one of the pieces. "It's like the artist captured the spirit of the place, not just the landscape."

Martin stood beside him, admiring the work. "It's amazing how much emotion can come through in art like this."

Luca nodded, his gaze never leaving the painting. "It reminds me of what we're trying to do at Château de Valmont, bringing the history to life in a way that resonates with people on a deeper level."

"Exactly," Martin said. "It's not just about preserving the physical structure. It's about telling the story, making people feel something."

They spent the next hour wandering through the gallery, discussing the various pieces and drawing parallels between the art and the work they were doing at the château. It was a conversation that flowed naturally, effortlessly, and Martin found himself feeling increasingly connected to Luca, not just as a collaborator on the project, but as a partner in this journey they were both on.

As they left the gallery and made their way back to the car, the sun was beginning to set, casting a warm glow over the town. The drive back to Chenonceaux was quiet but comfortable, both of them content with the day they had spent together.

When they arrived back at the château, the familiar sight of the grand estate greeted them, its stone walls bathed in the soft light of dusk. The workers had long since left for the day, leaving the château peaceful and still.

Martin and Luca walked side by side toward the château's entrance, their footsteps crunching softly on the gravel path.

"I'm glad we took the day off," Martin said, glancing over at Luca. "I feel like I have a clearer head now."

"Me too," Luca agreed. "Sometimes stepping away is the best way to find clarity."

They paused at the entrance, the massive wooden doors looming in front of them. Martin turned to Luca, his expression thoughtful.

"I've been thinking about what you said earlier," Martin began, "about how I've been working on myself. You're right, I've been confronting a lot of things lately. But I also realised something else today."

Luca tilted his head slightly. "What's that?"

"That I don't have to do it all alone," Martin said, his voice steady. "For so long, I've been used to handling things on my own, trying to figure it all out by myself. But now... I know that I don't have to. I have people around me; people like you, who are here to support me."

Luca's smile was soft, his eyes reflecting the fading light of the evening. "You're right. You don't have to do it alone."

Martin smiled back, feeling a sense of peace settle over him. For the first time in a long while, he felt like he was exactly where he needed to be, not just physically, but emotionally. He wasn't running from his past anymore, and he wasn't afraid of the future. He was here, in the present, with someone who understood him, and that was enough.

As they stepped inside the château, the quiet grandeur of the space enveloped them once again. But this time, Martin felt different. He wasn't just a visitor in this place, he was part of its story, just as it was now part of his.

And together, they were moving forward.

8

The morning sun struggled to pierce through the dense blanket of grey clouds that hung low over Château de Valmont. A fine mist clung to the air, draping the vineyards and gardens in a veil of melancholy. Martin stood on the terrace outside his office, a steaming cup of coffee cradled in his hands, his gaze fixed on the west wing of the château. Despite the serene beauty of the landscape, an undercurrent of tension gripped him, a knot of unease that had tightened since the engineering report had arrived the previous evening.

He took a slow sip, the bitter warmth of the coffee doing little to alleviate his concerns. The restoration project had been progressing smoothly, each phase unfolding with meticulous care and a shared sense of purpose among the team. But the latest findings threatened to unravel their hard work.

Footsteps echoed softly on the stone floor behind him. "Couldn't sleep either?" Sophie's voice was gentle, tinged with concern.

Martin turned to see her approaching, a cup of tea in her hands. Her eyes reflected the muted light of the overcast morning, mirroring the worry he felt. "Not much," he admitted, offering a wan smile. "The report kept me up."

She joined him at the balustrade, following his gaze toward the west wing. "I read it too. The structural issues are more severe than we anticipated."

He nodded grimly. "The foundations are compromised. The engineers estimate that without immediate reinforcement, we're at risk of a partial collapse. The repairs could cost upwards of two hundred thousand euros."

Sophie let out a low whistle. "That's a significant sum. Our budget can't absorb an expense like that."

"Exactly," Martin sighed, rubbing his temple. "We've already stretched our funds thin with the unexpected repairs in the east wing. This could halt the entire project."

She placed a reassuring hand on his arm. "We'll find a way. We've faced challenges before."

Before he could respond, Isabella emerged from the doorway, her tablet in hand and a purposeful stride in her step. "Morning," she greeted them, though her usual upbeat tone was subdued. "I've been crunching numbers since dawn."

"Any good news?" Martin asked, though his tone suggested he wasn't hopeful.

"Depends on your definition of good," she replied wryly. "I've identified some areas where we can cut costs, but it won't cover the amount we need for the structural repairs."

Sophie sipped her tea thoughtfully. "What about reallocating funds from the landscaping budget? We could postpone some of the garden restorations until we've addressed the critical structural issues."

Isabella nodded. "That would help, but we'd still be short by a significant margin."

Martin ran a hand through his hair, frustration evident in his expression. "We need to explore additional funding sources. Grants, sponsorships, anything."

"Most grant applications have long lead times," Isabella reminded him gently. "And we've already tapped into many of them. But perhaps we could consider hosting a fundraising event."

Sophie perked up at the suggestion. "An exclusive gala, perhaps? We could invite potential donors, showcase the progress we've made, and emphasise the château's historical significance."

Martin considered the idea. "It's ambitious, but it might be our best option. We'll need to act quickly."

Isabella was already jotting down notes. "I can start compiling a list of potential guests, patrons of the arts, business leaders, anyone with an interest in cultural preservation."

"I'll handle the event planning," Sophie offered. "Catering, entertainment, decor, we'll make it an evening to remember."

Martin felt a flicker of hope. "Thank you. Let's convene with the rest of the team and get started."

As they moved inside, the château's grandeur seemed to weigh heavier than usual. The ornate mouldings and high ceilings that once inspired awe now felt like a reminder of the immense responsibility resting on Martin's shoulders.

❖ ❖ ❖

In the conference room, the team assembled around the large oak table. The atmosphere was a mix of concern and determination. Luca arrived last, his sketchbook tucked under his arm, sensing the gravity of the meeting.

"Thank you all for coming on such short notice," Martin began, his tone serious. "As some of you are aware, we've encountered a significant structural issue with the west wing. The foundations are unstable, and without immediate intervention, we risk a catastrophic collapse."

A murmur rippled through the room. Marie, the archival expert, raised a hand. "What are our options?"

"We need to reinforce the foundations," Martin explained. "But the cost is substantial, over two hundred thousand euros. Our current budget can't cover this expense."

Isabella chimed in. "We're exploring ways to secure additional funding. One proposal is to host a fundraising gala to attract potential donors."

Luca leaned forward. "Perhaps we can incorporate an art exhibition into the event. Display works inspired by the château and its history. Art can be a powerful medium to connect with people emotionally."

Sophie smiled. "That's a wonderful idea. It would add a unique dimension to the gala."

Martin nodded appreciatively. "Agreed. Luca, would you be willing to curate the exhibition?"

"Of course," Luca replied. "I'll reach out to other artists who might contribute pieces."

"Excellent," Martin said. "We'll need everyone's efforts to make this a success. Let's divide the tasks and set deadlines."

As the meeting progressed, the team's spirits lifted, galvanised by a common goal. They brainstormed ideas, from themed performances to silent auctions, each suggestion building upon the last.

By the time the meeting adjourned, Martin felt a renewed sense of purpose. The challenges were daunting, but the collective enthusiasm of the team infused him with hope.

❖ ❖ ❖

Over the next few days, the château buzzed with activity. Invitations were meticulously crafted, featuring a watermark of the château's emblem, a rose entwined with a compass, a nod to the hidden histories they had uncovered. Isabella compiled an extensive guest list, leveraging contacts from previous projects and reaching out to influential figures in the arts and business communities.

Sophie transformed one of the grand salons into an event planning headquarters. Swatches of fabric, floral arrangements, and menu designs covered the tables. She coordinated with local vendors to source gourmet cuisine that highlighted regional specialties, ensuring that the event would be a feast for both the palate and the senses.

Luca immersed himself in curating the art exhibition. He spent hours in his studio, selecting pieces that embodied the château's spirit. His own artwork took on new depth, a series of paintings depicting the château through the ages, capturing its resilience and the stories embedded within its walls.

One afternoon, as the sun cast a warm glow over the courtyard, Martin found himself wandering toward Luca's studio. He knocked lightly on the open door.

"Come in," Luca called out without looking up, engrossed in his work.

Martin stepped inside, the scent of oil paint and turpentine filling the air. Canvases lined the walls, each one more captivating than the last. "These are incredible," he remarked, genuine admiration in his voice.

Luca turned; a hint of paint smudged on his cheek. "Thank you," he said modestly. "I'm trying to convey the château's essence, the layers of history, the emotions it evokes."

"You've succeeded," Martin replied, studying a painting of the château bathed in moonlight, its silhouette both haunting and majestic. "Your art will be the centrepiece of the gala."

Luca smiled softly. "I hope it resonates with the guests. We need them to feel connected to the château, to understand why it's worth preserving."

"Your work has a way of touching people," Martin said thoughtfully. "It's a gift."

A moment of comfortable silence settled between them, the unspoken appreciation deepening their connection.

"I wanted to thank you," Luca began hesitantly. "For believing in me, for giving me this opportunity."

Martin met his gaze. "You've brought a unique perspective to our team. Your passion is contagious."

Luca looked down, a faint flush colouring his cheeks. "It's easy to be passionate about something so meaningful."

They lingered a moment longer before Martin cleared his throat. "I should let you get back to it. Let me know if there's anything you need."

"Actually," Luca said, "I was wondering if you'd be willing to sit for a portrait. I think including a representation of our team would add a personal touch to the exhibition."

Martin raised an eyebrow. "Me? I'm not exactly model material."

Luca chuckled. "Nonsense. It would be an honour."

"Alright," Martin conceded. "But no promises on how it'll turn out."

"Leave that to me," Luca replied with a playful glint in his eye.

❖ ❖ ❖

As the date of the gala approached, the château transformed into a hive of preparation. The grand hall was adorned with elegant drapery and chandeliers that cast a warm glow over the polished marble floors. Tables were set with fine china and crystal, each place setting meticulously arranged.

Sophie oversaw every detail, her organisational prowess ensuring that nothing was overlooked. "Remember, first impressions are crucial," she reminded the staff during a final walkthrough. "We want our guests to be enchanted from the moment they arrive."

Isabella coordinated the logistics, arranging transportation and accommodations for out-of-town guests. She also secured media coverage, inviting journalists and critics who could amplify the château's story.

On the morning of the gala, the weather was idyllic. The sun shone brightly, a gentle breeze rustling the leaves of the ancient oaks that lined the driveway. Martin stood at the entrance, observing as staff made final adjustments.

"You look nervous," Sophie teased, approaching with two glasses of sparkling water.

"Just eager to get started," Martin replied, accepting the glass.

She gave him a knowing look. "Everything is in place. Trust in the team's efforts."

He took a sip, letting the effervescence settle his nerves. "I know. It's just, so much is riding on tonight."

"And we're all here to support you," she reassured him. "We've done everything we can. Now it's time to let the evening unfold."

❖ ❖ ❖

As evening descended, the château came alive with the arrival of guests. A procession of luxury cars wound up the driveway, depositing elegantly dressed attendees who were greeted by the soft strains of a string quartet positioned near the entrance.

Martin, now dressed in a tailored tuxedo, greeted guests alongside Isabella and Sophie. "Welcome to Château de Valmont," he said warmly, shaking hands and engaging in brief pleasantries.

Madame Dubois and Monsieur Lefevre arrived together, both radiating an air of dignified elegance. "The château looks magnificent," Madame Dubois remarked, her eyes sparkling with approval.

"An impressive turnout," Monsieur Lefevre added. "It's clear you've poured your heart into this event."

"Thank you both for coming," Martin replied sincerely. "Your support means a great deal."

Inside, the grand hall buzzed with conversation and laughter. The art exhibition drew significant attention, with guests marvelling at the array of works that depicted the château's history and the surrounding landscape.

Luca navigated the crowd with ease, engaging guests with anecdotes about the pieces. "This painting captures the château during the 17th century," he explained to a small group. "Notice the details in the architecture, which reflect the Baroque influences of the time."

An elegantly dressed woman, a patron of the arts named Madame Rousseau, was particularly taken with his work. "Your ability to convey emotion through landscape is remarkable," she praised.

"Thank you," Luca replied modestly. "I believe the environment holds the memories of those who have walked before us."

She glanced at Martin, who had joined the group. "You have a talented team, Mr. Longman. Their passion is evident."

"I'm fortunate to work with such dedicated individuals," Martin acknowledged.

Dinner was a sumptuous affair, featuring courses that celebrated local produce and culinary traditions. As dessert was served, a delicate lavender-infused crème brûlée, Martin stood to address the assembled guests.

"Ladies and gentlemen," he began, his voice steady despite the magnitude of the moment. "Thank you for honouring us with your presence tonight. Château de Valmont is not just a building; it is a custodian of history, a vessel of stories spanning centuries."

He spoke of the challenges they faced, the unexpected structural issues that threatened the project's continuation. "We stand at a crossroads," he continued. "To preserve the château for future generations, we need your support."

Martin's words were sincere, his appeal heartfelt. He shared anecdotes of their discoveries, the hidden chamber, the stories of refuge and resilience embedded within the château's walls. "This is a legacy worth saving," he concluded. "Together, we can ensure that Château de Valmont remains a beacon of culture and history."

The room erupted in applause; the guests visibly moved by his speech.

As the evening progressed, pledges of support began to flow. Madame Rousseau approached Martin with a generous offer. "I'd like to contribute fifty thousand euros toward your restoration efforts," she declared.

"Your generosity is deeply appreciated," Martin replied, gratitude evident in his expression.

Other guests followed suit, their commitments gradually bridging the funding gap. By the end of the night, they had surpassed their initial target.

Isabella approached Martin, her eyes shining with excitement. "We've done it," she whispered. "We've secured enough to proceed with the repairs."

He exhaled a breath he hadn't realised he'd been holding. "I can hardly believe it."

Sophie joined them, a satisfied smile on her face. "This is a testament to the power of collaboration."

Luca appeared at Martin's side. "Congratulations," he said softly. "Your leadership made this possible."

Martin turned to face him, their eyes meeting in a moment of shared accomplishment. "I couldn't have done it without all of you."

❖ ❖ ❖

Work on the west wing resumed in earnest. The engineering team began the painstaking process of reinforcing the foundations, their efforts bolstered by the newfound financial support. The château hummed with activity, the sounds of construction intermingling with the usual rhythms of daily operations.

One morning, as Martin reviewed progress reports in his office, his phone rang. The caller ID displayed an unfamiliar number with a Paris area code.

"Hello, this is Martin Longman," he answered.

"Good morning, Mr. Longman. This is Claire Duval from the Ministry of Culture. I hope I'm not calling at a bad time."

"Not at all, Ms. Duval," Martin replied, intrigued. "How can I assist you?"

"I wanted to discuss an opportunity," she began. "The ministry is launching a national initiative to promote heritage sites that exemplify exceptional preservation efforts. Château de Valmont has come to our attention, and we'd like to feature it prominently in our campaign."

Martin's eyes widened. "That's an incredible honour. We're humbled by your interest."

"The work your team has done is exemplary," Claire continued. "We believe showcasing the château could inspire similar projects across the country."

"Thank you," he said sincerely. "We would be delighted to participate."

They arranged a meeting to discuss details, and as Martin hung up the phone, a surge of excitement coursed through him. This recognition could elevate their project to new heights, attracting further support and ensuring the château's legacy.

He gathered the team to share the news. "This could be a game-changer," Isabella remarked, her enthusiasm palpable.

Sophie clapped her hands together. "Think of the educational programs we could expand, the outreach opportunities."

Luca smiled thoughtfully. "And the stories we can share with a broader audience."

❖ ❖ ❖

While the team celebrated the potential collaboration with the Ministry of Culture, whispers of concern began to surface among some villagers. The increased attention on the château raised fears about the impact of tourism on their quiet community.

At Le Clos des Roses, Martin overheard a conversation between two locals.

"All these outsiders," one man grumbled. "They'll overrun our village, change its character."

"Aye," his companion agreed. "We didn't sign up for this."

Martin felt a pang of concern. He had always valued the support of the community and didn't want to jeopardise their relationship.

He approached Madame Dubois, who was arranging flowers in the inn's foyer. "May I have a word?" he asked.

"Of course, dear," she replied, gesturing for him to sit.

"I'm hearing some reservations from the villagers about the increased attention on the château," he began carefully. "I want to address their concerns."

She nodded knowingly. "Change can be unsettling, especially when it feels imposed. Some fear that an influx of visitors will disrupt our way of life."

"I understand completely," Martin said earnestly. "I don't want the project to have a negative impact on the village. Perhaps we could organise a town meeting to discuss these issues openly."

"That's a wise approach," she agreed. "Transparency and inclusion are key."

❖ ❖ ❖

The town meeting was held in the village hall, a modest building that had hosted generations of community gatherings. The atmosphere was tense but respectful as residents filled the wooden pews.

Martin stood at the front, flanked by Sophie and Isabella. "Thank you all for coming," he began. "I value your perspectives and want to ensure that the château's development benefits everyone."

An elderly man named Jacques stood up, his weathered face etched with concern. "We're worried that our village will become a tourist trap," he said bluntly. "We cherish our peace and quiet."

A murmuring of agreement rippled through the crowd.

Martin nodded. "Your concerns are valid. Our intention is not to disrupt but to enhance. We propose implementing measures to manage visitor numbers and ensure that any growth is sustainable and respectful of the village's character."

Marie, the local schoolteacher, raised her hand. "Could we involve the community more directly? Perhaps by offering workshops or tours led by villagers."

"That's an excellent idea," Sophie interjected. "It would provide authentic experiences for visitors and empower residents to share their heritage."

Madame Dubois stood. "I propose forming a liaison committee, a bridge between the château team and the village. This way, decisions can be made collaboratively."

The suggestion was met with nods of approval.

Martin felt a sense of relief. "I wholeheartedly support this. Our goal has always been to work in harmony with the community."

By the meeting's end, tensions had eased, replaced by a spirit of cooperation. The formation of the liaison committee marked a new chapter in their relationship with the village.

❖ ❖ ❖

In the following weeks, the château's activities expanded to include community-led initiatives. Workshops on traditional crafts, agricultural practices, and local folklore were integrated into the visitor experience. The villagers took pride in sharing their knowledge, and the château became a vibrant hub of cultural exchange.

One afternoon, Martin received an unexpected email from David Thompson, his former colleague from Australia.

Martin,

I hope this message finds you well. I've been following the incredible work you're doing at Château de Valmont. It's truly inspiring.

We have an exciting opportunity here, a historical restoration project that aligns with your expertise. The board has authorised me to extend an offer for you to lead the initiative. It's a significant role with substantial resources.

Let's discuss further at your earliest convenience.

Best regards,

David

Martin stared at the screen, a mix of emotions swirling within him. The offer was flattering and professionally tempting, but his life had become deeply entwined with Chenonceaux and the château.

That evening, he confided in Luca as they walked along the riverbank, the setting sun casting a golden glow over the water.

"I received a job offer from Australia," he began, his tone contemplative. "A leadership position in a major restoration project."

Luca's expression remained neutral, though a flicker of apprehension crossed his eyes. "That's quite an opportunity."

"It is," Martin agreed. "But I'm conflicted. My work here feels more meaningful than anything I've done before."

They walked in silence for a moment, the gentle sounds of the river accompanying their thoughts.

"Do you want to go?" Luca asked quietly.

Martin considered the question. "No," he admitted. "My life is here now. With the château, the community... and you."

Luca looked at him, a softness in his gaze. "I'm glad to hear that."

Martin smiled, feeling a weight lift from his shoulders. "I wanted to be honest with you."

"Thank you," Luca replied. "Whatever you decide, I'll support you."

"I've already decided," Martin said firmly. "I'm staying."

❖ ❖ ❖

He penned a response to David, expressing his gratitude but declining the offer. The decision brought a sense of clarity and reaffirmed his commitment to the path he had chosen.

❖ ❖ ❖

As spring blossomed, the château prepared for a festival celebrating its restoration and the unity it had fostered. The event was a collaborative effort, with the villagers and château team working side by side.

On the day of the festival, the grounds were transformed into a vibrant tapestry of colour and activity. Stalls showcased local artisans, musicians performed traditional songs, and interactive exhibits highlighted the château's history.

Martin wandered through the crowds, his heart swelling with pride and contentment. He spotted Sophie teaching a group of children about historical artefacts, Isabella coordinating logistics with her characteristic efficiency, and Luca leading a painting workshop under a blooming cherry tree.

Madame Dubois approached him, her face radiant. "It's a marvellous sight, isn't it?"

"Indeed," Martin agreed. "A true embodiment of what we've worked toward."

She placed a hand on his arm. "You've brought something special to our village. We're grateful."

"Thank you," he replied, humbled. "But it's the collective effort that made it possible."

As evening fell, lanterns illuminated the pathways, and a communal feast brought everyone together. Laughter and conversation filled the air, the barriers between villagers and visitors dissolved in the shared celebration.

Martin stood to make a toast. "To community," he proclaimed, raising his glass. "To collaboration, and to the future we've built together."

"To the future!" the crowd echoed.

Luca sidled up beside him, a contented smile on his face. "It's been quite a journey."

"It has," Martin agreed, his gaze sweeping over the joyous scene. "And I wouldn't trade it for anything."

They clinked glasses, a silent acknowledgment of their shared experiences and the bond that had deepened between them.

❖ ❖ ❖

In the weeks that followed, the château continued to thrive. Educational programs flourished, and the partnership with the Ministry of Culture brought new opportunities. Martin was invited to join an international council on heritage preservation, allowing him to contribute on a broader scale while remaining rooted in Chenonceaux.

One afternoon, as he sat in his office reviewing plans for future projects, Sophie knocked on the open door. "Got a minute?"

"Always," he replied, gesturing for her to sit.

She settled into the chair opposite him. "I wanted to discuss expanding our outreach programs. There's interest from neighbouring communities to collaborate on cultural exchanges."

"That's fantastic," Martin said enthusiastically. "Let's set up a meeting to explore the possibilities."

She smiled. "It's exciting to see how far we've come."

"It is," he agreed. "And there's still so much potential."

❖ ❖ ❖

That evening, Martin and Luca sat on the terrace of their shared cottage, the twilight sky painted with hues of lavender and gold.

"Do you ever think about what might have been if you'd made different choices?" Luca asked softly.

"Sometimes," Martin admitted. "But I believe we're where we're meant to be."

Luca nodded, a serene expression on his face. "I'm glad our paths crossed."

"Me too," Martin said, reaching for his hand.

They sat in companionable silence, the gentle chorus of nighttime sounds enveloping them.

❖ ❖ ❖

In his journal, Martin reflected:

The challenges we've faced have forged us into a stronger, more cohesive community. The château stands not just as a monument to the past but as a beacon for the future. I've found fulfilment beyond professional success, in relationships, in shared purpose, in embracing the unexpected paths life presents. I am grateful for this journey and eager to see where it leads.

He closed the journal, a sense of peace settling over him.

As the stars emerged, casting a shimmering tapestry across the sky, Martin felt a deep contentment. The château, the village, the people, they were all part of a tapestry woven together by history, hope, and the enduring human spirit.

9

Martin sat in his office at Château de Valmont, his head in his hands, weighed down by the burdens of the past few weeks. The challenges now seemed insurmountable, the spiralling financial strain, resistance from the village, and the new discovery of structural issues that threatened to unravel everything. His meticulously crafted plans now seemed like fragments of a shattered puzzle. He had always prided himself on solving problems, but this time, he felt stuck.

His phone buzzed, breaking the oppressive silence in the room. It was a message from Sarah, his best friend in Sydney, reminding him of their scheduled video call. Martin hesitated for a moment, tempted to cancel. He wasn't sure he had the energy to talk, let alone share the chaos that had become his life. But something inside him knew he needed the familiarity of Sarah's voice, a lifeline to the world outside the château.

Martin clicked the video call link, and within seconds, Sarah's face appeared on the screen, her warm, easygoing smile instantly putting him at ease.

"There's my favourite architect!" Sarah laughed, her voice light, trying to lift his spirits. "You look... well, like you've been wrestling with ancient stone walls all day."

Despite everything, Martin chuckled. "You're not far off. It's been a rough few weeks."

"I figured as much," Sarah said, her tone softening. "Talk to me, Martin. What's going on?"

Martin leaned back in his chair and sighed deeply, rubbing his tired eyes. "Where do I even start? The structural issues in the west wing are worse than we thought, and we're already over budget. Every solution I come up with feels like it's just a temporary fix. And the village... there's this group, led by this guy Monsieur Lefevre, who's making everything harder. He's opposed to us including the château's LGBTQI+ history, saying it 'tarnishes' the legacy of the place. It's ridiculous, but he's managed to get a few people on his side, and now it's turning into a full-blown resistance."

Sarah frowned, shaking her head in disbelief. "That sounds tough. It must feel like you're fighting battles on all fronts."

"That's exactly what it feels like," Martin admitted, his voice heavy. "I'm trying to keep the project on track, but with the budget spiralling out of control and the villagers pushing back, I'm starting to wonder if I'm in over my head."

Sarah studied him through the screen, her expression thoughtful. She knew Martin better than anyone. She knew how much he valued control, how meticulously he planned every detail of his life and work. But she also knew how self-doubt could cripple him when things didn't go according to plan.

"You've been through tough times before, Martin," Sarah said gently. "Remember that project in Melbourne with the impossible deadline? You were convinced you wouldn't make it, but you did. You always find a way."

Martin's voice softened. "This feels different. This isn't just about meeting a deadline. It's about preserving something bigger than me, and I feel like I'm letting everyone down."

"You're not letting anyone down," Sarah said firmly. "You're doing your best with what you've got. But you can't do it all alone. You need to lean on your team, trust them to help you find a way forward."

Martin nodded, though the knot of anxiety in his chest remained. "I know you're right. I just... feel like I'm supposed to have all the answers. I'm the one who brought this project to life, and now it's slipping through my fingers."

"You don't have to have all the answers, Martin," Sarah reminded him. "It's okay to lean on other people."

Before Martin could respond, another call came through. It was Alex, his old gym buddy who had recently moved to Brisbane. Martin had meant to catch up with Alex, who had his own challenges, but time had slipped away. Perhaps now was the perfect moment to connect.

"Sarah, can I merge the call with Alex? He's calling in, and I could use both of you right now."

"Of course!" Sarah smiled. "The more, the merrier."

A moment later, Alex appeared on the screen, his familiar grin easing some of Martin's tension. "Hey, man. Long time no talk," Alex said, his voice upbeat despite the dark circles under his eyes. "Looks like I called at the right time. What's going on?"

Martin filled Alex in on the struggles with the château, the budget, the opposition from the village, and his feelings of inadequacy. By the time he finished, he felt lighter, as if sharing his burdens with Sarah and Alex had eased some of the pressure.

Alex leaned back in his chair, nodding thoughtfully. "It sounds like you've got a lot on your plate, man. But let me tell you something, this whole 'feeling like you're supposed to have all the answers' thing? I get it. I've been there. You know I've been dealing with my own stuff lately, with Jennifer and the wedding plans. I thought I had to have everything figured out, and if I didn't, I was failing. But sometimes, it's okay not to know. Sometimes, it's okay to let go of the plan."

Martin raised an eyebrow. "You? Letting go of a plan? That doesn't sound like the Alex I know."

Alex chuckled. "Yeah, well, I've had to learn that the hard way. But seriously, you've got a team there for a reason. Trust them. And trust yourself to adapt when things don't go the way you expect."

Sarah chimed in, her voice soft but steady. "Exactly. This project isn't just about you, Martin. It's about everyone involved, your team, the village, the history you're preserving. You've done an amazing job getting this far, but now it's time to let others help carry the load."

Martin listened, their words settling over him like a balm. He had been so focused on controlling every aspect of the project, so afraid of failure, that he had forgotten the value of leaning on others, of trusting his team. Sarah and Alex had always been his anchors, reminding him of what really mattered when he lost sight of it.

"Thanks, guys," Martin said, his voice quieter now. "I think I needed to hear that. It's just... hard to let go, you know? I've always been the one who has to keep everything together."

"We know," Sarah said with a gentle smile. "But that's what we're here for, to remind you that you don't have to do it all alone."

"Exactly," Alex added. "You've got this, man. And we're here whenever you need us."

For the first time in days, Martin felt a flicker of hope. The challenges were still there, the problems still unsolved, but somehow, they didn't feel quite as overwhelming. He wasn't in this alone. He had a team. He had friends. And he had the strength to keep moving forward.

After the call ended, Martin leaned back in his chair, staring out the window at the château's silhouette against the evening sky. The challenges ahead were daunting, but they weren't impossible. He didn't need all the answers right now. He just needed to keep moving, one step at a time.

❖ ❖ ❖

The next morning, Martin woke with a clearer head, though the weight of the project still hung over him. The conversation with Sarah and Alex had given him some much-needed perspective, but now the challenge was figuring out how to apply that wisdom. He couldn't keep moving forward as he had, trying to shoulder everything alone. It was time to start trusting the people around him, the ones who had supported him since day one.

As he walked through the quiet hallways of the château, the early morning light filtered through the tall windows, casting long shadows across the floor. The château, even with all its challenges, was beautiful, and despite everything, Martin still felt a deep connection to it. It had been a monumental undertaking, but he wasn't ready to give up, not yet. He just needed a new approach.

He was heading toward the main office for a morning briefing with Isabella and Sophie. Both women had been integral to the project, each bringing unique skills and perspectives. Isabella, with her sharp organisational mind, had kept the project on track, while Sophie, with her deep knowledge of the château's history, had unearthed countless stories that gave the place its soul.

Martin entered the office, where Isabella and Sophie were already seated, chatting over cups of coffee. They greeted him warmly as he sat down.

"Morning, Martin," Isabella said with a smile. "You look a little more rested today. I take it you got some sleep?"

Martin chuckled, appreciating her gentle teasing. "Yeah, I did. And I had a good chat with some friends last night, which helped a lot."

"That's great to hear," Sophie said, her kind eyes scanning his face. "You've been carrying a lot lately. It's good to see you taking care of yourself."

Martin nodded, though there was still a hint of hesitation in his expression. "Yeah, I guess I've been trying to do too much on my own. I've been so focused on fixing everything that I haven't let myself lean on the people around me."

Isabella leaned back in her chair, crossing her arms. "Well, you don't have to do it all alone. That's what we're here for. This project isn't just on your shoulders, Martin. It's a team effort."

"I know," Martin replied, his tone softer. "But it's hard to let go of control. I've always been the kind of person who needs everything planned out, and when things start going wrong… I feel like I'm failing."

Isabella exchanged a glance with Sophie before speaking. "We get it. But here's the thing, projects like this *always* go off-plan. There's no way to account for every little thing, especially with something as old and complex as Château de Valmont. You can't control everything, and you can't fix it all by yourself."

Martin sighed, running a hand through his hair. "I've been hearing that a lot lately."

"And for good reason," Sophie added gently. "This château has been here for centuries. It's seen changes, upheavals, restorations, and declines. It's not meant to be restored overnight, and certainly not by one person. What we're doing here is *preserving* its history, not forcing it into a perfect mould."

Martin leaned back, letting their words sink in. He had spent so much time obsessing over details, over trying to make the project flawless, that he had lost sight of the bigger picture. The château wasn't just a job, it was a living piece of history. It couldn't be controlled or manipulated into perfection. It had its own story, one that would continue long after the restoration was complete.

"You're both right," Martin admitted, a small smile tugging at the corners of his lips. "I've been trying to make this project fit my vision of what it should be, rather than letting it unfold naturally. I think I've been afraid of failure, but I'm starting to see that failure isn't necessarily bad. It's part of the process."

"Exactly," Isabella said, her smile widening. "Failure is how we learn and adapt. Speaking of adapting, I've been thinking about our approach to the budget and repairs."

Martin raised an eyebrow, intrigued. "Go on."

Isabella reached for a folder, revealing notes and calculations. "We've been trying to cover the costs of repairs in the west wing without blowing the budget, right? What if we stagger repairs, prioritise the most urgent issues first and spread the rest out over the next phases? That way, we keep the project moving without draining all our resources at once."

Martin leaned in, studying the notes closely. Isabella had broken down repairs into manageable sections, each with its timeline and cost estimate. It wasn't the all-at-once solution he had hoped for, but it was practical, and realistic.

"I like this," Martin said, nodding as he flipped through the pages. "It's not ideal, but it keeps the project moving without overwhelming us financially."

"Exactly," Isabella said. "And it'll give us breathing room to figure out other funding sources. Maybe apply for more grants or sponsorships once we show tangible progress."

Martin smiled, feeling a sense of relief. For the first time in weeks, he felt like they were back on solid ground, or at least heading in the right direction. "Thanks, Isabella. This helps a lot."

Sophie, who had been quietly sipping her coffee, chimed in. "There's something else I've been thinking about, too."

"What's that?" Martin asked, curious.

Sophie leaned forward. "We've been so focused on logistics, repairs, budgets, timelines, that we've almost forgotten the heart of the project. The *history* of the château is what makes it special, and I think we can use that to our advantage."

Martin tilted his head, listening closely. "Go on."

"We need to get the local community more involved," Sophie continued. "Monsieur Lefevre and his group have caused trouble, but I think part of the reason they're so resistant is because they don't feel part of this. If we can find a way to bring them into the project, to make them feel like they have a stake in it, we might be able to turn the tide."

Isabella nodded in agreement. "We've been so focused on the restoration that we haven't done enough to engage with the community. We need to build bridges, show them this project is as much for them as it is for us."

Martin thought, processing their ideas. Sophie was right, the château wasn't just an architectural landmark; it was part of the village's history. If they could make that connection more tangible, maybe they could change the narrative.

"Okay," Martin said slowly. "What if we organise an open house? We could invite the villagers to see the progress, showcasing the history we've uncovered, especially parts that tie directly to the local community."

"I love that idea," Sophie said, her eyes lighting up. "We could set up small exhibits with artefacts we've found, and maybe storytelling sessions sharing the château's personal stories."

"Exactly," Martin said, feeling a spark of excitement. "We could make it interactive, let the villagers share their own stories about the château. If we create a dialogue, it might help them feel more connected."

"That's a great approach," Isabella agreed. "It'll also give us a chance to address concerns, including the LGBTQI+ history. We can show them this isn't about rewriting history; it's about telling the full story."

Martin smiled, feeling renewed energy. The project still had challenges, but they were making progress, not just with restoration, but with the community as well.

"Let's do it," Martin said, standing and gathering his notes. "We'll plan the open house for next month. I'll work on a presentation, and we'll coordinate with the team."

Isabella and Sophie exchanged excited glances, clearly invigorated by the plan.

"You've got this, Martin," Isabella said. "We're all behind you."

"Yeah," Sophie added with a warm smile. "We're a team. We'll get through this together."

Martin nodded, feeling gratitude for those around him. The weight of the project didn't feel so heavy anymore, it felt manageable, even exciting.

❖ ❖ ❖

That afternoon, Martin found himself walking through the château's sunlit corridors, the tension of the past few weeks lifting. For the first time, he felt hope. The conversation with Sarah, Alex, Isabella, and Sophie had given him the clarity he needed.

But with hope came a realisation: if the project was to move forward, Martin needed to change. He couldn't keep pushing his team toward a rigid outcome. He had to learn to adapt, be flexible, and let go of his obsession with control. It was easier said than done, especially for someone like Martin, who had spent his entire career meticulously planning every detail.

Stopping at one of the large windows overlooking the gardens, Martin took a deep breath. The château, even with its challenges, was breathtaking. It had survived centuries of change, upheaval, and restoration. Perhaps it was time for Martin to take a lesson from the place he was restoring.

He thought back to his conversation with Sarah and Alex. They had urged him to let go, to embrace the uncertainty of the process, and to trust those around him. Isabella and Sophie had encouraged him to rely more on his team, to delegate and collaborate. It was clear now; this wasn't just about restoring a building. It was about restoring how Martin approached work and life.

Smiling, Martin decided to head back to his office and review the project plans. There were aspects of the restoration he had been stubbornly holding onto, despite knowing they weren't essential. Perhaps it was time to reevaluate those priorities.

Back in his office, Martin pulled up the restoration plans on his laptop. The timeline he had created was ambitious, too ambitious. He had aimed to complete the restoration in a year, but the château was vast, and its history complex. Rushing the process wasn't doing anyone any favours.

Scrolling through the plans, Martin highlighted areas for adjustment. The landscaping, for instance, while important in the long term, wasn't necessary right away. The same applied to decorative interior renovations. The real priorities were structural repairs and preserving the château's historical elements.

As he revised the timeline, Martin felt a sense of relief. Letting go of the need to accomplish everything at once wasn't just practical, it was liberating. For the first time in weeks, he felt like he could breathe. The project didn't have to be perfect, and it didn't have to happen all at once.

Martin glanced at the clock, realising it was nearing lunchtime. He grabbed his notebook and headed out to the garden, a favourite place to clear his head. The sun was warm, and the quiet atmosphere was just what he needed.

Sitting on one of the stone benches, Martin began jotting down ideas for approaching the project with more flexibility. He thought about involving his team more, encouraging collaboration and creative problem-solving. The château restoration was a shared effort, and by relying more on others, Martin could lighten his load.

He also thought about how to engage the community. Sophie's idea of an open house was a good start, but they needed to go deeper. Perhaps they could involve the villagers in the restoration, making them feel part of preserving their history.

As Martin scribbled down ideas, a soft voice interrupted his thoughts.

"Mind if I join you?"

Looking up, Martin saw Luca standing nearby, holding a sketchpad. He was on his way to draw in the garden, as he often did.

"Of course," Martin said, making room on the bench. "I could use the company."

Luca sat beside him, his sketchpad resting on his lap. "You seem deep in thought. Planning something?"

"More like re-planning," Martin replied with a smile. "I've been going over some of the project timelines, trying to figure out how to be more flexible. I've been holding onto this idea that everything needs to be perfect and on time, but that's not realistic. I need to let go a little."

Luca nodded, his eyes thoughtful. "That makes sense. This place has been here for centuries, it's not going anywhere. Sometimes I think the most important things take the longest to come together."

Martin smiled at Luca's wisdom. There was something about his calm, steady presence that always put things in perspective.

"That's what I'm starting to realise," Martin said. "I've been so focused on controlling every detail that I've forgotten to enjoy the process. This château is special, and I want to make sure we're doing it justice, not just restoring it physically, but honouring its history."

Luca smiled softly. "You're doing more than justice to this place, Martin. You're bringing it back to life. And that's something that can't be rushed."

Martin nodded, feeling the truth of Luca's words. The château, like all things of value, couldn't be forced into a rigid timeline. It had its own rhythm, its own story to tell. And Martin's role was to guide, not control, the restoration.

"Thanks, Luca," Martin said after a moment of reflection. "You always know what to say."

Luca shrugged modestly. "I just see things differently, I guess."

They sat in companionable silence for a while, each lost in thought. Martin glanced at Luca's sketchpad, noticing the blank page.

"Not drawing today?" Martin asked.

Luca smiled sheepishly. "I was going to, but I guess I got distracted. Listening to you talk made me think about the stories this place holds. There's so much history here, so many layers. It's hard to capture it all in one drawing."

Martin nodded. "Maybe we're not supposed to capture it all at once. Maybe it's something that unfolds over time."

Luca looked at him, thoughtful. "Yeah. It's like we're part of the story too, just one chapter in a much bigger book."

Martin smiled. That was exactly it. They were all part of the château's story, everyone working on the restoration, everyone who had lived there in the past, and everyone who would come after them. It wasn't about finishing the project quickly or perfectly. It was about adding their piece to history, knowing the story would continue long after they were gone.

As the sun began to set, casting golden light over the garden, Martin felt a renewed sense of purpose. He had been so focused on controlling the outcome that he had forgotten to appreciate the journey. But now, with Luca's quiet wisdom and the support of his team, he was ready to embrace the changes ahead, both in the project and in himself.

10

The morning after the open house, Château de Valmont was quiet again. The echo of footsteps and conversations that had filled its grand hall the day before had given way to a calm, peaceful silence. The first light of dawn streamed through the tall, arched windows, casting soft shadows over the stone floors. Martin stood at the entrance of the hall, gazing out at the now empty space that had been filled with life, energy, and, most importantly, connection.

The event had gone better than any of them had expected. As Martin walked through the château, taking in the exhibits that remained on display, he replayed the events of the day in his mind. The conversations, the curious faces, the way people had reacted to the stories of the château's past, it was all still sinking in. What had started as a project to restore a crumbling building had turned into something much more profound. The château had come back to life, not just physically, but emotionally, and the villagers were starting to see it as part of their shared history once again.

He made his way to the courtyard, where the team was already gathering for a debrief. Sophie, Isabella, Jean-Claude, and Luca had all contributed in their own ways to making the event a success, and today was a moment to reflect on that success and plan their next steps. The sun was just beginning to warm the stones of the courtyard, and the air was filled with the scent of lavender from the nearby gardens.

"Morning, everyone," Martin greeted the group as he approached. The team, though tired from the long day before, looked energised and satisfied. The open house had been a major milestone for them all.

"Morning," Sophie said, smiling brightly as she stretched her arms. "I can't believe how well it went. I mean, I knew we'd put in the work, but seeing the villagers actually engage with the history like that, it was amazing."

Martin nodded in agreement. "It was. I think we managed to reach more people than we thought we would. Even some of the sceptics seemed to be interested."

Isabella, ever practical, pulled out her notebook and began listing off points to discuss. "We should go over what worked and what we can improve for next time. But first, let's just take a moment to acknowledge what we achieved yesterday. I think we exceeded all expectations."

Jean-Claude, who had been overseeing the workshops during the event, grunted his approval. "The workshops were a hit. People were genuinely interested in learning about the traditional restoration techniques. I had kids and adults alike getting their hands dirty, and it seemed to make them feel more connected to the château."

Isabella added, "That hands-on experience was key. People don't want to just be told about history, they want to feel like they're part of it. And by giving them a chance to work on the restoration themselves, even in small ways, we showed them that they *are* part of it."

Martin smiled as he listened to his team's reflections. They had done something important yesterday, something that would have a lasting impact on the village. The château had always been a symbol of history and culture, but for many villagers, it had also been a symbol of something distant and inaccessible. Now, for the first time in years, it felt like the people were starting to see it as their own.

Luca, who had been quietly listening, finally spoke up. "I was really nervous about how people would react to the installation, but… it seemed like it connected with them. I saw people standing in front of it for a long time, talking about it. That meant a lot."

Martin turned to Luca; his expression filled with pride. "Your installation was incredible, Luca. *The Reach* captured the spirit of what we've been trying to do here, showing the château as a place of connection, of longing for something greater. It resonated with people on a deep level."

Luca smiled shyly, his fingers brushing over his sketchbook as he thought about the impact his artwork had made. "It's funny, I didn't expect people to see themselves in the figures, but so many of them told me that they did. I guess we all feel like we're reaching for something at times."

Sophie nodded, her eyes soft with understanding. "That's the power of art, Luca. It gives people a way to connect with their own emotions, even when they don't realise it. Your work made the château's history personal for them, and that's a huge achievement."

Martin couldn't agree more. The success of the event had hinged on making the château's past feel relevant and personal to the people who lived in the village today. It wasn't enough to simply restore the building; they had to restore its place in the hearts and minds of the community. And Luca's installation, along with the personal stories shared through Sophie's carefully curated exhibits, had done exactly that.

Isabella, always focused on moving forward, tapped her pen against her notebook, drawing everyone's attention back to the task at hand. "So, what's next? We've got momentum now, and we need to keep building on it."

Martin thought for a moment before answering. "We need to continue involving the community in the restoration process. The workshops were a great start, but I think we should organise more of them, maybe even invite people to contribute to specific parts of the project. If they feel like they're helping to rebuild the château, they'll feel more connected to it."

Jean-Claude nodded in agreement. "We could expand the workshops to cover different restoration techniques, stonework, woodwork, even painting. Give people more ways to get involved."

Sophie added, "And we should keep telling the personal stories of the château. There are still so many untold stories hidden in the archives, and we can use those to keep people engaged. Every time we uncover something new, we can share it with the village."

Isabella made notes as they spoke, her mind already racing ahead to the next phase of the project. "I'll start planning the next set of workshops and public events. We should also think about inviting more media coverage now that we've had some success. The more attention we can bring to the château, the more support we'll get."

Martin agreed, but his thoughts were still lingering on the emotional impact of the event. It wasn't just about the logistics or the next steps, it was about the connection they had created between the château and the village. For years, the building had stood as a reminder of a distant past, but now it felt alive again, filled with stories and people who cared about its future.

Eventually, as the sun rose higher and the day began in earnest, the team wrapped up their meeting. Martin stayed behind in the courtyard for a few moments, watching as Sophie, Isabella, Jean-Claude, and Luca went their separate ways, each one preparing for the tasks ahead.

He took a deep breath, letting the fresh morning air fill his lungs. The open house had been a success, but there was still much to be done. The next steps would be crucial in maintaining the momentum they had built. But for now, Martin allowed himself a moment of quiet satisfaction. They had brought the château back to life, not just as a building, but as a living part of the village's identity.

As he turned to head back inside the château, Martin's phone buzzed in his pocket. It was a message from Alex, a reminder that while things were going well here, his friend was struggling with his own battles back home. Martin read the message, feeling a mix of concern and empathy for Alex. He made a mental note to call him later, knowing that no matter what was happening with the château, he would always be there for his friend.

With one last glance at the courtyard, Martin walked back into the château, ready to face whatever came next. The journey was far from over, but for the first time in a long time, he felt like they were on the right path.

Martin had just settled into one of the reading chairs in the château's library, planning to spend a quiet hour reviewing some of the personal journals they had uncovered, when his phone buzzed. He glanced down at the screen, seeing Alex's name flash across. It had been a while since they had spoken in-depth, and though they often exchanged messages, Martin could tell from the timing and tone of the last few that something wasn't quite right.

Swiping to answer, Martin leaned back in the chair. "Hey, Alex, how's it going?"

There was a pause on the other end, and then Alex's voice, low and tense, came through. "Hey, Martin. I... needed to talk. Do you have a few minutes?"

"Of course," Martin said, his tone immediately softening. "What's going on?"

Alex sighed heavily, the sound of someone carrying the weight of too much for too long. "It's Jennifer... and the wedding. Things aren't going well. I don't know what to do anymore."

Martin frowned slightly, the comforting stillness of the château around him contrasting sharply with the turmoil he could hear in his friend's voice. "What's happening? You guys were in full wedding planning mode last time we talked."

"We were," Alex said, but his voice lacked any of the enthusiasm that would have normally accompanied that statement. "But it's like... the closer we get, the worse it feels. I've been having doubts, Martin. Serious doubts. And when I brought up the idea of postponing the wedding, Jennifer completely shut it down."

Martin sat up a little straighter, feeling the tension in his own shoulders as Alex's words sank in. "Postponing the wedding? Wow, that's... that's a big step. What made you feel like that?"

There was another heavy pause. "It's a lot of things," Alex began, sounding as though he were struggling to put his thoughts into words. "I love Jennifer, but the more we plan this wedding, the more I feel like I'm just going along with everything to keep her happy. She's so dead set on how everything needs to be. She doesn't compromise, not on the big things and not on the little things. It's like she has this vision of the perfect wedding, and the perfect marriage, and if anything challenges that, she shuts it down."

"That sounds... tough," Martin said, choosing his words carefully. He wanted Alex to feel heard, but he also wanted to understand what was driving these doubts.

Alex's frustration was palpable even through the phone. "Tough doesn't even begin to cover it. It's suffocating. Every time I try to express that I need more time, or that I'm feeling overwhelmed, she just brushes it off. It's like delaying the wedding isn't even an option for her. She said it would be 'embarrassing' to change the date now, and that we've already invested so much into the planning that it's too late to turn back."

Martin's heart went out to his friend. He knew Alex wasn't someone who made decisions lightly, and if he was bringing up the idea of postponing the wedding, it meant that the doubts he had were serious. "Have you two talked about why you want to postpone? I mean, have you been able to have an actual conversation about it?"

Alex let out a dry laugh, though there was no humour in it. "Conversation? If you can call it that. I've tried to tell her that I'm not ready, that maybe we need to step back and reassess where we're at before moving forward. But every time, she just gets defensive. She doesn't see it as a sign that we need to work on things; she sees it as me not being committed enough. She keeps saying things like, 'If you loved me, you'd just go through with it.' And it's not like I don't love her, but... I don't know. I just feel like I'm drowning."

Martin's stomach clenched as he listened. He had been through enough difficult moments in his own relationships to know that feeling, when everything seemed to be pushing you toward a decision you weren't ready to make, when it felt like you were on a track with no way to slow down or get off. It sounded like Alex was on that same track now, and Jennifer wasn't giving him the space he needed to figure things out.

"I'm so sorry you're going through this, Alex," Martin said gently. "It sounds like she's really focused on the wedding itself, but marriage is about more than the wedding day. It sounds like you're asking for the time to make sure the marriage is right."

"That's exactly it," Alex said, his voice rising slightly with the frustration of not being understood by the person closest to him. "But every time I try to bring that up, she acts like I'm attacking her. She says things like, 'Why would you even suggest postponing unless you don't think we're going to work out?' But I'm not saying that, I'm just saying we need to slow down and make sure we're ready for this huge step."

Martin nodded, even though Alex couldn't see him. "That makes sense. Have you thought about couples therapy? Sometimes having a neutral party can help with these kinds of conversations."

Alex sighed again, the weight of the suggestion clear in his exhale. "I've thought about it, but I don't know if Jennifer would go for it. She's so determined to prove that we're perfect, that everything's fine, that I'm afraid suggesting therapy would make things worse."

"That's tough," Martin said, feeling for his friend. He could tell how much Alex wanted to make this work, but without compromise from Jennifer, it didn't seem like there was much room for Alex's needs in the relationship. "What about you, though? What do you need right now?"

For a moment, Alex didn't say anything. Then, in a quieter voice, he answered, "I need time, Martin. I need space to figure out if this is what I really want, or if I'm just going through the motions because it's what's expected. I thought I could do it, just push through, but the closer we get to the wedding, the more I feel like I'm losing myself."

Martin felt his chest tighten in empathy. "You're not wrong for feeling that way, Alex. It's important to listen to that part of yourself. Marriage isn't something you should feel pressured into, and if you're having these doubts, it's okay to ask for more time. You shouldn't have to sacrifice your own peace of mind just to meet someone else's expectations."

"I know," Alex said, his voice softening as though he were finally admitting it to himself. "But Jennifer... she won't budge. She keeps telling me that delaying the wedding would be humiliating, that people will talk. I get that it's important to her, but it's like she's not even considering what I need in this."

"That sounds really one-sided," Martin said carefully, not wanting to outright criticise Jennifer but needing to be honest. "If she's not willing to listen to you now, that's a big problem, Alex. Marriage is about compromise, about being able to meet each other's needs."

"I know, I know," Alex said, his voice breaking slightly with the weight of it all. "That's what scares me the most. If we can't even compromise on this, what does that mean for the rest of our marriage? I keep thinking about what it'll be like after the wedding, and I'm just... I'm scared, Martin. Scared that I'm making a mistake."

The rawness in Alex's voice hit Martin hard. He had always seen Alex as the strong, confident one, the one who had it all figured out. But hearing him so vulnerable, so unsure, reminded Martin of just how complex relationships could be. It was clear that Alex was struggling, and it was equally clear that Jennifer wasn't giving him the space to process his feelings.

"I can hear how much you're hurting, Alex," Martin said softly. "It sounds like you're carrying a lot of this on your own, and that's not fair. You shouldn't feel like you have to push through something just because you're worried about what other people will think."

Alex was quiet for a moment before responding. "I guess I just feel trapped. Like I don't have any options. I want to make things work with Jennifer, but not like this. Not when it feels like I'm losing myself in the process."

Martin could feel the heaviness in his friend's words. "You do have options, Alex. You always have the option to take care of yourself first. If that means postponing the wedding or even stepping back entirely, that's okay. You have to prioritise your own well-being, because if you don't, it's going to be even harder to be the partner you want to be."

"I know you're right," Alex admitted, his voice barely above a whisper. "It's just hard to accept that. I don't want to hurt her, but I also don't want to wake up one day and realise I'm in a marriage that isn't right for me."

"That's a tough balance," Martin agreed. "But sometimes, the hardest decisions are the ones that are best for both people. If Jennifer can't understand that you need more time, that's something you need to think about. You deserve a partner who respects your needs as much as their own."

"Yeah," Alex said, his voice filled with uncertainty. "I just don't know what to do next."

Martin paused, thinking carefully before responding. "Maybe the next step isn't making a final decision. Maybe the next step is just taking a breath. Give yourself permission to step back for a moment and really think about what you want, not just what Jennifer wants or what other people expect."

"I wish it were that simple," Alex said, but there was a note of appreciation in his tone. "I don't know how I'd get through this without you, Martin. I'm lucky to have you as a friend."

Martin smiled softly, though Alex couldn't see it. "You're not alone in this, Alex. I'm here for you, whatever you decide. And remember, it's okay to put yourself first. It's not selfish, it's necessary."

They talked for a little while longer, with Martin listening as Alex shared more of his worries. Though Alex wasn't ready to make any final decisions about his relationship with Jennifer, it was clear that he was reaching a breaking point. Martin could only hope that Alex would take the time he needed to figure things out, even if Jennifer wasn't giving him that space.

By the time they ended the call, Martin felt a mix of concern and helplessness. He wanted to do more for his friend, but he knew that Alex had to come to his own conclusions. Still, Martin made a mental note to check in with him regularly, knowing that this kind of emotional burden wasn't something Alex should have to carry alone.

As he put his phone down, Martin leaned back in his chair, his mind still on Alex's struggles. It reminded him of how important it was to listen to your own needs, even when it was hard, even when it meant making difficult decisions. He hoped Alex would find the strength to do just that.

Later that afternoon, after the team had dispersed to work on various tasks, Martin found himself in the château's garden, soaking in the late afternoon sun. The air was crisp, and the smell of freshly turned earth mixed with the faint fragrance of the blooming lavender. It was a moment of peace in the midst of the ongoing work and the emotional weight of the conversation he'd had with Alex earlier. The open house had been a success, but the pressures of the project were still very much present.

Martin had come to love these quiet moments in the garden, where he could reflect on the progress they'd made and the relationships that had formed since the project began. As he wandered through the rows of neatly trimmed hedges, his thoughts turned to Luca. The young artist had been instrumental in connecting the villagers to the project in ways Martin hadn't anticipated, but there was more to Luca than just his art. There was something deeper, a quiet vulnerability that Martin sensed, but that Luca rarely spoke about.

As if on cue, Martin spotted Luca sitting on a low stone wall near the far end of the garden, his sketchbook balanced on his lap. His head was bowed, his pencil moving softly across the page in smooth, deliberate strokes. He seemed deep in thought, his usually animated expression subdued.

Martin approached slowly, not wanting to interrupt. When he was a few steps away, Luca looked up, his expression shifting from concentration to a small, shy smile.

"Hey," Martin said, sitting down beside him on the wall. "What are you working on?"

Luca glanced down at his sketchbook, tilting it slightly so Martin could see. It was a rough sketch of a new concept, perhaps a follow-up to *The Reach*. Two figures, similar to those in his installation, were emerging from a dense forest, their hands still outstretched but with more distance between them than in the original piece. The figures seemed almost hesitant, unsure if they were moving toward each other or drifting apart.

"It's something new I've been thinking about," Luca said quietly, brushing a strand of hair away from his face. "It's still in the early stages."

Martin studied the drawing, struck by how much emotion Luca managed to convey even in the simplest lines. "I like it. It feels... tentative, like they're not sure what's going to happen next."

Luca nodded, his gaze dropping back to the sketch. "That's kind of what I was going for. I've been thinking a lot about what happens after you reach for something, what happens when you're not sure if the connection is really there, or if it's just something you've imagined."

Martin frowned slightly, sensing that there was more to Luca's words than just artistic inspiration. "Is everything okay? You seem... quieter than usual."

Luca hesitated, his fingers tightening slightly around his pencil. For a moment, it seemed like he might brush off the question, but then he sighed, closing his sketchbook and setting it aside.

"I guess I've just been thinking about a lot of things lately," Luca admitted, his voice low. "The open house was incredible, and seeing people connect with my installation, it meant the world to me. But it also made me realise how much of myself I poured into that piece. *The Reach* wasn't just about the château's history. It was about me."

Martin turned to face him, giving Luca his full attention. "I had a feeling there was something personal behind it. Do you want to talk about it?"

Luca exhaled slowly, glancing out at the garden. "It's just... for most of my life, I've felt like I was always on the outside looking in. Like I was always reaching for something I couldn't quite grasp. Growing up, I never really felt like I belonged, whether it was with my family, my friends, or even in my own skin. I think that's why I connected so much with the château's story. It's been a place of refuge for people who didn't fit in, who didn't belong anywhere else."

Martin's heart ached at the vulnerability in Luca's voice. He had suspected that there was more to Luca's connection to the project, but hearing him talk about his feelings of isolation made it all the more poignant.

"I'm really sorry you felt that way," Martin said softly. "It's hard to feel like you don't belong, especially when it comes to your family."

Luca nodded, his expression tightening slightly as he thought back to his family. "Yeah, my family's... complicated. They love me, but they've never really understood me. They're very traditional, and when I came out, it was like the ground shifted beneath us. They didn't reject me, but they didn't accept me fully either. It's like they're always holding me at arm's length, like they're not sure how to relate to me anymore."

Martin felt a surge of empathy for Luca. It was a feeling he had encountered in his own life, that sense of distance between who you are and what people expect you to be. "That sounds incredibly difficult. It's like you're always walking a tightrope, trying not to fall on either side."

Luca glanced at him, his eyes softening. "Exactly. It's exhausting sometimes. And I think that's why I gravitated toward art. It was the one place where I could express everything I was feeling without having to explain it. When I created *The Reach*, it was like I was trying to show people what it's like to be always reaching for connection, for belonging, but never quite getting there."

Martin took a deep breath, feeling the weight of Luca's words. It made sense now, why the installation had resonated with so many people, why it had such a profound emotional impact on the villagers. Luca hadn't just been telling the château's story; he had been telling his own.

"I'm really proud of you, Luca," Martin said, his voice filled with sincerity. "What you've done here is incredible. You've taken something deeply personal and turned it into something that speaks to so many people. That's not easy to do."

Luca's cheeks flushed slightly at the compliment, but his smile was tinged with sadness. "Thanks. It feels good to know that people connected with it, but it also scares me a little. I've always been afraid of letting people see too much of me. I guess I didn't realise how much of myself I put into *The Reach* until people started reacting to it."

"That's the power of art," Martin said gently. "It allows you to communicate things you might not be able to say out loud. And sometimes, it reveals things about yourself that you didn't even know were there."

Luca nodded, his expression thoughtful. "Yeah, I guess it does. I just... I don't know. Part of me feels like I've exposed too much. Like, what if people don't like what they see?"

Martin shook his head, offering Luca a reassuring smile. "I don't think you need to worry about that. The people who matter will see you for who you are and appreciate it. And for the ones who don't, well, that's on them, not you."

Luca sighed softly, his shoulders relaxing just a little. "I wish it were that simple. But I've spent so long trying to fit into boxes that other people created for me. It's hard to shake that feeling, you know?"

"I do know," Martin said, his voice steady. "I've been there too. It took me a long time to figure out that I didn't have to live up to other people's expectations, that I could define my own life and my own happiness. It's not easy, and sometimes it feels impossible, but it's worth it."

Luca looked at him, his eyes searching Martin's face as if trying to gauge the truth of his words. "You really think so?"

"I do," Martin said with conviction. "And you've already taken the first step by creating something as honest and raw as *The Reach*. You've shown people a part of yourself, and instead of pushing you away, they connected with it. That's powerful, Luca."

For the first time in their conversation, Luca's expression softened into something resembling hope. He still looked uncertain, still weighed down by the years of trying to fit in, but there was a glimmer of belief in his eyes, a belief that maybe, just maybe, he could be accepted for who he truly was.

"Thanks, Martin," Luca said quietly, his voice thick with emotion. "That means a lot. I guess I just needed to hear it."

Martin reached out and placed a hand on Luca's shoulder, giving it a gentle squeeze. "You're not alone in this, Luca. You've got a whole team here who believes in you. And more importantly, you're starting to believe in yourself."

Luca smiled, a small but genuine smile that lit up his face in a way Martin hadn't seen before. "Yeah, I guess I am."

They sat in companionable silence for a few moments, watching the sun dip lower in the sky, casting long shadows across the garden. There was a sense of peace in the air, a quiet understanding between them that went beyond words.

As the evening light began to fade, Luca picked up his sketchbook again, his pencil moving softly across the page as he added more details to the figures in his new concept. Martin stayed beside him, not saying much, but offering the quiet support that only a true friend could give.

Luca might still be reaching for connection, but today, in this moment, it felt like he was getting closer.

11

It was a warm, sunny morning, and the restoration work at Château de Valmont was in full swing. The team had been making significant progress over the past few weeks, and the scaffolding along the château's northern façade was filled with workers diligently attending to the stonework that had crumbled over the years. There was a sense of rhythm to the day as the sound of hammers, chisels, and the occasional hum of conversation floated through the air.

Martin stood near the entrance of the château, observing the activity with a sense of satisfaction. After the success of the open house, the restoration project had gained momentum, and the villagers' growing support had brought new life to the worksite. The team was operating like a well-oiled machine, and Martin was beginning to feel that they were truly on the right track.

He glanced over at Antoine, one of the château's most experienced stonemasons, who was perched high up on the scaffolding, carefully working on a section of the château's stone façade. Antoine was meticulous in his craft, always insisting on doing things the old-fashioned way, and Martin had come to appreciate his dedication to preserving the château's authenticity. Antoine moved methodically, chiselling away at the stone, focused and steady.

It was a calm morning, and nothing seemed out of place. Martin exchanged a few words with Sophie and Isabella, who were reviewing some architectural plans near the main entrance, and then he decided to take a walk around the château grounds. As he walked, he felt the warmth of the sun on his back and allowed himself a moment of peace. Everything was progressing as it should.

But then, just as Martin reached the garden at the back of the château, a sudden, sharp crack echoed through the air. It was the sound of wood splintering, followed by the unmistakable noise of metal clanging against stone. Martin froze, his heart immediately jumping into his throat.

He turned and sprinted back toward the château, his eyes scanning the scaffolding as he tried to assess what had happened. Workers were shouting, and Martin's pulse quickened as he saw several people rushing toward the northern façade. The scaffolding, specifically the section where Antoine had been working, was collapsing.

"Antoine!" someone shouted, and Martin's stomach dropped.

When he reached the scene, Martin's worst fears were confirmed. A portion of the scaffolding had given way, and Antoine had fallen from his position high above the ground. He lay sprawled on the stone pathway below, motionless, his tools scattered around him. Several workers were already kneeling beside him, trying to assess his condition, while others were frantically calling for help.

Martin felt a wave of nausea wash over him as he ran toward the group, his mind racing. How had this happened? The scaffolding had been inspected multiple times, and Antoine had always been so careful.

When Martin reached Antoine, he knelt beside him, his breath coming in quick, shallow bursts. Antoine was conscious, but he was clearly in pain, his face pale and his breathing laboured. His leg was bent at an awkward angle, and there was blood on his hands and arms where they had scraped against the stone during the fall.

"Antoine," Martin said urgently, his voice tight with concern. "Can you hear me?"

Antoine groaned in response, his eyes fluttering open briefly before closing again. He was clearly in shock.

"Stay with us, Antoine," one of the workers said, gently holding his hand. "Help is on the way."

Martin felt his heart pounding in his chest as he stood up, taking a few steps back to allow the others to tend to Antoine. He could see that one of the workers had already called for an ambulance, and the sound of sirens could be heard faintly in the distance.

His mind raced, trying to make sense of what had happened. Everything had seemed fine, there were no warnings, no signs that the scaffolding was unstable. But now, Antoine was lying injured on the ground, and the restoration work had come to an abrupt halt.

As the minutes ticked by, Martin's guilt began to build. He was the project leader; he was the one responsible for ensuring that everything ran smoothly, that every precaution was taken to keep the workers safe. How had he missed this? How had this happened under his watch?

The ambulance arrived within minutes, and the paramedics quickly took over, stabilising Antoine and preparing him for transport to the nearest hospital. As they carefully loaded him onto the stretcher, Martin stood back, feeling helpless. Antoine had always been one of the most resilient workers on the team, and seeing him in such a vulnerable state was a blow to Martin's confidence.

Once the ambulance had driven away, taking Antoine to the hospital, the workers gathered around, the shock of the accident still hanging heavily in the air. There was a sombre silence, broken only by the occasional murmur of concern. The restoration had come to a sudden stop, and Martin could see the worry etched on everyone's faces.

Isabella approached Martin, her expression a mixture of concern and urgency. "We need to investigate what happened with the scaffolding," she said quietly. "It looked like it collapsed without warning."

Martin nodded, his throat tight. "Yeah, we need to figure out what went wrong. I just... I can't believe this happened."

Isabella placed a reassuring hand on his shoulder. "Accidents happen, Martin. We've been so careful, but sometimes things go wrong that we couldn't have predicted. Don't blame yourself."

But Martin did blame himself. As the project leader, he felt responsible for every aspect of the restoration, including the safety of his team. Antoine's injury weighed heavily on him, and the guilt gnawed at his insides like a slow-burning fire.

They spent the next hour assessing the damage. The section of scaffolding where Antoine had been working was in ruins, the wooden beams and metal supports twisted and broken. It was clear that something had gone wrong with the structure, but the cause wasn't immediately apparent. They would need to conduct a thorough investigation to determine whether it had been a fault in the materials or an oversight in the setup.

As the day wore on, Martin's sense of responsibility only grew. He replayed the morning in his mind over and over, wondering if there had been something, anything, he could have done to prevent the accident. The worksite had always been meticulously maintained, and safety protocols had been followed to the letter, but it hadn't been enough.

By late afternoon, Martin gathered the workers together to address the situation. His voice was heavy with emotion as he spoke.

"I know today has been difficult," Martin began, looking around at the group of tired, anxious faces. "Antoine is being treated at the hospital, and from what I've heard, his condition is stable, but he's going to need time to recover. I want to thank all of you for acting so quickly to help him. We did everything we could in the moment, and I'm grateful for that."

He paused, taking a deep breath before continuing. "But we also need to figure out what went wrong. I know we've been careful with the scaffolding and with our safety protocols, but something went wrong today, and we need to make sure it doesn't happen again."

The workers nodded, their expressions sombre. Martin could see the fear and uncertainty in their eyes. Accidents like this could shake the confidence of even the most experienced workers, and he knew it was up to him to reassure them that they would find answers.

"I'm going to conduct a full investigation into the scaffolding collapse," Martin continued. "We'll work with the safety inspectors to determine what happened, and we won't resume work on the scaffolding until we're absolutely sure that it's safe. In the meantime, I want all of you to take care of yourselves. If anyone needs time to process what happened today, don't hesitate to ask for it."

There was a murmur of agreement from the workers, but the tension in the air was palpable. Everyone was on edge, and Martin knew that this setback could have lasting effects on the project. They had been making such good progress, and now everything felt like it was hanging in the balance.

As the workers began to disperse, Martin stood alone for a moment, staring up at the château's stone façade. The sun was beginning to set, casting long shadows across the building, and for the first time since the restoration began, Martin felt a sense of doubt creeping in.

He had been so sure of himself, so confident that they were on the right path. But now, with Antoine injured and the scaffolding in ruins, he wasn't sure anymore. The weight of the responsibility he carried felt heavier than ever, and he couldn't shake the feeling that he had let his team down.

Isabella approached him once more, her expression gentle but firm. "You can't carry this on your own, Martin," she said quietly. "We're a team, and we'll get through this together. Don't let this setback define the entire project."

Martin nodded, though the doubt still lingered in his mind. He wanted to believe that they could move past this, that they could continue the restoration without further incidents. But for now, all he could think about was Antoine lying in that hospital bed, and the fear that this accident was only the beginning of more challenges to come.

❖ ❖ ❖

After the accident, the château's restoration site had fallen into an eerie quietness. What had once been a bustling scene of workers chipping away at old stone and discussing the next steps of the restoration now felt heavy with unease. The once-welcoming hum of progress had been replaced by hushed voices, strained conversations, and an overwhelming sense of guilt that seemed to hang in the air like a thick fog.

For Martin, that fog felt suffocating. He couldn't shake the memory of Antoine lying on the ground, injured and in pain, surrounded by a scene of chaos that felt like it could have been avoided. As project leader, the weight of responsibility sat squarely on his shoulders, and it wasn't something he could easily brush aside. The guilt gnawed at him relentlessly, a constant reminder that under his watch, things had gone wrong.

Back in his makeshift office at the château, Martin sat at his desk, staring blankly at the safety reports scattered in front of him. His mind kept drifting back to the accident, replaying the moment the scaffolding had collapsed and Antoine had fallen. No matter how much he tried to focus on the reports and the steps they had taken to ensure safety, he couldn't escape the nagging feeling that it was somehow his fault.

"Should I have double-checked the scaffolding? Was there something I missed during the inspections?" he muttered to himself, his hands gripping the edges of his desk.

His thoughts spiralled as he recalled every decision he had made in the days leading up to the accident. The team had been moving quickly, eager to make up for lost time after a few unexpected delays. Had he pushed them too hard? Had he been too focused on meeting deadlines and impressing the village, rather than prioritising the workers' safety? Every question fed into his growing sense of doubt, making the weight of guilt even heavier.

There was a knock on the door, pulling Martin out of his thoughts. He looked up to see Sophie standing in the doorway, concern etched across her face.

"Mind if I come in?" she asked softly, her usual energetic tone subdued.

Martin nodded, grateful for the company, even if he wasn't quite ready to talk about what was really bothering him. Sophie walked in and sat down across from him, eyeing the safety reports strewn across the desk.

"How are you holding up?" she asked after a moment, her gaze gentle but probing.

Martin sighed and leaned back in his chair, running a hand through his hair. "Honestly? Not great. I can't stop thinking about the accident. It feels like I should have done more, like I should have seen it coming. Antoine's hurt, and I keep thinking that if I'd been more careful, this wouldn't have happened."

Sophie's expression softened. She leaned forward, resting her arms on the desk. "I get it. But Martin, you can't blame yourself for this. Accidents happen, even when we're doing everything by the book. You've always been meticulous about safety; you've put everything in place to make sure this project runs smoothly."

Martin shook his head, the self-doubt still gnawing at him. "But I missed something, Sophie. I know I did. The scaffolding shouldn't have collapsed like that. We did the inspections, we followed protocol, but…"

Sophie reached out and placed a hand on his arm, cutting him off gently. "You did everything you could, Martin. No one's perfect. Sometimes things go wrong even when we're being as careful as we can be. You can't shoulder all the blame for this."

Martin sighed again, though Sophie's words offered some comfort. Still, the guilt lingered. He knew that no matter how much preparation they had done, no matter how closely they had followed protocol, Antoine was still injured, and the project had ground to a halt.

"I just keep thinking about what could have been done differently," Martin said after a pause. "I've spent so much time trying to make sure everything was perfect. But now… I don't know if I'm cut out for this. Maybe someone else should be leading the project."

Sophie's eyes widened slightly, and she shook her head firmly. "No, Martin. Don't even think that. You're the reason this project has come as far as it has. The village was on the verge of giving up on the château before you stepped in. You're the one who's brought the team together, who's made sure we've stayed true to the château's history. Don't let one accident make you question everything you've accomplished."

Martin wanted to believe her, but the doubt still weighed heavily on his mind. "I don't know, Sophie. What if there's another accident? What if someone else gets hurt? I couldn't handle that."

Sophie leaned back in her chair, crossing her arms as she studied him. "Look, I'm not going to pretend that this isn't a serious setback. It is. But it's just that, a setback. It's not the end of the project, and it's not the end of your leadership. If you quit now, who's going to take over? Someone who doesn't care about the château the way you do? Someone who's just in it for the money or the recognition? That's not what this project needs, and you know it."

Martin frowned, the weight of her words sinking in. She was right, of course. He had invested so much of himself into the château, not just as a building, but as a symbol of the village's history and a place of refuge. Walking away now, because of one accident, would mean abandoning the very thing he had worked so hard to protect.

But the guilt still lingered, a heavy presence that refused to be shaken. He looked down at his hands, which were resting on the desk, and exhaled slowly. "I just... I don't know how to move forward from this."

Sophie offered him a small, encouraging smile. "You don't have to figure it all out right now. Take a breath. We'll investigate what went wrong with the scaffolding, and we'll make sure it never happens again. But don't make any decisions while you're feeling like this. You've been carrying so much responsibility for so long, and this accident has shaken you. That's normal. But we'll get through it, together."

Martin nodded, though the guilt still weighed on his heart. He appreciated Sophie's support, but he couldn't shake the feeling that he had let his team down. The trust he had placed in the safety protocols, the confidence he had in the restoration process, it all felt fragile now, like it could crumble at any moment.

As Sophie stood to leave, she paused at the doorway, glancing back at him. "Don't be too hard on yourself, Martin. You're doing an incredible job. And no matter what, we're here to support you. You're not in this alone."

Martin offered her a weak smile, grateful for her words, even if he wasn't sure he fully believed them. "Thanks, Sophie."

After she left, Martin sat in silence for a long time, staring at the reports in front of him without really seeing them. His mind was still clouded with guilt, and no matter how many reassurances he received, he couldn't escape the feeling that he had failed his team.

Later that evening, after most of the workers had gone home, Martin wandered through the château's halls, his footsteps echoing against the stone floors. The quietness of the château, usually a source of comfort, now felt heavy. He passed by the section where the scaffolding had collapsed, the broken pieces of wood and metal still strewn across the ground like the remnants of a shattered dream.

He stood there for a long time, staring at the scene of the accident, his heart heavy with the weight of responsibility. Antoine's fall replayed in his mind, and he couldn't help but think that he could have prevented it somehow. The doubts continued to creep in, whispering that maybe he wasn't the right person for this project after all.

But as the minutes passed, Martin took a deep breath and closed his eyes. He knew that this guilt couldn't be his guide. Yes, mistakes had been made, and yes, the accident had been serious. But quitting now wouldn't solve anything. It would only leave the team leaderless, and the project without the vision it needed to succeed.

With that realisation, Martin turned away from the collapsed scaffolding and made his way back to his office. The weight of guilt was still there, but he was beginning to understand that it didn't have to control him. He would investigate what went wrong, make the necessary changes, and continue leading the project with the same care and dedication he had shown from the start.

As he sat back down at his desk, Martin picked up the phone to check on Antoine's condition at the hospital. He owed it to his team, and to Antoine, to make sure they moved forward with caution, but with renewed determination.

❖ ❖ ❖

The days following the accident at the château were a blur for Martin. Antoine's injury weighed heavily on his mind, and the restoration project had come to an abrupt halt. The scaffolding had been dismantled, and work on the northern façade had ceased while they waited for a full investigation into the accident. The château, which had been buzzing with energy and progress, now felt like a ghost of its former self. The team, too, was subdued. The optimism that had fuelled their efforts after the successful open house seemed to have dissipated.

Martin spent most of his time in his office, poring over safety protocols, reviewing the incident reports, and trying to understand what had gone wrong. He found himself overwhelmed by a sense of responsibility, not just for the project, but for the people who worked under him. Antoine's absence was keenly felt, and Martin knew the rest of the team was worried, both about their colleague's health and the future of the project.

It wasn't long before word of the accident spread through the village. Martin had been so focused on the internal investigation and his own guilt that he hadn't considered how the villagers might react. To his surprise, the first sign of the community's response came just two days after the accident, when Madame Dubois knocked on his office door early in the morning.

"Martin, dear, I heard about Antoine's accident," she said as she entered, her arms laden with bags of food. "I've brought some meals for you and the team. You've all been working so hard, and I know how stressful it must be with everything on hold."

Martin blinked in surprise, momentarily taken aback by her kindness. He stood and helped her set the bags on the table in the corner of the office. The smell of freshly baked bread and hearty stews filled the room, and for the first time in days, Martin felt a small sense of relief. It wasn't much, but the simple gesture reminded him that they weren't as isolated in their struggle as he had thought.

"Thank you, Madame Dubois," Martin said, his voice soft with gratitude. "This is incredibly kind of you."

She waved off his thanks, brushing a few strands of grey hair behind her ear. "Nonsense. You and your team have done so much for this château and for the village. It's the least we can do. How is Antoine, by the way?"

Martin sighed, running a hand through his hair. "He's stable, but he'll need time to recover. They're still doing tests to make sure there aren't any complications. We're just hoping for the best."

Madame Dubois's face softened with concern. "I'm sure he'll pull through. He's a strong one, that Antoine. If there's anything we can do to help, please don't hesitate to ask."

Martin nodded, still touched by her offer. After she left, he sat back at his desk, feeling the weight on his shoulders lift ever so slightly. He had expected backlash from the village after the accident, more criticism, more doubt, but instead, he was met with support. It was something he hadn't anticipated, and it gave him a small spark of hope.

Later that same day, as the team gathered in the château's dining area for lunch, Martin shared the food that Madame Dubois had brought. The mood in the room was still sombre, but the presence of the meals, and the reminder that the village was behind them, seemed to lift the team's spirits a little. Sophie and Isabella exchanged a few quiet words of encouragement, while Jean-Claude cracked a rare smile as he bit into a piece of freshly baked bread.

"This is good," Jean-Claude muttered through a mouthful of food. "Leave it to Madame Dubois to know exactly what we needed."

Martin chuckled softly, grateful for the moment of levity. "She's been amazing. And apparently, she's not the only one who's offered help."

That afternoon, Martin received another unexpected visit, this time from Monsieur Dubois, the village historian. Dubois was a quiet, thoughtful man who had always been supportive of the project, though he kept mostly to himself. He entered Martin's office with a stack of old documents in hand, his expression as serious as ever.

"I heard about the accident," Dubois said, settling into a chair across from Martin's desk. "I wanted to offer my help, if there's anything I can do. I know this is a difficult time for the restoration team."

Martin leaned back in his chair, surprised yet again by the community's outreach. "Thank you, Monsieur Dubois. I didn't expect so many people to come forward after what happened. We've had to pause the work while we investigate the scaffolding failure, but we'll be back on track soon."

Dubois nodded, setting the documents on the desk. "I brought these from the village archives. They might not help with the investigation, but they contain some detailed records of the château's earlier restorations. I thought they might be of interest to you, particularly since those projects faced setbacks as well."

Martin raised an eyebrow, intrigued. "Setbacks?"

Dubois smiled faintly, a rare expression for him. "The château has always been a place of challenges. Even in the 1800s, when the first major restoration took place, the workers faced accidents, material shortages, and delays. But they pressed on. I suppose it's a reminder that even the grandest projects have their stumbling blocks."

Martin ran his fingers over the aged papers, feeling a connection to the past. It was a comforting thought, that others had faced similar obstacles before him, yet had managed to complete the work. The château had endured many challenges over the centuries, and perhaps this was just one more that they would overcome.

"Thank you, Dubois," Martin said sincerely. "I appreciate this. And the reminder that we're not the first to face difficulties here."

Dubois nodded again, standing to leave. "The village is behind you, Martin. We may not always show it, but we care about the château. And we care about the people who are working to restore it."

As Dubois left, Martin felt a warmth spread through his chest. The quiet historian's words meant more to him than he could express, and it was clear that the village's support wasn't just a one-time gesture. They were in this together, and that realisation gave Martin a renewed sense of determination.

❖ ❖ ❖

Over the next few days, more members of the village came forward to offer their help. A local baker sent over trays of pastries for the workers, and one of the farmers donated fresh vegetables for the team's meals. Even the village mechanic, who had once been one of the most vocal critics of the restoration project, stopped by to offer his services if any of the machinery needed repairs.

But the biggest surprise came when Monsieur Lefevre arrived at the château. Martin had heard that Lefevre had softened slightly after the open house, but he hadn't expected to see the older man at the site, let alone offering help.

Lefevre approached Martin in the courtyard, his hands clasped behind his back, his expression as stern as ever. "I heard about Antoine's accident," Lefevre said gruffly, his tone brusque but not unkind. "I suppose you'll be needing more hands now that he's out of commission."

Martin blinked, momentarily caught off guard. "Yes, we're short-staffed at the moment. But we're managing."

Lefevre snorted softly, as if the idea of "managing" wasn't quite good enough. "Managing isn't going to finish the restoration. I've got some experience with stonework from my younger days. I could lend a hand for a few hours a week, if you need it."

Martin stared at him, stunned. Of all the people he had expected to offer assistance, Monsieur Lefevre had been at the bottom of the list. Lefevre had been the most resistant to the project, adamantly opposed to the direction the restoration was taking, particularly when it came to the château's LGBTQI+ history. And yet, here he was, standing in the courtyard, offering to help.

"That would be... greatly appreciated," Martin managed to say, still processing Lefevre's unexpected gesture.

Lefevre grunted in response. "Don't get any ideas. I'm not doing this because I've come around to your way of thinking. I just don't want to see the château fall apart. It's part of our history, and if you're determined to restore it, I'd rather see it done right."

Martin nodded, understanding Lefevre's position. It wasn't an outright endorsement, but it was a step forward, and Martin wasn't about to turn down the help.

As Lefevre walked away, Martin felt a sense of pride swelling in his chest. The village, despite its initial scepticism, was rallying behind the restoration project. It wasn't just about the château anymore, it was about the community, the shared history, and the future they were all working toward.

❖ ❖ ❖

Despite the community's outpouring of support, Martin couldn't shake the heavy burden of responsibility weighing him down after Antoine's accident. The sight of Antoine lying injured on the ground haunted him, replaying in his mind every time he closed his eyes. It wasn't just the accident that troubled him; it was the creeping realisation that he might not be the leader the project needed. No matter how many people reassured him that accidents happen, that the village was behind him, Martin felt like he had failed.

A few days after the accident, the château was quieter than usual. Work had slowed considerably while the team investigated the scaffolding collapse, and the temporary halt had given Martin too much time to think. He wandered the château's halls, passing by the scaffolding site where the collapse had happened, and each time he walked past it, the doubts gnawing at him grew louder. The excitement and drive that had once fuelled his work on the project felt like it had evaporated. Now all he felt was guilt.

One evening, after the workers had left for the day and the château was bathed in the golden light of dusk, Martin found himself sitting in his office, staring blankly at a report he hadn't touched in hours. The quiet of the château, usually a source of solace, now seemed oppressive. The silence pressed down on him, amplifying his inner turmoil.

He had spent so much time convincing himself that he was the right person to lead the restoration of Château de Valmont, that his passion for history, architecture, and the château's legacy would carry him through the challenges. But Antoine's injury had shaken that belief to its core. Martin wasn't just second-guessing himself; he was seriously considering whether stepping down was the right thing to do.

The door creaked open, and Isabella stepped into the room, her eyes immediately falling on Martin's hunched figure. She had been checking on the progress of the investigation into the scaffolding collapse but had noticed that Martin hadn't left his office all day. Concern clouded her face as she approached.

"Martin?" she asked gently, taking a seat across from him. "You've been in here for hours. What's going on?"

Martin didn't look up at first, but the tension in his shoulders spoke volumes. He ran a hand through his hair, letting out a long, tired sigh. "I don't know if I can do this, Isabella," he said quietly, his voice laced with uncertainty. "I'm starting to think I'm not the right person for this project."

Isabella frowned, leaning forward in her chair. "What are you talking about? You've been the driving force behind this entire restoration. You've brought us all together. Without you, we wouldn't have made it this far."

Martin shook his head, still not meeting her gaze. "Antoine's accident… it shouldn't have happened. I was the one overseeing everything, and I missed something. I don't know what, but I missed it. And now Antoine's in the hospital because of me. I can't stop thinking about what could have been done differently."

Isabella sat back in her chair, her expression softening as she listened to Martin pour out his guilt. She had known him long enough to understand that he carried the weight of the project on his shoulders, perhaps too much. Martin had always been meticulous and detail-oriented, but this level of self-blame wasn't like him.

"Martin, I get that you're feeling responsible for what happened," Isabella said gently. "But you need to understand that you can't control everything. We've done everything we can to ensure the safety of the workers, but accidents happen. It doesn't mean you failed. It means we need to learn from this and move forward."

Martin finally looked up, his eyes tired and filled with doubt. "But what if I'm not the right person to lead us forward? What if someone else could do a better job? Someone with more experience leading a project like this?"

Isabella frowned, not understanding where this was coming from. "You're not seriously thinking about quitting, are you?"

Martin didn't answer immediately, but his silence was enough to confirm Isabella's suspicion. She leaned forward again, her voice firmer now. "Martin, quitting isn't the answer. I know this accident was a setback, and I know you're feeling responsible for what happened to Antoine, but stepping down won't solve anything. If anything, it'll leave the project leaderless at a time when we need strong leadership more than ever."

Martin stared at her, the conflict evident in his expression. He had been battling these thoughts for days now, and while part of him knew that Isabella was right, the guilt and doubt still lingered.

"I don't want to make another mistake," Martin said quietly. "I don't want to be the reason someone else gets hurt. If I'm not the right person for this, then stepping down is the responsible thing to do."

Isabella's gaze softened as she saw the depth of Martin's fear. She had always known him to be someone who took his responsibilities seriously, but now she realised just how deeply he was internalising the accident.

"You're human, Martin," she said gently. "You care about this project, and you care about the people involved. That's what makes you a good leader, not because you're perfect, but because you're willing to take responsibility when things go wrong and find a way to move forward."

Martin leaned back in his chair, his gaze drifting toward the window where the light from the setting sun cast long shadows across the floor. "I don't know if I can move forward from this. I feel like I've lost sight of why I'm even doing this in the first place."

Isabella sat in silence for a moment, thinking carefully before she responded. "Do you remember why you took this project on in the first place?" she asked softly. "Because I do."

Martin glanced at her, his curiosity piqued despite his mood. "Why do you think I took it on?"

Isabella smiled, though it was tinged with sadness. "Because you wanted to bring this place back to life. You saw the history in these walls, the stories that had been forgotten, and you wanted to give the château a future. You believed that restoring this place would bring the village together, that it could be more than just a crumbling relic of the past. And you've done that, Martin. You've already brought so much life back to the château."

Martin sighed, rubbing his temples. "But at what cost? If someone gets hurt again…"

"That's a risk in any project like this," Isabella said, her voice steady. "But we take precautions, we learn from our mistakes, and we keep going. You're the one who brought us all together, Martin. If you walk away now, we lose more than just a leader. We lose the heart of the project."

Her words hung in the air, and Martin felt the truth of them sinking in. He had been so focused on his own guilt, on his fear of making another mistake, that he had forgotten why he had started this project in the first place. The château had always been more than just a building to him. It was a symbol of resilience, of history, and of community. And now, it was a symbol of his own journey.

After a long silence, Martin finally spoke, his voice quiet but more certain than it had been in days. "You're right," he said. "I can't walk away from this. But I need to figure out how to move forward without letting this guilt control me."

Isabella smiled, relieved to see a glimmer of the old Martin returning. "That's the first step. And you're not alone in this. We're all here to help. You don't have to carry the weight of this project on your own."

Martin nodded, feeling a small sense of relief. He still didn't have all the answers, and he knew there would be challenges ahead, but Isabella's words had reminded him of why he had taken on the restoration in the first place. It wasn't just about the building, it was about the people, the community, and the legacy they were preserving together.

For the first time since the accident, Martin allowed himself to believe that they could move forward. It wouldn't be easy, and the guilt would take time to fade, but he wasn't ready to give up. Not yet.

As Isabella stood to leave, she paused at the door, her expression thoughtful. "Remember, Martin, leadership isn't about being perfect. It's about facing the hard moments and finding a way through them. And I know you can do that."

Martin gave her a small, grateful smile. "Thanks, Isabella. I'll do my best."

After she left, Martin remained in his office for a while longer, staring out at the château's grounds as the sun dipped below the horizon. The weight of guilt still lingered, but it was no longer as suffocating. He had a long road ahead, but for the first time in days, he felt like he could breathe again.

And maybe, just maybe, he could still lead the project to success.

❖ ❖ ❖

After days of doubt and introspection, Martin knew the time had come to make a choice. The accident had shaken his confidence to its core, but the guilt that had threatened to consume him was slowly starting to ease. Thanks to Isabella's words, he had begun to see that quitting would be a temporary escape rather than a solution. And yet, moving forward still felt like an uphill battle.

The following morning, the team gathered outside the château to discuss the next steps for the project. The sky was overcast, with a light breeze brushing through the trees, but there was an air of quiet determination amongst the group. The scaffolding had been taken down, and the site where Antoine had fallen was now cordoned off. Safety inspectors were due to visit later in the day to assess the situation, but in the meantime, Martin had called the meeting to talk openly with the team about what had happened, and how they could move forward.

As the workers assembled, Martin felt a familiar wave of anxiety rise in his chest. He had always prided himself on being a steady leader, someone who could guide the team through both the highs and the lows of the project. But now, standing in front of them, he felt exposed. This wasn't the confident leader they had come to expect. This was someone who had been knocked down and was still figuring out how to get back up.

But Martin knew he couldn't hide from the team. They deserved transparency, and more importantly, they deserved a leader who was willing to face the difficult moments head-on.

Taking a deep breath, Martin addressed the group.

"I know the last few days have been tough," he began, his voice steady but soft. "Antoine's accident was a shock to all of us, and it's left me with a lot of questions, questions about our safety protocols, our processes, and about my role as your leader."

The workers shifted slightly, their faces attentive and concerned. Martin could see the toll the accident had taken on them, too. They were a close-knit team, and Antoine's injury had affected everyone.

"I want to start by saying that I take full responsibility for what happened," Martin continued. "As the project leader, it's my job to ensure the safety of everyone on this site, and I feel like I let you down. We've always prided ourselves on following safety protocols, but clearly, something went wrong. I'm working with the safety inspectors to figure out exactly what happened, and we won't resume work on the scaffolding until we're absolutely certain it's safe."

There was a murmur of agreement from the group, and Martin felt a small sense of relief. He knew that the team needed to hear him acknowledge his role in the accident, but he also knew that this was just the first step.

"But beyond the logistics," Martin continued, his tone softening, "I want to talk about how we move forward from this, how *I* move forward from this. I won't lie to you. After the accident, I seriously considered stepping down from my role. I questioned whether I was the right person to lead this project."

There was a collective intake of breath from the group, and Martin saw a few surprised glances exchanged between the workers. He hadn't told anyone about his internal struggle, not even Sophie, who stood just a few feet away with a furrowed brow.

"But after some long conversations and a lot of reflection, I've come to a decision," Martin said, his voice growing more confident. "I'm not going to step down. I'm staying on as your leader, because I believe in this project, and I believe in all of you."

A wave of relief seemed to wash over the group, and Martin saw a few nods of encouragement from the workers.

"I know we've faced setbacks," Martin continued, "and I know this accident has shaken our confidence. But this project is about more than just restoring a building. It's about bringing life back to something that has been forgotten for years. It's about creating a legacy, not just for us, but for the village and for future generations. And I want to see it through, *with* all of you."

Sophie, who had been listening quietly, gave Martin a small, supportive smile. It was the kind of smile that told him she had known he would come to this decision, even if he hadn't realised it himself.

Jean-Claude, who had been standing at the back of the group, crossed his arms and grunted in approval. "Glad to hear it, Martin. We need you here. You're the one who's kept us going this far."

There was a murmur of agreement from the rest of the workers, and Martin felt a warmth spread through his chest. He hadn't realised just how much he needed their support, too.

"Thank you," Martin said, his voice filled with gratitude. "We'll get through this, and we'll come out stronger for it. But I want to make one thing clear: If anyone needs to talk about what happened, if you're feeling unsure or unsafe, please come to me. We're a team, and I don't want anyone to feel like they have to carry this alone."

The group nodded, and Martin could see the tension in their faces begin to ease. It was clear that Antoine's injury had affected more than just the physical work on the project; it had shaken their sense of security. But now, standing together in the shadow of the château, Martin felt a renewed sense of purpose.

After the meeting, the workers dispersed to their various tasks, and Martin found himself standing alone in the courtyard. The weight of the last few days still lingered, but it was no longer as suffocating. He had made his decision, and now it was time to move forward.

Just as Martin was about to head back to his office, Sophie approached him, her arms crossed and her expression a mix of concern and admiration.

"You really had us worried there for a minute," she said, her tone light but serious. "I didn't know you were thinking about stepping down."

Martin nodded, a faint smile tugging at the corners of his mouth. "I didn't tell anyone. I guess I needed to figure it out for myself before I said anything."

Sophie studied him for a moment, then reached out and placed a hand on his arm. "I'm glad you're staying. This project needs you. *We* need you."

Martin felt a wave of emotion well up inside him, but he kept his expression composed. "Thanks, Sophie. I'm not going anywhere."

Sophie gave him a nod of approval before heading back to join the other workers, leaving Martin standing in the courtyard, his mind racing with thoughts of the future.

As the day wore on, Martin busied himself with tasks that had been piling up over the last few days. He reviewed the safety inspector's preliminary report, which confirmed that the scaffolding collapse had likely been caused by a combination of structural weakness in the materials and the strain from recent heavy winds. It was a relief to know that it wasn't a result of negligence on their part, but Martin still felt responsible for not catching the potential issue earlier.

In the afternoon, as the sun began to cast long shadows across the château's stone walls, Martin took a walk around the site. The workers were busy again, focusing on tasks that didn't involve the scaffolding, and there was a renewed sense of purpose in the air. Even though they were short-staffed without Antoine, the team had rallied together, their determination unwavering.

As Martin passed by the site of the scaffolding collapse, he paused for a moment, looking up at the now-empty space where the scaffolding had once stood. The area had been cleared, and new materials would be arriving soon to replace the faulty ones. But the memory of the accident still lingered in the air, a reminder of how quickly things could change.

He stood there for a long time, thinking about everything that had happened, Antoine's fall, his own doubts, and the decision to stay on as the project leader. It hadn't been an easy decision, but it was the right one. This project was more than just a job; it was a part of him now. The château's story, its history, and its future were all intertwined with his own journey, and he wasn't ready to walk away from that.

As the sun dipped lower in the sky, casting a golden glow across the château, Martin felt a sense of peace wash over him. He wasn't perfect, and there would be more challenges ahead, but he was ready to face them, alongside his team, the village, and everyone who had come to believe in the project.

With a deep breath, Martin turned away from the site of the accident and made his way back to the château, his steps lighter and his resolve stronger. The road ahead would be long, but for the first time in days, Martin knew he was ready to lead them through it.

12

The morning air around Château de Valmont was crisp and cool, with the faint scent of earth and stone mixing in the breeze. After days of halted work following Antoine's accident, the château had finally come back to life. New scaffolding had been erected on the northern façade, this time with extra precautions taken, and the workers moved with a renewed sense of purpose and caution. The buzz of conversation among the team was quieter than usual, but there was an undercurrent of determination that hadn't been there before. Everyone was focused, more focused than ever, as if they were all holding the weight of Antoine's fall in their minds and hearts.

Martin stood just outside the main entrance, watching as the team prepared to resume work on the exterior walls. His hands rested in his pockets, his eyes scanning the site for any signs of lingering doubt or hesitation. He could sense the tension still hanging over the group, but it was different now. The accident had changed things, not just physically but emotionally as well. The team was working together in a way that felt more deliberate, more thoughtful. Each movement seemed measured, every tool carefully placed, and each step taken with full awareness of its consequences.

It had taken days to repair the damage caused by the collapsed scaffolding, and even longer to put together a solid safety plan that the entire team could trust. The accident had been a wake-up call for everyone, not just Martin. But now, after long conversations and planning sessions, they were ready to move forward.

As the workers gathered to begin the day, Martin felt a wave of pride surge through him. It wasn't just the work that they were doing on the château, it was the way they were doing it. The accident had left everyone shaken, but instead of retreating, the team had rallied together. There was a sense of solidarity that hadn't been as strong before, and Martin could see it in the way the workers interacted with one another. They checked in more often, asking about each other's well-being, offering help without hesitation. The camaraderie that had always been there had deepened, forged by the challenges they had faced.

Martin stepped forward, clapping his hands to gather the group's attention. The workers turned toward him, their faces attentive but weary. They had been through a lot, and Martin knew they were still processing the accident in their own ways. He, too, was still carrying the weight of what had happened, but today, he felt more determined than ever to lead them through this next phase of the restoration.

"Good morning, everyone," Martin began, his voice carrying across the courtyard. "First, I just want to thank you all for your patience and hard work over the last few days. I know it hasn't been easy, but we've made a lot of progress in getting everything back on track."

There was a murmur of agreement from the group, and Martin could see a few nods of acknowledgment. Sophie, always energetic and upbeat, stood at the front of the group, her arms crossed as she listened closely. Jean-Claude, the lead stonemason, was leaning against a stack of materials, his expression as serious as ever. Despite his gruff exterior, Martin knew Jean-Claude cared deeply about the project, and his quiet leadership had been a source of strength for the team.

"I want to remind everyone that safety is our top priority," Martin continued, his tone firm but encouraging. "We've gone over the new protocols, and I'm confident that we've addressed the issues that led to the accident. But if anyone has any concerns, at any time, please don't hesitate to speak up. We're a team, and we need to look out for each other."

The workers exchanged glances, some of them giving small nods of approval. It was clear that they were ready to move forward, but the memory of the accident still lingered. Martin knew it would take time for everyone to fully trust the new systems in place, but he was confident that they would get there.

As the team broke off into smaller groups to begin the day's tasks, Martin made his way over to Sophie and Jean-Claude. They were discussing the logistics of the stone repairs, with Sophie pointing out sections of the façade that needed immediate attention. Jean-Claude, ever the perfectionist, was scrutinising the stone with his usual intensity, but there was a newfound sense of caution in his movements.

"How are we looking today?" Martin asked as he approached, his hands still tucked in his pockets.

Sophie glanced up, flashing him a quick smile. "We're good. The new scaffolding is holding up, and we're going to start on the higher sections of the façade this morning. I've got the team split into smaller groups to make sure we're not overcrowding any one area."

Jean-Claude nodded, still focused on the stone in front of him. "We'll need to be careful with this section," he said, his voice gruff but steady. "The stone here is more fragile than the rest. It's going to take time to do it right."

Martin nodded, appreciating Jean-Claude's thoroughness. "Take as much time as you need. I'd rather we go slow and get it right than rush and risk anything."

Jean-Claude grunted in agreement, his eyes never leaving the stone. It was one of the things Martin admired most about him, his dedication to the craft, his insistence on quality over speed.

As they talked, Martin couldn't help but notice how seamlessly the team was working together. The accident had forced them to reassess not just their safety measures, but how they communicated and collaborated. There was an unspoken understanding among the workers now, a mutual respect that had deepened in the face of adversity.

Isabella approached from the direction of the main entrance, a clipboard in hand and a look of quiet focus on her face. She had been instrumental in coordinating the new safety protocols, and Martin was grateful for her organisational skills and level-headedness. As she joined the group, she gave Martin a nod of approval.

"Everything seems to be going smoothly so far," Isabella said, glancing around the site. "The inspectors were satisfied with the changes we made, and I've sent them the final report. We should be in the clear to continue at full capacity."

Martin exhaled a small sigh of relief. Knowing that the inspectors had signed off on the safety measures was a huge weight off his shoulders. It was one thing to implement changes, but having them officially approved gave him a renewed sense of confidence in the project's progress.

"That's great to hear," Martin said, offering Isabella a grateful smile. "I really appreciate everything you've done to make sure we're back on track."

Isabella smiled back, her expression softening. "It's a team effort. We've all had to step up in different ways, but we're getting there."

As the morning wore on, the worksite hummed with quiet efficiency. The workers moved with precision, their focus sharpened by the challenges they had faced. Martin walked around the site, checking in with different groups, offering support where needed, and keeping an eye on the progress being made. Everywhere he looked, he saw people working together, not just as colleagues but as a team united by a shared goal.

It wasn't just the restoration of the château that bound them, it was the sense of purpose that had developed over time. The accident had been a harsh reminder of the risks involved, but it had also strengthened the team's resolve. They weren't just restoring a building; they were rebuilding trust, both in each other and in the project itself.

As Martin watched the teamwork, he reflected on how much they had grown since the early days of the restoration. When they had first started, there had been a sense of excitement, but also uncertainty. The villagers had been sceptical, the workers had been adjusting to a new rhythm, and Martin himself had been grappling with the enormity of the task ahead. But now, after everything they had been through, that uncertainty had been replaced by a quiet determination. They had faced setbacks, and they would likely face more, but they were stronger for it.

Around midday, the workers broke for lunch, gathering in the courtyard where tables had been set up with food provided by the villagers. It had become a daily tradition, one that Martin cherished. The villagers, once hesitant and distant, had become an integral part of the project, offering not just food but encouragement and support. The sense of community that had developed around the château was something Martin hadn't anticipated, but it was one of the most rewarding aspects of the work.

As the workers sat down to eat, Martin joined them, taking a seat next to Jean-Claude and Sophie. The conversation was light, with the workers sharing stories and jokes, the tension of the morning giving way to a more relaxed atmosphere. Martin listened, occasionally chiming in, but mostly just enjoying the sense of togetherness that had formed among the group.

It was during these moments, away from the work and the responsibilities, that Martin truly appreciated what they were building, not just a restored château, but a community. The relationships they had formed, the bonds that had strengthened, were as much a part of the project as the stone and mortar they were using to rebuild the walls.

As lunch ended and the workers prepared to return to their tasks, Martin stood up, taking a moment to look around the courtyard. The sun had risen higher in the sky, casting a warm glow over the château's weathered stone walls. It was a reminder that, despite the challenges, they were moving forward. The accident had been a setback, but it hadn't broken them. If anything, it had made them stronger.

Martin knew there was still a long way to go before the restoration was complete, but for the first time in days, he felt a sense of optimism that he hadn't felt since before Antoine's accident.

They were on the right path, and with the collective effort of the team and the village, they would see the project through to the end.

The sense of camaraderie that had grown amongst the restoration team at Château de Valmont was undeniable. The accident that had nearly derailed their progress had, in many ways, brought them closer. As they resumed work with renewed caution, the workers shared not just the responsibility of restoring the château, but the emotional weight of what they had been through. The small, day-to-day interactions began to feel more meaningful, as if the work they were doing was no longer just about fixing the stone walls or repairing damaged sections, it was about the connections they were forging in the process.

It was during one of their midday breaks, as the sun beat down gently over the château, that the personal connections among the team began to deepen even more. The villagers had, as usual, provided food for the team, and the workers gathered around the long tables in the courtyard, shaded by the large trees that bordered the property. The buzz of conversation was more relaxed than it had been in days, with laughter punctuating the air as workers exchanged stories.

Luca, usually quiet and reserved during these moments, was sitting at the far end of one of the tables, flipping through his sketchbook while he ate. His artistic nature had always made him something of an outsider among the more physically demanding workers, but over time, he had found his place. His art had become an integral part of the restoration project, particularly his contributions to the open house and the historical exhibition they had planned for the village. However, there was still an air of mystery around Luca, his past, his struggles, and the deeper motivations behind his art.

Martin, noticing Luca sitting somewhat apart from the others, decided to join him. He grabbed his plate and made his way over, sitting down across from the young artist. Luca glanced up briefly, offering a small smile before returning to his sketches.

"What are you working on?" Martin asked, nodding toward the sketchbook.

Luca hesitated for a moment, then turned the sketchbook around so Martin could see. The page was filled with delicate drawings of the château's interior, but there was something more abstract in the background, figures emerging from the shadows, their faces indistinct, as if they were part of the château itself.

"It's... just an idea," Luca said quietly. "I've been thinking about how the château is more than just a building. It holds so many stories, so many lives, and I wanted to capture that in some way."

Martin studied the drawing, struck by the depth of emotion in Luca's work. The figures seemed to represent not just the people who had lived in the château, but also those who had passed through it, seeking refuge, belonging, or perhaps something more. It was a hauntingly beautiful portrayal of the way history lived on in the walls of the château, even after the people were gone.

"I love it," Martin said sincerely. "You've captured something really powerful here. The way the figures blend into the stone, it's like they're part of the château itself."

Luca looked up, his eyes soft with gratitude. "Thanks. I wasn't sure if it was too... abstract. But that's what I was going for, this idea that the people who lived here left a part of themselves behind, and now we're carrying that forward."

Martin nodded, appreciating the thoughtfulness behind Luca's words. "That's exactly what we're doing here. We're not just restoring a building; we're preserving the stories of the people who came before us. And you're helping us tell those stories in a way that's really moving."

Luca's expression softened further, but there was still a hint of uncertainty in his eyes. It was clear that he was proud of his work, but there was something holding him back, something that kept him from fully embracing the connection he had made with the project.

After a few moments of silence, Luca closed his sketchbook and set it aside. "You ever feel like you don't quite fit in?" he asked, his voice quieter now, as if he wasn't sure he should be asking.

Martin was taken aback by the question, but he understood the feeling immediately. "Yeah," he said after a moment. "I think we all feel that way sometimes. Especially when we're doing something that doesn't fit the mould of what people expect from us."

Luca nodded, his gaze dropping to his plate. "I've felt that way for most of my life. Growing up, I was always the odd one out. I didn't like the things other kids liked. I wasn't interested in sports, or the usual stuff. Art was the only thing that made sense to me, but it made me different. And when I came out... well, that made me even more of an outsider."

Martin's heart ached at Luca's words. He knew what it was like to feel like an outsider, to be different from what people expected. And he knew how isolating that could be. "I'm sorry you felt that way," Martin said quietly. "It's hard when the things that make you who you are also make you feel like you don't belong."

Luca nodded, but there was a sadness in his eyes that told Martin the feeling hadn't entirely gone away. "That's part of why I came here," Luca admitted. "When I heard about the château's history, about the people who had lived here, I felt this weird connection to it. Like maybe if I could help restore this place, I'd be restoring something in myself, too."

Martin sat back, taking in Luca's words. It was a deeply personal admission, one that resonated with Martin more than he had expected. The château had been a place of refuge for so many people throughout its history, and now, it was becoming a place of healing for the people working to restore it.

"I think you're doing that," Martin said softly. "You're not just helping to restore the château; you're bringing your own story into it. And that's important. Your art, your perspective, it's all part of what makes this project so special."

Luca smiled, though it was still a little shy. "Thanks. I guess I've been so used to feeling like an outsider that it's hard to believe I could actually belong somewhere."

"You do belong here," Martin said firmly. "We all do. This project has brought together people from all social classes, and that's what makes it so powerful. We're not just restoring a building; we're building something new together. A new community, a new future."

Luca nodded, but his expression remained thoughtful, as if he was still processing the weight of Martin's words.

As they continued to talk, Sophie and Jean-Claude joined them at the table, their conversation flowing easily as they ate and shared stories from the week. Sophie, always the optimist, regaled the group with a story about a near disaster involving a stray cat and a pile of freshly mixed cement, while Jean-Claude chimed in with his usual dry humour. The atmosphere was light, but there was an underlying sense of connection that hadn't been there before.

At one point, Sophie turned to Luca, her eyes bright with curiosity. "You know, Luca, I've been meaning to ask you about your art. It's so beautiful, and I can see how much of yourself you put into it. Where do you get your inspiration?"

Luca hesitated for a moment, glancing at Martin before answering. "A lot of it comes from my own experiences, I guess. My childhood, the places I've been, the things I've felt. But this project, it's been a big source of inspiration, too. The history of the château, the people who lived here… it all speaks to me in a way I didn't expect."

Sophie smiled warmly, clearly moved by Luca's response. "That's amazing. It's clear that you've poured your heart into your work. And you've become such an important part of this project. I don't think we'd be where we are without your contributions."

Luca's cheeks flushed slightly at the compliment, but there was a genuine smile on his face now. "Thanks. That means a lot."

As the group continued to talk, the conversation shifted from work to more personal topics. The workers shared stories about their families, their childhoods, and their struggles. It was a rare moment of vulnerability, and Martin could see how the events of the past few weeks had brought them all closer. They weren't just colleagues anymore, they were a community, bound together by their shared experiences.

For Martin, it was a moment of realisation. The work they were doing wasn't just about the château, it was about the people. The bonds they were forming, the personal connections they were making, were just as important as the physical restoration of the building. And in some ways, those connections were even more powerful.

As the lunch break ended and the workers began to disperse, Martin felt a renewed sense of purpose. The challenges they had faced hadn't broken them; they had made them stronger. And as they continued their work on the château, Martin knew that they were building something much more lasting than just walls and stone.

They were building a community. And that was something worth fighting for.

As the afternoon sun hung low over Château de Valmont, casting a golden hue across the stone walls, Martin found himself lost in the rhythm of the workday. The renewed sense of purpose in the project had filled him with a quiet optimism. After the setbacks and the weight of responsibility following Antoine's accident, the restoration was once again moving forward. The camaraderie among the team was stronger than ever, and for the first time in days, Martin allowed himself to feel that they might actually pull this off.

He was overseeing the masonry work near the northern façade when his phone buzzed in his pocket. Pulling it out, he noticed a message from Alex. It was short and unexpected: *In town. Can we talk?*

Martin's brow furrowed in surprise. Alex hadn't mentioned any plans to visit, and after their last conversation about his relationship with Jennifer, Martin had assumed Alex was still caught up in the mess of trying to postpone the wedding and navigate his conflicting feelings. Curious, and a little concerned, Martin texted back quickly: *Of course. Where are you?*

The response came almost immediately: *Outside the château.*

Martin blinked and turned, looking toward the front entrance. Sure enough, standing at the gate was Alex, looking both weary and relieved to see him. Without a second thought, Martin excused himself from the workers and made his way across the courtyard, his boots crunching against the gravel as he approached his old friend.

"Alex?" Martin called out, a mixture of surprise and concern in his voice. "What are you doing here?"

Alex, with his hands shoved deep into the pockets of his jacket, offered a small, tired smile. His usually well-kept appearance was a bit rumpled, and there were dark circles under his eyes, telling Martin that whatever had brought him here, it hadn't been easy.

"I needed to get away," Alex said quietly, his voice carrying a note of exhaustion. "I couldn't stay in Sydney any longer."

Martin frowned, sensing the weight of whatever Alex was dealing with. He motioned toward the front gate. "Come inside. We can talk in the office."

Alex nodded, and the two made their way inside the château, the cool air of the stone interior providing a welcome respite from the warmth outside. Martin led Alex to his small office, tucked away in one of the château's side wings, where they could have some privacy. Once inside, Alex sank into a chair with a sigh, rubbing his face as if he hadn't slept in days.

Martin sat across from him, watching with concern. "What happened, Alex? I didn't expect to see you here."

For a moment, Alex didn't answer. He seemed to be gathering his thoughts, his hands clasped together as he stared at the floor. Finally, he spoke, his voice heavy with emotion.

13

The days had begun to blur together as the restoration of Château de Valmont approached its final stages. What had once been a dilapidated ruin now stood tall, its majestic stone walls reborn, no longer hidden beneath layers of decay. The scaffolding that had clung to the château like a skeleton was being dismantled, piece by piece, revealing the grandeur of a structure that had once been left for dead. The scent of freshly cut stone mingled with the earthy perfume of the château's gardens, a reminder of how far they had come.

Progress was evident everywhere. The once-overgrown gardens now bloomed with a riot of colours, thanks to Isabella's landscaping team. The sound of chisels and hammers had given way to the more delicate tones of final changes, polishing wood, hanging tapestries, restoring period furniture. The team moved like a well-oiled machine, their rhythm a testament to months of relentless dedication. Despite the sense of urgency in the air, as they worked to prepare for the grand reopening, Martin found himself increasingly drawn to moments of solitude, moments where he could reflect on the personal journey he had embarked on during the restoration.

One of those moments found Martin wandering through the château's sprawling gardens. The sun hung low in the sky, casting a warm golden glow over the hedges and wildflowers that framed the paths. The neat rows of lavender and the wild sprigs of jasmine filled the air with a sweet, calming fragrance, while bees hummed lazily from bloom to bloom. Martin inhaled deeply, letting the peacefulness of the gardens wash over him. The château had once been a monument to neglect and decay, but now it stood like an old friend, battered by time, yet resilient and renewed.

The irony wasn't lost on him. The château's restoration had mirrored his own personal journey in ways he had never anticipated. He had always been someone who thrived on control, on structure and meticulous planning. When he had first taken on the project, he had approached it with a rigid vision of how things should unfold. He had drawn up detailed blueprints, set precise timelines, and orchestrated every aspect of the restoration. Yet the reality had been far messier, much more complex than the lines and numbers on his plans. Life, as he had learned, didn't fit neatly into a blueprint.

The accident with Antoine had been one of the first cracks in his carefully laid plans, a jarring reminder that no matter how much he tried to control, some things would always be beyond his grasp. Antoine had been injured while inspecting the scaffolding, a small misstep that led to a fall, leaving the project in limbo for weeks. Martin had spent days questioning his decisions, wondering if he could have done something differently, if he could have prevented it. But in the end, he had realised that no amount of planning could account for the unpredictability of life.

Antoine's accident had been the catalyst for a shift in Martin's thinking. Standing there in the garden, with the cool breeze ruffling his hair, Martin let the memories wash over him. The accident had shaken him to his core, forcing him to confront something he had long avoided: the unpredictability of life, and his own need for control. In those early days of the project, every deviation from his plan had felt like a personal failure, a crack in the façade of the meticulous world he had constructed around himself.

But now, standing in the garden, he could see how much he had grown. The château had taught him that restoration, whether of a building or of oneself, wasn't about erasing imperfections. It was about embracing them, about understanding that the cracks and flaws told a story. The château's crumbling walls, and weathered stones had been a testament to its history, just as his own struggles and challenges had shaped who he was.

The project had been about more than saving a building. It had been about saving himself.

Martin let his feet carry him deeper into the gardens, past the rows of lavender and jasmine, toward a quiet corner where an old stone bench sat beneath the shade of an ancient oak tree. The bench was weathered, its surface worn smooth by time and the elements, much like the château itself. He sat down, resting his hands on the cool stone, and looked out at the château in the distance. The late afternoon light bathed the building in a soft, golden glow, illuminating the intricate stonework that Jean-Claude and his team had painstakingly restored.

Jean-Claude. The thought of the master stonemason brought a smile to Martin's lips. The gruff, no-nonsense craftsman had been one of the project's unsung heroes. In the early days, Jean-Claude had been a difficult man to read, his face often set in a stoic expression, his words very rare. But over time, Martin had come to appreciate the quiet passion that fuelled Jean-Claude's work. Every stone the man touched seemed to come alive under his skilled hands. The façade of the château, once crumbling and weathered, now gleamed with new life, each stone a testament to Jean-Claude's meticulous craftsmanship.

Martin closed his eyes and leaned back against the bench, letting the peace of the garden wash over him. The sense of contentment that settled over him was a stark contrast to the constant mental and emotional juggling he had done in those early months. Back then, he had been so focused on the physical restoration of the château, on its crumbling walls, its damaged stone, its forgotten history, that he hadn't realised how much of his own internal structure needed mending.

His thoughts drifted back to the beginning of the project, to the rigid and unyielding mindset that had defined him. Every detail of the restoration had been meticulously planned, from the sourcing of materials to the hiring of contractors. Martin had approached it like he approached everything in life, with a need for control. But the château, like life, had proven to be far less predictable than he had anticipated. The constant adjustments to the restoration plans, the challenges of managing a diverse team, and the unexpected setbacks had forced him to confront something he had long avoided: the reality that life couldn't be controlled, only navigated.

The accident with Antoine had been the breaking point, the moment when everything Martin thought he could control slipped through his fingers. It had been a humbling experience, one that left him questioning not only his leadership but his ability to continue leading the project. But that breaking point had also been a turning point. The accident had forced Martin to reevaluate not just how he approached the restoration, but how he approached life.

He had realised that no matter how much he planned, no matter how carefully he tried to orchestrate every detail, there would always be things outside of his control. It was a humbling realisation, but one that had ultimately freed him from the self-imposed pressure to be perfect. Perfection, he had come to understand, wasn't the goal. It was the cracks in the walls, the imperfections in the stone, that told the story of the château's past. And it was those same imperfections in his own life that made him who he was.

Sitting on the stone bench, Martin realised that he had grown more comfortable with the unknown. The need for rigid control that had once defined him had softened. He still valued organisation and planning, but he had learned to leave space for flexibility, for spontaneity, and for the unexpected turns that life inevitably took. He had learned to trust his team, to delegate, and to rely on the people around him instead of trying to shoulder everything on his own. And in doing so, he had become a better leader, and a better person.

His thoughts drifted to the people who had been with him on this journey, Sophie, with her boundless energy and optimism; Jean-Claude, whose meticulous craftsmanship had brought so much beauty back to the château; Isabella, whose calm and steady presence had been a constant source of support. And of course,

Alex, whose unexpected arrival had deepened Martin's understanding of friendship and the importance of emotional connection.

Martin thought back to the late-night conversations he'd had with Alex over the past few weeks. They had talked about everything, from their careers to their relationships, to their fears and hopes for the future. For Alex, the château had become a place of refuge, a space where he could heal from the emotional wounds left by his breakup with Jennifer. For Martin, those conversations had reminded him of the importance of vulnerability, of being open with the people who cared about him.

In the past, Martin had often kept his emotions close to his chest, preferring to deal with his problems on his own. But the château had shown him the value of community, of leaning on others when the weight of responsibility became too much to bear alone. He had seen it in the way the villagers had rallied around them after Antoine's accident, offering their support and resources without hesitation. He had felt it in the way his team had come together, not just as co-workers, but as friends, each of them contributing their unique strengths to the project.

Martin smiled to himself as he thought about Luca. The young artist had undergone a remarkable transformation over the course of the project, and Martin couldn't help but feel a sense of pride in the role he had played in helping Luca find his voice. When Luca had first arrived at the château, he had been quiet and unsure of himself, his art a reflection of his internal struggles. But as the project progressed, Luca had grown more confident, both in his abilities and in his place within the team. His art had become a central part of the restoration, and the passion he poured into his work had been inspiring to everyone around him.

Luca's growth had been a reminder to Martin of the importance of embracing one's true self, of not shying away from the things that made him different or unique. In a way, the restoration of the château had mirrored the restoration of each person who had worked on it. They had all come to the project with their own histories, their own cracks and imperfections, and through the process of working together, they had each found a way to heal and grow.

Martin leaned back against the bench, closing his eyes for a moment as he soaked in the quiet peace of the garden. The château stood tall and proud in the distance, no longer a symbol of the daunting task that lay ahead, but a testament to what they had accomplished together. It was a place of history, of stories both forgotten and remembered, and now, it was a place of new beginnings.

For Martin, this project had been a turning point. He had entered the restoration with a clear idea of who he was and what he wanted out of life, but the château had shown him that there was so much more to discover. He had learned to let go of the need for control, to embrace the unexpected, and to find strength in vulnerability. And in doing so, he had not only helped restore the château, but he had also restored himself.

As the sun began to dip lower in the sky, casting a warm golden light across the garden, Martin stood up from the bench and made his way back toward the château. There was still work to be done, both on the building and within himself, but for the first time in a long time, he felt ready for whatever came next.

The future was uncertain, and for once, Martin was okay with that. He had learned that sometimes, the best things in life came from the moments you couldn't plan for, from the cracks in the walls and the imperfections that told the story of who you were.

And now, as he walked back toward the château, he felt more grounded and at peace than he had in years. The restoration of Château de Valmont had been about more than just bringing a building back to life, it had been about bringing people together, about healing, and about growth. And in that process, Martin had found something far more valuable than he had ever expected.

The château restoration project had not only transformed the building itself but also the lives of those who had been part of it. Among the most striking changes Martin had witnessed was the personal and artistic growth of Luca. When Luca first arrived at Château de Valmont, he had been a shy, reserved young man who kept to himself, his quiet presence a contrast to the more outgoing members of the team. But over the months, as the walls of the château were rebuilt, so too were the walls Luca had placed around himself.

Luca had come to the project as an artist, recruited to capture the historical essence of the château in his sketches. At first, his contributions seemed modest, small illustrations of the building's architecture and its interior. Martin had noticed Luca's artistic talent early on but sensed that there was much more beneath the surface than what Luca was showing. There was a depth to his sketches, an emotional resonance that hinted at something more personal. As the project progressed, it became clear that Luca wasn't just documenting the restoration; he was pouring his heart into his work.

One afternoon, as the team took a break from their labour, Martin found Luca sitting alone in one of the château's grand rooms, his sketchbook resting on his knees. The light streaming in through the tall windows cast a warm glow over the room, illuminating the dust particles floating in the air. Luca's head was bent over his sketchbook, his pencil moving swiftly as he captured the intricate details of a nearby fireplace. His concentration was intense, his brow furrowed in thought, and Martin, not wanting to disturb him, quietly sat down beside him.

For a few minutes, they sat in silence, the only sound being the soft scratching of Luca's pencil on paper. Eventually, Luca seemed to sense Martin's presence and looked up, offering him a small smile.

"Sorry, I didn't hear you come in," Luca said, closing his sketchbook as if to hide what he was working on.

"No need to apologise," Martin replied, returning the smile. "I didn't want to interrupt. You looked like you were in the zone."

Luca nodded, but there was a hint of discomfort in his eyes. He had always been hesitant to share his work, even though Martin and the rest of the team had been nothing but supportive. It was as if Luca didn't fully trust that his contributions were valuable or meaningful enough.

Martin had noticed this hesitancy early on, and he had made it a point to encourage Luca whenever he could. But it wasn't until recently that Luca had started to open up, both as an artist and as a person. His sketches, once focused solely on the physical restoration of the château, had begun to take on a new dimension. They were no longer just technical drawings; they had become deeply personal expressions of Luca's inner world.

"Can I see what you're working on?" Martin asked gently, nodding toward the closed sketchbook in Luca's hands.

Luca hesitated for a moment, then slowly opened the book to the page he had been working on. What Martin saw took his breath away. The sketch was of the fireplace in the room they were sitting in, but it wasn't just a simple rendering of the stone and the ornate carvings. Luca had imbued the drawing with a sense of history and life. There were faint figures in the background, almost like ghosts, their faces turned away as if they were caught in a moment of passing through time. The detail was astonishing, but it was the emotion in the piece that struck Martin the most.

"This is incredible," Martin said, his voice filled with genuine admiration. "You've captured something here that goes beyond just the physical structure. It's like you've brought the château's history to life."

Luca's cheeks flushed slightly at the compliment, but there was a flicker of pride in his eyes. "Thanks. I've been thinking a lot about the people who lived here, the stories these walls have seen. I wanted to show that, somehow."

"You've done more than that," Martin said, still studying the sketch. "This feels personal, Luca. Like you've poured something of yourself into it."

Luca's expression softened, and he nodded slowly. "I have. This project has made me think a lot about my own story, about where I fit into things. At first, I thought I was just here to document the restoration, but it's become something more for me. I've been trying to figure out who I am as an artist, and I guess… as a person, too."

Martin nodded, understanding exactly what Luca meant. The château had become a place of transformation for all of them, not just in the physical sense, but in a deeply personal way. The project had pushed them all to confront parts of themselves they might have otherwise ignored. For Luca, it had been about finding his voice as an artist, and perhaps even more importantly, finding his sense of belonging.

"You've found something here," Martin said softly. "I've seen the way your work has evolved, and it's incredible to watch. You've gone from documenting history to creating it. Your art is going to be a part of this château's story, and that's something really special."

Luca looked down at his sketchbook, his fingers tracing the edge of the page. "I never really thought of it that way," he admitted. "I've always felt like my work wasn't… I don't know, important enough. Like I didn't really have anything meaningful to say."

Martin frowned, surprised by Luca's self-doubt. "You've got more to say than you realise. Look at this," he gestured to the sketch. "This isn't just a drawing of a fireplace. It's a reflection of the château's past, of its life, and in a way, it's a reflection of your own journey too. You've grown so much, Luca, both as an artist and as a person."

Luca's eyes softened, and for the first time, Martin saw a glimmer of belief in the young artist's expression. It was as if the weight of self-doubt he had been carrying for so long was starting to lift.

"I've been thinking a lot about that," Luca said quietly. "About how much I've changed since I came here. When I first arrived, I wasn't sure I belonged. I've always felt like I was on the outside looking in, like I didn't quite fit anywhere. But being here, working with all of you, it's made me feel like I'm part of something bigger. Like maybe I do belong after all."

Martin smiled warmly, feeling a surge of pride for Luca. He had watched the young man transform over the past few months, watched as he went from someone who was unsure of his place to someone who had found his voice, both artistically and personally. It was a beautiful thing to witness, and Martin couldn't help but feel that the château had played a part in that transformation.

"You absolutely belong, Luca," Martin said firmly. "And not just here. You belong wherever your art takes you, wherever you want to go. You've got something unique, something important to share with the world."

Luca smiled, and this time, it was a genuine, confident smile. "Thanks, Martin. That means a lot coming from you."

They sat in silence for a while longer, the weight of the conversation settling between them. Martin couldn't help but reflect on his own journey as he sat there with Luca. Like Luca, he had come to the château with his own set of doubts and uncertainties, but the project had changed him. It had pushed him to grow, to let go of his rigid need for control, and to embrace the unexpected. And in the process, he had found a deeper sense of purpose.

Luca's journey was still unfolding, but Martin could see that he was on the right path. The young artist had found his place within the project, but more importantly, he had found his place within himself. His art had become a reflection of his own growth, a visual representation of the internal transformation he had undergone.

As the afternoon light shifted, casting long shadows across the room, Luca closed his sketchbook and stood up, a sense of calm and contentment in his movements.

"I think I'm going to head outside for a bit," Luca said, slinging his sketchbook under his arm. "I want to capture the light before it fades."

Martin nodded, watching as Luca made his way toward the door. There was a lightness to his step that hadn't been there before, a confidence that had been hard-won over the course of the project.

As Luca disappeared down the hallway, Martin sat back in his chair, feeling a deep sense of satisfaction. The château restoration had been about more than just repairing walls and rebuilding structures, it had been about rebuilding people. Luca's transformation was just one example of the personal growth that had taken place within the team, and Martin couldn't help but feel grateful to have been part of it.

The journey wasn't over yet, but as he sat there in the quiet of the château, Martin knew that they were all headed in the right direction, toward something new, something better. And Luca, with his art and his newfound sense of self, was proof of just how powerful that journey could be.

14

As the morning sun cast its first light over Château de Valmont, the reality of the project's end began to settle in. The celebration from the night before had been full of joy, music, and camaraderie, but now, the château grounds were quiet. Only the soft rustle of the wind through the trees and the distant chirping of birds could be heard as the team prepared to go their separate ways. It was a bittersweet moment, marked by the pride of having completed something monumental, but tinged with the sadness of saying goodbye to the people who had made it all possible.

Martin stood at the entrance to the château, watching as the final preparations for departure were underway. Sophie was carefully packing up some last-minute items, her movements efficient but a little slower than usual, as if she, too, was reluctant to leave. Jean-Claude was overseeing the workers who were dismantling the temporary scaffolding, his usual stern expression softened by what Martin knew was satisfaction at a job well done. Luca was standing near the garden, staring at his own artwork, which had become an integral part of the château's new identity.

It was hard for Martin to believe that their time here was ending. The château had been a place of transformation, not just for the building, but for all of them. They had come together as strangers, each with their own skills and stories, but had become something much more, a team, a family of sorts. And now, it was time to say goodbye.

Sophie was the first to approach him, her eyes bright with unshed tears. She was usually the most upbeat and energetic of the group, always bringing a sense of joy and light-heartedness to the work, but today, even she seemed subdued.

"Well, boss," she said with a half-smile, "I guess this is it."

Martin smiled back, though his heart felt heavy. "It doesn't seem real, does it? After all this time, it feels strange to think about leaving."

Sophie nodded, her gaze drifting to the château behind them. "It's been such an incredible experience. I've worked on a lot of restoration projects, but this one… this one was different. There was something special about this place, about this team. I'm going to miss it."

Martin felt a lump form in his throat. "I'm going to miss it too. And I'm going to miss working with you. You've been such an important part of this project. I couldn't have done it without you."

Sophie's eyes shimmered with emotion as she reached out and pulled Martin into a hug. "You're not getting rid of me that easily," she said with a laugh, though her voice wavered slightly. "We'll stay in touch. And who knows? Maybe we'll get the chance to work together again on another project."

Martin hugged her tightly, grateful for her friendship and the incredible energy she had brought to the team. "I hope so," he said softly. "I really do."

When they pulled apart, Sophie wiped at her eyes with a laugh. "Okay, enough of this emotional stuff. You've got other goodbyes to make." She gave him a wink before turning to help pack up the last of her supplies.

Next, Martin spotted Jean-Claude, who was standing near one of the restored archways, watching the workers finish dismantling the scaffolding. His arms were crossed over his chest, and his face was set in its usual serious expression, but Martin could see the glimmer of pride in his eyes. Jean-Claude was not a man of many words, but his craftsmanship had spoken for him throughout the project. The château's restoration had been as much his success as anyone else's.

Martin walked over to him, feeling a sense of gratitude for the man's skill and dedication. "Jean-Claude," he began, "I just wanted to thank you again for everything you've done. The château wouldn't be what it is today without your work."

Jean-Claude glanced at him, his lips twitching slightly as if he was fighting a smile. "We did good work," he said simply, his voice gruff. "You had the vision. I just made sure it was done right."

Martin chuckled. "You more than did that. Your attention to detail, your commitment to making sure everything was historically accurate, it's why this project has been such a success."

Jean-Claude nodded, but then turned his gaze back to the château, his expression softening. "I've worked on a lot of old buildings," he said quietly. "But this one…

it's different. This place has a soul. And now, thanks to the work we've done, it can breathe again."

Martin felt a swell of emotion at Jean-Claude's words. Coming from a man who was usually so reserved, it meant even more. "I couldn't have said it better myself," Martin replied. "You've been incredible, Jean-Claude. Thank you."

Jean-Claude gave a small nod, clearly uncomfortable with the sentimentality of the moment. "You're a good leader, Martin. You kept us on track, even when things got tough. That's not easy to do."

Martin smiled, feeling a deep sense of pride and gratitude. "I had a great team to back me up."

Jean-Claude reached out and shook Martin's hand, his grip firm and reassuring. "If you ever need another craftsman for a project, you know where to find me."

"I'll keep that in mind," Martin said with a smile. "Take care of yourself, Jean-Claude."

With that, Jean-Claude turned and walked away, his figure disappearing into the morning light as he went to oversee the last of the workers. Martin watched him go, feeling the weight of their shared experiences settle over him.

Finally, Martin turned his attention to Luca, who was still standing by the garden, staring at his artwork with a contemplative expression. The young artist had come so far since the beginning of the project, when he had been uncertain of his place and unsure of his talent. Now, his artwork was a central part of the château's identity, a tribute to its past and a reflection of the people who had lived within its walls.

Martin approached him slowly, not wanting to interrupt what was clearly a reflective moment for Luca. "You did it," Martin said softly as he reached his side. "Your art is a part of this château now. It's a part of its story."

Luca turned to him, his eyes wide with emotion. "I can't believe it," he said quietly. "I never thought… I never thought my work would be part of something like this. It's like a dream."

Martin smiled, feeling a swell of pride for the young artist. "You've earned it, Luca. Your talent, your vision, it's brought this place to life in a way that nothing else could have. You should be proud."

Luca looked back at his artwork, a small, shy smile spreading across his face. "I am. I really am. And I'm so grateful to you, Martin. You gave me this opportunity, and you believed in me when I didn't believe in myself."

Martin placed a hand on Luca's shoulder, giving it a reassuring squeeze. "You did all of this on your own, Luca. I just gave you the space to show the world what you're capable of. And you've proven that you're capable of incredible things."

Luca's eyes shimmered with emotion as he nodded. "Thank you. For everything."

They stood in silence for a moment, both of them taking in the significance of the moment. It was a farewell, yes, but it was also a new beginning for Luca. The young artist had already been approached by a local gallery interested in showcasing his work, and Martin had no doubt that this was just the start of a long and successful career.

As they stood there, the soft sound of footsteps approached, and Martin turned to see Alex walking toward them. His expression was calm, but Martin could sense the same bittersweet emotion lingering beneath the surface.

"You ready to go?" Alex asked, his voice quiet.

Martin nodded, though the weight of the goodbyes still pressed on his heart. "Almost," he replied, glancing around at the château one last time. "Just taking it all in."

Alex stepped closer, standing beside Martin and Luca as they looked out over the château. The three of them stood in companionable silence, the gravity of the moment sinking in.

"This place," Alex said after a while, "it's going to stay with us. No matter where we go next, or what we do, this place will always be a part of us."

Martin nodded, feeling the truth of Alex's words settle deep within him. The château wasn't just a building, it was a part of their story now, a chapter that had shaped them all in ways they couldn't have imagined when they first arrived.

"Yeah," Martin said softly. "It will."

There was a long pause, each of them lost in their own thoughts, before Alex finally spoke again. "I'm going to miss this, you know. The work, the team… everything. But I also feel ready for what's next."

Martin looked over at his friend, feeling a deep sense of pride. Alex had come to Château de Valmont unsure of himself, uncertain of his path, but now he stood beside Martin, more grounded, surer of what he wanted from life. The journey hadn't been easy, but it had been transformative.

"I'm going to miss it too," Martin admitted. "But like you said, I think we're all ready for what comes next."

Alex gave him a small smile, a glimmer of excitement in his eyes. "Whatever it is, I think it's going to be good."

Luca nodded in agreement; his eyes still focused on his artwork. "Yeah. I think so too."

The three of them stood there for a little while longer, watching as the last of the workers packed up and the château settled into its new life. The future was wide open, filled with possibility, and though their time at Château de Valmont was ending, they knew that this was just the beginning of something new.

Finally, Martin turned to his friends, feeling a sense of peace wash over him. "Let's go," he said softly, and together, they walked away from the château, ready to face whatever the future held.

After the emotional goodbyes with Sophie, Jean-Claude, Luca, and Alex, Martin found himself standing alone in the courtyard of Château de Valmont. The early morning sun was rising higher, casting a golden hue over the grand façade of the château, making the restored stonework glow with warmth. It was as if the building itself was alive, basking in the sunlight and embracing its new chapter with pride. The once empty and crumbling structure now stood strong, a symbol of resilience, history, and transformation.

But now, with the team gone and the celebration over, the château felt quiet. Not the eerie silence of abandonment it had once held, but a peaceful, reflective stillness. Martin's heart was full, but it was also heavy. The end of the project, though long anticipated, left him with an unexpected sense of loss. He had poured so much of himself into the restoration that it felt strange to think about moving on. What was next for him? He wasn't entirely sure.

Martin slowly wandered through the now-empty château, his footsteps echoing softly against the stone floors. The grand halls that had been filled with life and laughter just the night before now stood silent. But instead of feeling lonely, Martin felt a deep sense of calm. This silence wasn't the emptiness of the past, it was the calm after the storm, a moment to reflect and breathe.

As he walked through the familiar rooms, Martin paused in front of the large windows in the grand salon, gazing out at the gardens that Luca and the landscaping team had so lovingly restored. The flowers swayed gently in the breeze, their vibrant colours standing out against the backdrop of the meticulously trimmed hedges and perfectly placed trees. The gardens, once overgrown and neglected, now mirrored the château itself, vibrant, alive, and full of potential.

Martin had always been a planner. Throughout his career, he had prided himself on his ability to foresee challenges, anticipate problems, and map out solutions with meticulous detail. But Château de Valmont had taught him something invaluable: sometimes, the best moments in life weren't the ones you planned for. Sometimes, the unexpected could lead to the most profound transformations.

He thought back to when he had first arrived at the château. Back then, his focus had been solely on the project, on the logistics of the restoration and the demands of preserving history. He had come to the château with a clear vision and an even clearer plan of how everything should unfold. But as the months had gone by, the project had become more than just a professional endeavour. It had become personal, a journey of growth, connection, and discovery.

The team, the community, the château itself, all of it had shifted something inside him. The rigid structure he had once relied on had softened, allowing room for spontaneity, collaboration, and even a little chaos. And in that space, Martin had found something he hadn't even realised he was missing: balance.

For so long, Martin's life had revolved around his work. Project after project, deadline after deadline, he had always moved from one goal to the next, barely pausing to reflect or rest. But the château had forced him to slow down, to adapt, to relinquish control at times. And in doing so, it had given him a new perspective, not just on his career, but on life itself.

Martin moved deeper into the château, his hands brushing lightly against the stone walls as he passed. Each room held a memory, each corridor a moment of triumph or challenge. He remembered the late nights spent pouring over architectural plans with Sophie, the quiet moments of reflection with Luca in the library, and the camaraderie that had developed over shared meals and hard work. These weren't just professional memories; they were personal, emotional, and deeply meaningful.

When he reached the library, Martin paused again, stepping inside and letting the familiar smell of old books wash over him. This room had been one of his favourite places in the château, a sanctuary of knowledge and history. It had been where he and the team had uncovered so much about the château's past, piecing together its story bit by bit. Now, the library stood fully restored, its shelves lined with books that had been carefully catalogued and preserved.

Martin walked over to one of the bookshelves, his fingers trailing over the spines of the volumes. So much of his identity had been tied to this project, and now that it was over, he was faced with the question that had been lingering in the back of his mind for weeks: What comes next?

In the past, the answer would have been simple. He would have moved on to the next project, the next challenge. But something had shifted inside him during his time at the château. He didn't feel the same urgency to jump into the next big thing.

For the first time in years, Martin felt like he could take a breath, like he could give himself permission to slow down and reflect.

He pulled a book from the shelf and sat down in one of the plush armchairs near the window. The sun streamed in, casting a warm glow over the pages as he flipped through them absentmindedly. His mind drifted to the possibilities that lay ahead. He could take on another restoration project, maybe even something abroad. He had offers coming in, after all. But the idea didn't spark the same excitement it once had. Instead, it felt like more of the same, another project, another deadline, another cycle of work.

Martin closed the book and set it aside, gazing out the window. The gardens were peaceful, and for a moment, he imagined himself staying here at the château, making it his home. But as much as he loved this place, he knew that staying wasn't the answer either. The château had been a chapter in his life, one filled with growth and transformation, but it wasn't where his future lay.

His thoughts shifted to the idea of taking some time off, something he had never seriously considered before. Travelling, exploring new places without the pressure of work, experiencing life in a way that wasn't tied to deadlines and expectations. The idea intrigued him. Maybe he could spend some time in Europe, explore the art and architecture of cities he'd only ever visited for brief work trips. Or perhaps he could go somewhere completely different, somewhere where he could disconnect, recharge, and find inspiration.

For so long, Martin had defined himself by his work. He had been successful, yes, but he had also been consumed by it. The château had reminded him that there was more to life than the next big project. There were connections to be made, stories to be told, and experiences to be had that didn't revolve around work. And now, with the château project complete, he had the freedom to explore those possibilities.

As Martin sat there, lost in thought, he heard the faint sound of footsteps approaching. He looked up to see Alex standing in the doorway, a small smile on his face.

"Thought I'd find you in here," Alex said, stepping into the library.

Martin smiled, gesturing for him to sit. "It's one of my favourite spots."

Alex took a seat in the armchair opposite him, leaning back and letting out a contented sigh. "This place really is something special, isn't it?"

Martin nodded, his gaze drifting back to the window. "Yeah, it is. It's going to be strange not coming here every day."

There was a brief silence, and then Alex spoke again, his voice thoughtful. "So, what's next for you? Any big plans?"

Martin chuckled softly. "Funny you should ask. I was just thinking about that." He paused, running a hand through his hair. "I don't know yet. For the first time in a long time, I don't have a plan."

Alex raised an eyebrow. "No plan? Now that *is* surprising."

"I know, right?" Martin said with a laugh. "But honestly, it feels good. I think I need a break, a real break. I've been moving from one project to the next for so long that I've forgotten what it's like to just… be."

Alex nodded in understanding. "I get that. I've been thinking a lot about what's next for me too. After everything with Jennifer, I'm starting to realise that I need to figure out what I really want. Not just what other people expect from me, but what makes me happy."

Martin looked at his friend, feeling a deep sense of connection. They were both at a crossroads, both figuring out what came next. "It sounds like we're both in the same boat," Martin said quietly. "Trying to figure out what's next, but not feeling the same pressure to jump into something right away."

Alex smiled. "Yeah, it's a weird feeling, isn't it? But also, kind of liberating."

They sat in comfortable silence for a while, the weight of their conversation hanging between them. Martin felt a sense of peace knowing that he wasn't alone in this transition. Alex, like him, was navigating the uncertainty of what came next, but they both knew that whatever it was, it didn't have to be rushed.

After a few moments, Alex leaned forward, his expression more serious. "You know, Martin, you've done something incredible here. Not just with the château, but with how you've changed. I've seen it, you've let go of a lot of the pressure you used to put on yourself. You're more open, more... balanced."

Martin felt a warmth spread through his chest at Alex's words. "Thanks, Alex. That means a lot coming from you."

Alex grinned, leaning back in his chair. "It's true. And I think whatever you decide to do next, it's going to be amazing. Whether it's another project or something completely different, you're going to make it count."

Martin smiled, feeling a sense of clarity start to form. Alex was right, whatever came next, he didn't have to rush into it. He had time to explore, to figure out what truly made him happy. And for the first time in a long time, he was okay with not having all the answers.

"I think I will," Martin said, his voice filled with quiet determination. "I think I will."

As the sun continued to rise outside the château's windows, casting a warm glow over the gardens and the stone walls, Martin felt a deep sense of peace settle over him. The future was uncertain, yes, but it was also full of possibility. And whatever came next, Martin knew he was ready for it.

The château had given him more than just a successful project, it had given him the space to grow, to reflect, and to rediscover what mattered most. And as he and Alex sat there in the quiet of the library, Martin realised that the best was yet to come.

Martin's return to Sydney was marked by a comforting yet disorienting sense of familiarity. The city was the same, bustling and vibrant, filled with the noise of people going about their daily lives. But Martin felt different. The experience of restoring Château de Valmont had shifted something fundamental inside him, and as he stepped off the plane and took his first breath of the Sydney air, he realised that he was seeing his home through new eyes.

The drive from the airport to his flat felt surreal. The streets were lined with familiar landmarks, places he had passed countless times over the years. But now, they seemed almost foreign, as if they belonged to a past version of himself that he could barely recognise. It wasn't that Sydney had changed, it was Martin who had changed.

When the taxi pulled up in front of his building, Martin paid the driver and took a moment to stand on the pavement, taking it all in. The tall, modern structure of his flat building contrasted sharply with the centuries-old architecture of the château.

The clean, sharp lines of the building, once a source of pride for Martin as a symbol of his success, now seemed almost sterile compared to the rich history and intricate details of Château de Valmont.

He made his way up to his flat, feeling a strange mix of anticipation and nostalgia. He hadn't been home in months, and while he was eager to settle back into the rhythm of his life, there was also a part of him that wondered how much of that old rhythm still fit him.

As soon as he opened the door to his flat, the familiar scent of home greeted him. Everything was just as he had left it, immaculate, organised, and perfectly in place. Yet, standing in the middle of his living room, Martin felt a sense of disconnect. His space, once a refuge of control and order, felt almost too rigid now, lacking the warmth and spontaneity he had grown to appreciate during his time in France.

Before he had too much time to dwell on the feeling, his phone buzzed. It was a message from Sarah: *Welcome home, stranger! Can't wait to see you. Dinner at mine tonight, 7 PM. Be there, or I'll never forgive you.*

Martin smiled to himself, feeling a surge of affection for his best friend. Sarah had been a constant in his life for years, always there with her infectious energy and unwavering support. He had missed her more than he'd realised while he was away, and the thought of seeing her again filled him with warmth.

That evening, Martin made his way to Sarah's place, carrying a bottle of wine he'd picked up from a small French vineyard near the château as a gift. As he approached her front door, he could already hear the familiar sounds of music and laughter coming from inside. Sarah had always had a way of making her home feel alive, and tonight was no different.

Before Martin could even knock, the door swung open, and there she was, Sarah, with her bright smile and sparkling eyes, looking just as radiant as ever.

"Martin!" she exclaimed, throwing her arms around him in a tight hug. "You're finally back! I missed you so much."

Martin laughed, hugging her back just as tightly. "I missed you too, Sarah. It's good to be home."

She pulled back, looking him over with a mischievous grin. "You look... different. France has done something to you, hasn't it?"

Martin chuckled, shaking his head. "Maybe. It was definitely an experience."

"Well, come on in!" Sarah said, grabbing his hand and pulling him inside. "I want to hear everything. Every single detail."

The moment Martin stepped inside; he was enveloped in the warmth of Sarah's home. The smell of cooking filled the air, something savoury and delicious, and the soft glow of candlelight flickered from the dining table, which was already set for two. Sarah had always been an incredible host, and tonight was no exception.

They settled at the table with glasses of wine in hand, and Martin found himself relaxing for the first time since he'd returned. The familiarity of Sarah's presence, the ease of their conversation, it was exactly what he needed.

"So," Sarah began, leaning forward with a playful grin, "tell me everything. What was it like living in a château? Was it as glamorous as it sounds?"

Martin laughed, shaking his head. "Not exactly glamorous. More like a lot of hard work, long days, and unexpected challenges. But it was... transformative."

"Transformative?" Sarah raised an eyebrow, her interest piqued. "That sounds deep. How so?"

Martin took a sip of his wine, considering how to explain it. "I went there thinking it was just another project, restoring an old building, preserving history. But it became so much more than that. The people I worked with, the connections we made, the stories we uncovered… it changed me. I'm not sure I even realised how much until now."

Sarah's expression softened, her eyes filled with curiosity and warmth. "I can see it. You seem… lighter somehow. Like you've let go of something."

Martin smiled, appreciating her insight. "I think I have. I've always been so focused on my work, on the next project, the next goal. But the château taught me to slow down, to let go of control a little. To appreciate the moments that don't go according to plan."

Sarah nodded, her smile widening. "That sounds like exactly what you needed. I'm so happy for you, Martin. It's good to see you like this."

They spent the rest of the evening talking, laughing, and sharing stories. Martin told her about Sophie, Jean-Claude, and Luca, about the challenges they faced during the restoration and the bonds they had formed along the way. Sarah listened intently, her face lighting up with every new detail.

As the night wore on, Sarah poured them another glass of wine and leaned back in her chair with a contented sigh. "I'm really glad you're back, Martin. Things just aren't the same without you."

Martin smiled, feeling a deep sense of gratitude. "I'm glad to be back too. But I have to admit, I'm not quite sure what's next for me."

Sarah raised an eyebrow. "No big plans yet?"

Martin shook his head. "Not really. For the first time in a long time, I'm not in a rush to jump into the next project. I think I need some time to figure things out."

Sarah nodded thoughtfully. "That makes sense. You've been going full throttle for as long as I've known you. Maybe it's time to take a breath, see where life takes you."

Martin smiled, feeling a sense of calm settle over him. "Yeah. I think you're right."

As the evening drew to a close, Sarah walked him to the door, giving him one last hug before he left. "Whatever you decide, I know it's going to be amazing," she said softly. "You always find a way to make things work."

Martin nodded, feeling the warmth of her words. "Thanks, Sarah. I needed to hear that."

He stepped outside into the cool night air, feeling a strange mix of nostalgia and anticipation. Being back in Sydney felt both comforting and unfamiliar, as if the city had stayed the same while he had changed. But for the first time in a long while, Martin wasn't anxious about the future. He wasn't rushing to plan or control what came next. Instead, he was ready to embrace whatever life had in store for him.

As he walked back to his flat, the sounds of the city fading into the background, Martin allowed himself to simply be in the moment. His time at Château de Valmont had changed him, and now, back home, he was ready to start building something new, something that reflected the person he had become.

The days after his return from Château de Valmont passed in a blur of readjustment. Martin found himself falling back into familiar routines, but everything felt slightly off, as if the pieces didn't quite fit the way they used to. His morning runs through the nearby park, his carefully curated work schedule, and even the time he spent at his favourite cafés, none of it held the same allure it once had. It wasn't that he no longer enjoyed these things; it was more that he had changed, and now he was seeing his life through a new lens.

One afternoon, as Martin sat in his living room, surrounded by silence, he found himself thinking about the lessons he had learned at Château de Valmont. His journey there had been about more than just restoring an old building; it had been about rediscovering what truly mattered to him. And now, back in Sydney, those revelations were slowly coming into focus.

He poured himself a cup of tea and settled into the couch, thinking about his conversations with Alex at the château. Alex had been struggling with his own sense of identity and fulfilment, and their late-night talks about life, purpose, and happiness had struck a chord with Martin. In many ways, Martin had been wrestling with the same questions, though he hadn't fully realised it until now.

For years, Martin's life had been defined by his work. He was proud of his career; of the projects he had completed and the successes he had achieved. But over time, his work had become all-consuming, leaving little room for anything else. The pressure to constantly achieve, to always be working toward the next goal, had left him feeling drained, even if he hadn't admitted it to himself at the time.

Château de Valmont had forced him to slow down. The challenges they had faced there, the unexpected setbacks, the tight deadlines, the need to adapt on the fly, had taught Martin that he couldn't control everything. And, more importantly, he had learned that he didn't need to. There was freedom in letting go, in allowing life to unfold naturally rather than forcing it into a predetermined plan.

Martin sipped his tea, his thoughts drifting back to the final weeks at the château. He had grown so much during his time there, not just as a professional, but as a person. He had learned to trust his team, to delegate and collaborate in ways he hadn't before. He had allowed himself to be vulnerable, to admit when he didn't have all the answers. And in doing so, he had forged deeper connections with the people around him, connections that had changed him in profound ways.

One of those connections, of course, was with Alex. The two of them had bonded over their shared uncertainties, over their desire to find a deeper sense of purpose in their lives. Alex had been candid about his struggles, about his failed relationship with Jennifer and his growing realisation that he had been living a life that wasn't truly his own. In many ways, Alex's journey had mirrored Martin's, though their paths had been different.

A knock at the door pulled Martin from his thoughts. He stood and made his way over to the door, opening it to find none other than Alex standing on the other side, a sheepish grin on his face.

"Surprise," Alex said with a laugh. "I figured I'd drop by. Hope that's okay?"

Martin smiled, genuinely happy to see his friend. "Of course, come in," he said, stepping aside to let Alex enter.

As Alex walked into the flat, Martin could see that his friend seemed more relaxed than he had been in the final days at the château. There was an ease to his movements, a calmness in his expression that hadn't been there before.

"You look good," Martin said, closing the door behind him. "How have you been?"

Alex shrugged, sitting down on the couch. "I've been... better," he admitted, his smile soft but genuine. "It's been weird, though, adjusting to life after the château. I feel like everything's different, but also the same, you know?"

Martin nodded, sitting across from him. "I know exactly what you mean. It's strange being back, trying to fit into the old routines when you feel like you've changed so much."

"Exactly," Alex said, leaning back against the couch. "But I've been doing a lot of thinking since we got back. I've realised that I've been living my life trying to meet other people's expectations. With Jennifer, with my job, even with myself. I kept telling myself that I needed to keep everything in order, to follow this path I thought I was supposed to be on. But the château made me see things differently."

Martin listened intently, feeling a deep connection to what Alex was saying. "I've been thinking about that a lot too," he said. "For so long, I've been driven by my work, by this need to achieve and succeed. But I don't think that's enough for me anymore. There's more to life than the next project or the next goal."

Alex nodded, his expression thoughtful. "Exactly. I've been thinking a lot about what makes me happy, what I really want out of life. And I think it's time I stop trying to fit into a mould that doesn't suit me."

Martin smiled, feeling a deep sense of pride for his friend. "That's a big step, Alex. I'm really happy for you."

"Thanks," Alex said with a grin. "I'm happy for you too, you know. It seems like you've found a lot of clarity as well."

Martin nodded, his smile softening. "I think I have. I'm still figuring things out, but I know I want to approach my life differently now. I want to prioritise the things that matter, the people I care about, the experiences that bring me joy, the work that aligns with my values."

"That sounds perfect," Alex said, his eyes bright with enthusiasm. "I think we both needed the château more than we realised."

Martin laughed softly. "Yeah, I think you're right."

They sat in comfortable silence for a while, both of them reflecting on how far they had come. It was clear that their time at the château had been transformative, not just in terms of their careers, but in terms of their personal growth.

After a while, Alex leaned forward, his expression serious. "You know, Martin, I just wanted to say... thank you. For everything. You've been a huge part of my journey, and I don't think I would have gotten through all of this without your support."

Martin felt a lump form in his throat at Alex's words. "You don't need to thank me, Alex. We've been there for each other. That's what friends do."

Alex smiled; his eyes filled with gratitude. "Still, I appreciate it. You've helped me realise that it's okay to not have all the answers. That it's okay to take things one step at a time."

Martin nodded, feeling a deep sense of connection to his friend. "We're both figuring it out, one step at a time."

As they continued to talk, Martin realised just how much his time at Château de Valmont had changed him. The pressure he had once felt to constantly achieve, to always be in control, had faded. In its place was a newfound sense of balance, a willingness to embrace the unknown, to let life unfold naturally, and to prioritise the things that truly mattered.

Martin knew he still had a lot to figure out, but for the first time in years, he wasn't anxious about the future. He wasn't rushing to plan or control what came next. Instead, he was ready to let life take its course, knowing that whatever happened, he had the support of people like Alex and Sarah by his side.

As the afternoon sun streamed through the windows, casting a warm glow over the room, Martin smiled, feeling a deep sense of peace. The château had given him more than just professional success, it had given him the clarity and the courage to build a life that truly fulfilled him. And for that, he was eternally grateful.

The days following his return to Sydney were filled with reflection for Martin, but soon enough, the world of work began to creep back in. His inbox, which had been blessedly quiet while he was in France, began to fill with emails, requests from colleagues, offers for new projects, and inquiries from clients who had heard about the success of the Château de Valmont restoration. It didn't take long for his phone to start buzzing again, bringing with it the familiar hum of responsibility and expectation.

Yet, something was different this time.

In the past, Martin would have leaped at every opportunity, eager to prove himself and tackle the next big project. His identity had been so intertwined with his work that the thought of turning something down had always seemed unthinkable. But now, as he scanned the messages and proposals, he felt no urgency. The excitement he once felt at the prospect of another high-profile project wasn't there anymore. Instead, there was a calmness, a sense of clarity that he hadn't experienced before.

Martin leaned back in his chair, staring out the window of his flat. The city skyline stretched out before him, a reminder of the bustling, fast-paced life he had built for himself here. But as he thought about the château, its quiet gardens, the sense of history that permeated its walls, he realised that the life he had built might no longer fit the person he had become.

One email in particular caught his eye. It was from a well-known architectural firm that specialised in large-scale commercial projects. They had heard about his success with the château and wanted him to come on board for a new, ambitious development in the city. In the past, Martin would have been thrilled by the offer, it was prestigious, high-paying, and would undoubtedly enhance his reputation even further. But as he read through the details of the project, he felt a growing sense of unease.

The project was huge, an impressive, modern skyscraper that would require months of intense work, tight deadlines, and a lot of time away from anything else. It was exactly the kind of project he had once thrived on, but now, it felt like a step back into the same cycle he had just broken free from. Martin closed the email, leaning back in his chair again, deep in thought.

Did he really want to go back to that?

His phone buzzed again, but this time, it wasn't another email. It was a message from Sophie, one of his closest friends and colleagues from the château project. Sophie had been an integral part of the restoration, and they had grown close during their time working together. The message was short, but it made Martin smile: *Have you decided what's next yet? I have some ideas...*

Martin laughed softly, shaking his head. Sophie had always been full of ideas, always thinking ahead to the next challenge. But there was something different about her projects, Sophie's ideas weren't about prestige or recognition. They were about passion, about making a meaningful impact. She had a way of seeing potential in the smallest things and turning them into something beautiful and significant.

Intrigued, Martin opened the message and responded: *Not yet. What do you have in mind?*

It didn't take long for Sophie to reply, her excitement palpable even through the screen: *How do you feel about sustainable design and cultural preservation? There's this small town in regional New South Wales that's looking to revitalise its old town centre. Lots of heritage buildings, lots of potential for combining restoration with modern sustainable practices. It's not a skyscraper, but it could be something special.*

Martin stared at the message for a long moment, feeling a flicker of something he hadn't felt in a while: genuine excitement. This wasn't the kind of project that would land him on the cover of architecture magazines or earn him a massive paycheque, but it sounded exactly like the kind of work he wanted to do now. Something that aligned with his values, something that blended history with innovation, something that made a real difference to a community.

He messaged Sophie back: *Tell me more.*

As the details came through, Martin felt a growing sense of clarity. The project in New South Wales was small in comparison to the kinds of work he had done before, but it was rich in meaning. The town's historical buildings were in desperate need of restoration, but the community also wanted to incorporate sustainable design elements, making the project a unique blend of old and new. It was the perfect opportunity to apply everything he had learned at Château de Valmont, to take the lessons of balance, flexibility, and collaboration, and put them to use in a way that truly mattered.

Martin felt a surge of excitement as he imagined walking through the old town centre, talking to the locals, hearing their stories, and finding ways to bring their vision to life. It reminded him of the early days at the château, when everything had seemed uncertain but full of possibility. And just like at the château, this project wasn't about building something grand and flashy. It was about preserving something important, about honouring the past while embracing the future.

For the first time in weeks, Martin felt a sense of purpose stirring inside him. This was what he wanted, to work on projects that aligned with his values, that allowed him to make a real impact, and that gave him the freedom to approach his work with the balance he had learned to cultivate.

He sat up straighter, suddenly filled with energy. The skyscraper project in the city could wait. In fact, it didn't need to happen at all. He opened the email from the architectural firm again, his finger hovering over the "Reply" button. With a deep breath, Martin began typing:

Thank you for the offer, but I've decided to pursue a different direction with my work. I appreciate the opportunity, and I wish you the best with the project.

With a sense of finality, Martin hit "Send."

It was a small moment, but it felt monumental. In that instant, he had made a choice, a choice to prioritise what mattered to him, rather than what was expected of him. He had chosen the project that spoke to his heart, the one that would allow him to continue building on the foundation he had laid at Château de Valmont.

As the message disappeared from his screen, Martin leaned back in his chair, a smile playing at the corners of his lips. He wasn't rushing headlong into the next big thing, but he wasn't standing still either. He was taking the lessons he had learned, the growth he had experienced, and using them to shape a future that felt authentic to who he was now.

His phone buzzed again, another message from Sophie: *You're in, right? This is going to be amazing!*

Martin grinned as he typed his response: *I'm in.*

And just like that, a new chapter began.

As the weeks passed, Martin found himself settling into a new rhythm. The days of high-pressure deadlines and constant stress were behind him, replaced by a sense of calm and purpose. He had officially accepted Sophie's offer to work on the sustainable restoration project in New South Wales, and while the project was still in its planning stages, the anticipation of diving into meaningful work felt exhilarating. For the first time in years, Martin felt like he was moving at his own pace, not bound by external expectations.

The project in New South Wales wasn't like the sprawling, high-profile developments he had been used to. It was smaller, more intimate, but its potential was immense. The town, with its faded heritage buildings and rich history, was eager for revitalisation. The community wanted to breathe new life into their beloved but neglected town centre, and Martin was determined to ensure that this project would preserve the soul of the place while also integrating modern, sustainable practices.

But as excited as he was about the project, Martin knew that it was about more than just the work. It was about continuing the journey of self-discovery that had started at Château de Valmont. His time in France had taught him that success wasn't measured solely by accolades or financial rewards, but by the connections he made and the impact his work had on people and communities.

One evening, as he sat on his balcony overlooking the city, his thoughts drifted to Alex. They hadn't spoken in a few days, but their friendship had deepened since their return from the château. Alex had undergone his own transformation, breaking free from the expectations he had placed on himself and making the difficult decision to postpone his wedding with Jennifer. It had been a hard choice, but Martin admired Alex for recognising that he needed time to focus on his own happiness before committing to a life that wasn't fully aligned with his true self.

Martin reached for his phone, sending Alex a quick message: *How's everything going? Up for a catch-up sometime this week?*

The reply came almost instantly: *Definitely. Let's grab coffee tomorrow. Need to talk about some big decisions I've made.*

Intrigued, Martin smiled to himself, wondering what Alex had been up to. The two had been supporting each other through their respective journeys, and Martin had a feeling that Alex's next steps would be just as transformative as his own.

The following afternoon, they met at a small café near the harbour, a place they had frequented before Martin's trip to France. The café was quiet, the sound of the water gently lapping against the pier adding a peaceful background to their conversation. Alex looked more relaxed than Martin had seen him in months, and as they sat down with their coffees, there was an unmistakable sense of excitement in the air.

"So," Martin began, leaning forward with a grin, "what's this big decision you've made?"

Alex took a deep breath, his eyes shining with a mixture of excitement and nerves. "I've decided to call off the wedding completely," he said, his voice steady but full of emotion. "It wasn't an easy choice, but after everything that's happened, I realised that I was trying to fit into a life that didn't really suit me. Jennifer and I, we were going down different paths, and I couldn't keep pretending that it was going to work."

Martin nodded, understanding the weight of Alex's decision. "That's huge, Alex. I'm proud of you for making that choice, it couldn't have been easy."

Alex smiled, though there was a hint of sadness in his expression. "It wasn't. But I've been thinking a lot about what we talked about at the château, about finding what really makes me happy. And the more I thought about it, the more I realised that I wasn't being fair to myself or to Jennifer. We both deserve to be with someone who's fully committed, and I wasn't. Not in the way that mattered."

Martin reached across the table, giving Alex's arm a reassuring squeeze. "It sounds like you made the right decision, even if it was a tough one. What's next for you?"

Alex leaned back in his chair, a slow smile spreading across his face. "That's the exciting part. I've decided to take a break from the corporate world for a while. I've been doing a lot of thinking about what I want out of life, and I realised that I need to take some time for myself. Travel, maybe work on some personal projects. I don't know exactly where I'm headed yet, but I feel like I'm finally on the right path."

Martin felt a surge of pride for his friend. Alex's journey had been a long and difficult one, but he was finally taking control of his life in a way that felt authentic. "That's amazing, Alex. I'm really happy for you. You've earned this time to figure things out."

"Thanks," Alex said, his smile widening. "And what about you? How's everything with the project in New South Wales?"

Martin's eyes lit up as he started to describe the plans for the sustainable restoration. "It's still in the early stages, but I'm really excited about it. It's the kind of project I've been wanting to do for a long time, something that combines my passion for history with my commitment to sustainability. It feels like the perfect balance."

Alex listened intently, nodding along as Martin spoke. "It sounds like you've found your groove. This project seems like the exact right fit for where you're at now."

"I think so," Martin agreed, feeling a sense of peace settle over him. "It's not about the size or the recognition anymore, it's about the impact. I want to work on projects that mean something, both to me and to the communities I'm working with. And this feels like the right step."

They talked for hours, sharing their hopes for the future, their excitement about what lay ahead. As the sun began to set over the harbour, casting a warm, golden glow over the water, Martin realised just how far he and Alex had come. They had both faced their fears, let go of the need for control, and embraced the unknown. And in doing so, they had opened themselves up to new possibilities, possibilities that felt far more fulfilling than the paths they had once thought they had to follow.

As they stood to leave, Alex gave Martin a heartfelt hug. "Thanks for always having my back, man. I don't think I could have made it through all of this without you."

Martin smiled, feeling the warmth of their friendship. "Same goes for you. We've both grown a lot, and I'm really excited to see where we go from here."

They parted ways, and as Martin walked along the harbour, the cool evening breeze ruffling his hair, he felt an overwhelming sense of gratitude. He had come so far from the person he had been before Château de Valmont, and now, as he looked toward the future, he knew that he was on the right path.

There would be challenges ahead, of course. There always were. But Martin no longer felt the pressure to have everything perfectly planned out. He was ready to embrace the journey, wherever it might lead him, knowing that he was grounded in a sense of purpose and balance that he hadn't had before.

Looking out over the shimmering water, Martin smiled to himself. The future was wide open, and for the first time in years, he felt ready to face it with an open heart and a clear mind.

Printed in Great Britain
by Amazon